CODENAME ROMEO

Rogues and Rescuers Book One

LUCY LEROUX

DISCLAIMER

This book is a work of fiction. All of the characters, names, and events portrayed in this novel are products of the author's imagination. Any resemblance to actual events or persons, living or dead, is entirely coincidental.

This eBook is licensed for your personal enjoyment only and may not be re-sold or given away to other people. If you would like to share this book with someone else, please send them to the author's website, where they can find out where to purchase a copy for themselves. Free content can be downloaded at the author's free reads page.

Thank you for respecting the author's work. Enjoy!

Codename Romeo © 2019 Lucy Leroux

❀ Created with Vellum

TITLES BY LUCY LEROUX

The Millionaire's Mechanic
Burned Deep - Coming Soon

Writing As L.B. Gilbert
The Elementals Saga
Discordia, A Free Elementals Story
Fire
Air
Water
Earth

A Shifter's Claim
Kin Selection
Eat You Up*
Tooth and Nail
The When Witch and the Wolf - Coming Soon

Charmed Legacy Cursed Angel Watchtowers
Forsaken

as Lucy Leroux

CHAPTER ONE

Ethan resisted the urge to slam his phone against the counter. It was bad enough his so-called best friend had to fly home instead of helping him out, but now he was telling Ethan he hadn't even dealt with their squatter?

"Are you *f-ing* kidding me?" he gritted out from behind set teeth. "You're the one who talked me into buying this damn money pit in the first place. I agreed on one condition—that you clear the girl out. I don't even know if she can even be here, legally speaking, while we're renovating."

He wasn't sure. Ethan was an FBI agent, not a general contractor.

"I'm sure it's fine. You're living there," Mason pointed out.

"That's different." Ethan spun on his heel, taking in the barren expanse that was supposed to be the sunken living room of his new apartment. It was right across from Mason's unit, or it would be once the idiot came around to finish the new insulation and plumbing on his future place.

"I'm one of the owners. Anything that happens to me doesn't count," he continued with a scowl. "But tenants are another story. If anything goes wrong, they can sue the shit out of you. I don't want to lose my shirt on this. I'm overextended as it is."

Yes, thanks to his connections, he'd been able to get an excellent term on his loans, but he still needed this venture to succeed if he wanted to be in the clear before the FBI's mandatory retirement age.

"The woman is not going to sue. She's not like that."

Ethan sighed. Despite his profession, Mason could be a sucker sometimes.

Mason worked for a private firm that specialized in overseas mission support and security in high-risk environments. That was how the company's webpage described it. In laymen's terms, he was a mercenary and one of Ethan's closest friends—aside from his partner Jason at the bureau.

Mason Lang had been his best friend since grade school. They grew up tearing up the backroads in Tennessee, and they'd enlisted in the army together. Later—during a brief stint in med school, Ethan had met Donovan Carter, their third investor. Donovan was off in Africa somewhere, saving the world with *Doctors Without Borders*.

Mason was the bastard who'd talked him and Donovan into buying an entire apartment building. Ethan had gone to visit Mason in L.A. to decompress after Peyton Carson's not-quite wedding a few months out. The visit had landed Ethan in his current predicament.

Losing his shot at the girl he'd been crushing on for years had been more of a blow than Ethan had anticipated. Not that he blamed her for it or anything. Peyton had been spoken for when he'd met her. But it had taken that dick Liam Tyler a few years to wake up and claim her. It had been a near thing, though. For a little while, Ethan had fooled himself into thinking…well, it worked out for her in the end. He didn't exactly get Peyton's new lifestyle, but she was happy. And he liked Peyton enough to be happy for her. Mostly.

Ethan's grousing about the extravagant island nuptials had moved Mason to suggest it. If guys like them wanted quality women like Peyton, they needed more to offer them. Since Ethan had been rubbing shoulders with a lot of entrepreneurs and hoteliers, he'd proposed a major investment they could go in on together. They were going to be real estate moguls.

It had seemed like a good idea when they'd been drunk on mid-range bourbon. And for some insane reason, all three were still excited about it the next morning. Six months later, surrounded by the crumbling plaster of their 'investment', Ethan was starting to realize how truly stupid the whole enterprise was.

Mason sighed across the line. "I'm sorry, man. I wish I could be there, but this thing came up."

Damn it, Ethan should have known better than get into business with a merc. "I understand if you got called up for a job."

There was a beat of silence. "It's not a job. It's a girl."

Ethan counted to ten. "Are you telling me you blew off the renovations for a piece of ass?"

Mason wasn't what one would call a womanizer. As a mercenary, he couldn't afford to get distracted by a relationship, or so his excuse went.

"It's not like that. I haven't—it's not like that."

"Then what is it like?" Ethan was exasperated. "Tell me, because I truly want to know what would make you abandon your best friend to do a massive job like this on his own? Not to mention conveniently forgetting to evict the building's last tenant."

That latter was what he was pissed about, and Mason knew it.

"It's a short delay. Well, I hope it is. I have to check something out for a couple of days, then I'll be on the next flight out."

"And the girl downstairs? What the hell am I supposed to do with her?"

More silence. "I sort of told her she could stay until after the renovation."

"You did *what?*"

What the hell was Mason thinking? "You know this place isn't up to code. I barely got my room livable. None of the others are anywhere near ready for occupation."

"Look, she was the last one to sign a lease with that slumlord before we took over the place. She's new in town, and she didn't know where else to go. Cash is obviously an issue, too. Plus, she's got that little kid…"

Ethan hadn't seen a kid. Crap, this kept getting better and better. "Since when are you a sucker for a hard-luck story?"

"The girl was renting the basement room—the damp one we were sure had mold. It's not a story if she was willing to live there."

Ethan raised a brow. "She's not in the basement room now."

"I shifted her to the first-floor studio. It needed the least work at the time."

Perfect. "Why didn't you give her one of the suites up on the top floor with us? I'm sure Donovan won't mind arriving home from his mission of mercy to find squatters in his place."

Actually, knowing Donovan, he'd probably be fine with it.

"She's paying rent," Mason offered as if that would convince Ethan. "You should collect that by the way. I told her to put it in your mail slot…although you should know I knocked fifty bucks off what she was paying the slumlord."

The rent itself was chump change compared to what they'd paid for the building. This wasn't about the money, but he was still dripping sarcasm like acid when he replied. "Of course you did."

"She needs the cash for diapers and shit. It's a baby, man."

Ethan was going to get a headache from grinding his teeth so hard. He didn't like dealing with people. Criminals and colleagues—he was great. But families with kids were a big nope. That was why he was an FBI agent and not a doctor like Donovan.

"She can stay until we renovate that floor," he said after a long silence. Since they were working from the top down, that would give the woman a little time to find a new place.

"Good enough." Mason was relieved. "Just make sure she has a little warning. Moving with a kid can't be easy when you hardly know the language."

Ethan bit his tongue to keep from swearing. "What language does she speak?"

"Spanish, I think. Or at least the accent is Mexican. She knows enough English to get by, or that dive bar on the corner wouldn't have hired her as a waitress."

"How do you know where she works?"

"I wanted a beer after fixing the furnace, and I saw her waiting tables there. Listen, I'm sorry about the delay. I can get some professional contractors out there to give you a hand if you want. I'll pay for it."

"No." Ethan had already lost this argument. Guilting Mason into forking over more cash wasn't going to change that. Besides, this whole project might bankrupt them yet. He wasn't convinced they weren't going to have to replace the plumbing on the ground floor the way Mason was. They needed to save wherever they could.

"We agreed to do the rough stuff ourselves, then bring in the pros to polish everything up after," he continued. "Let's stick to that until we're forced to do otherwise."

"All right. And, Ethan, I *am* sorry."

And he was. Ethan knew that, but Mason was still throwing a wrench in their plans, so it was hard for Ethan to be sanguine. "Just finish what you are doing, then hurry back before I get to the first floor. I would much rather you deal with the girl."

Mason agreed before clicking off. Ethan got back to work, wondering how he had missed the fact the girl downstairs had a baby.

CHAPTER TWO

Two weeks later

The snowy weather was wreaking havoc with the traffic. Ethan got into the apartment much later than he'd intended—well after the blizzard hit.

He stamped his boots to remove the snow before tugging his wool coat off. *Thank frigging God I fixed the heaters last week.*

Over the past couple of weeks, he and Jason, his partner at the bureau, had ripped out the old dysfunctional radiators in Ethan's apartment and replaced them with a state-of-the-art central heating system. He was looking forward to spending the night watching an old New Zealand rugby game while eating frozen pizza in his toasty new living room—as long as the power didn't go out.

I may have to think about a portable generator if these storms get any worse. It could be a wise investment. But at least his food wouldn't rot if the power failed. All he had to do was store his perishables in the nearest snowbank.

Ethan rested his wool coat across the banister, then took off his gloves. Hunkering down with an old rugby game sounded a lot less lame earlier when he'd turned down an offer from his partner Jason to wait out the storm at the Caislean, a five-star hotel in town. His partner lived there with his wife as she was part owner.

How his geeky partner had managed to land a rich and hot hotel heiress still made his head spin, but there was no accounting for taste. Maggie was cool, though. Not as hot as her best friend Peyton, but still way out of Jason's league.

If Ethan had gotten snowed in at the Caislean, he could have had his pick of the hotel's empty rooms to crash in. Gourmet meals served by a courteous staff, his run of the gym—all for free. Most people would give their eyeteeth for a deal like that, but hanging at the hotel seemed too pathetic now that Peyton was off on her honeymoon.

Frozen pizza, it is. Good thing he'd finally convinced the local grocery store to deliver. They had thought the building was condemned—or at least that was what the snide teenager answering the phone had said.

Ethan sniffed. That shitty delivery kid could shove it. The building was starting to shape up. As Mason had declared, it had excellent bones. Most of the remaining work was cosmetic. Once they got rid of the crumbling stucco on the exterior and restored the original brickwork, it would look great. And his double-pane weatherproofed windows would be an amazing place to watch the storm.

He shoved his fleece-lined leather gloves into his pocket to open his mailbox. *Damn it.* The envelope was back.

Yesterday, he'd found it in his slot. It had been filled with grubby tens, twenties, and a whole lot of singles. The envelope contained rent from the building's last resident, the girl Mason hadn't kicked out because he felt sorry for her.

Ethan had given the rent back yesterday…along with an extra two hundred out of his own wallet. He'd stuffed it into a manila envelope, then shoved it under the corner studio's door with a warning to vacate by the first of next month.

In theory, that should have given the girl enough time to find a new place. But that was before the blizzard hit. It was supposed to last the better part of the week. The weather would hamper apartment hunting, which meant he might have to give the woman an extra couple of weeks. However, getting the envelope back was a bad sign. What if she didn't understand English enough to read his note?

Damn it. He was going to have to talk to her in person.

Ethan wasn't afraid of crushing someone. He did it to criminals in the interrogation room regularly, but this was different. For fuck's sake, it was a single mom.

Trying not to swear aloud, he turned the corner instead of heading for the stairs. Maybe he would finally catch his sneaky little tenant at home this time. The woman had been avoiding him for weeks. And he was fairly certain she was turning out the lights and pretending not to be home whenever she heard him in the hall.

Not this time. This couldn't go on. Ethan needed to look the girl in the eye to get a verbal agreement she would start searching for a new place. He didn't want this hanging over his head anymore.

What the hell was the woman's name again? He squinted at the envelope, but he hadn't written it down. The only identifying information was the apartment number drawn in a script so precise it could have been typed. *Doesn't matter.* He didn't need to know her name.

Ethan turned the corner of the short hallway leading to the first-floor units. Stopping short, he stared.

There was a tiny figure in the middle of the hall. He blinked, but the apparition didn't fade or disappear. In front of him, there was a living breathing child, standing there like an oversized garden gnome.

Not oversized by much. The child seemed too small to be standing upright. Ethan eyeballed the tiny being. It couldn't be more than a year old. The toddler was wearing a puffy hot pink snowsuit, the kind that was so thick it forced its arms out like the *Stay Puft* marshmallow man. Ethan couldn't tell if it was male or female, despite the color of the suit, though he'd bet on a girl. Then again, the suit could have been a hand-me-down. The patches indicated it was used.

"Hey...kid," he finished lamely. "Where's your mom?"

It—*her?*—raised its head, a pair of huge dark eyes blinking up. The child tottered, turning around to face the other way. Ethan relaxed as another small but adult-sized figure came toward him and the child.

It had to be the tenant girl, although he would have found it impossible to guess if he'd seen her on the street. She was wrapped in too many layers. The woman's body was covered in two coats, and a multitude of scarves obscured half her face. Nothing appeared thick enough for the current weather, which was presumably why she'd layered up.

"Hi. I'm glad I finally caught you," he said, cocking his head as she marched down the hall toward him.

Her mittened hand ran along the wall. Behind her and the kid, he could see the studio door, open at last. A brown bag partially filled with groceries rested on the floor outside.

The girl reached for the kid so slowly Ethan wondered if she were drunk. That was how the inebriated moved—extremely carefully.

She didn't acknowledge his words—only picked up the child and turned around.

Fuck. That was rude. "Did you hear me?"

How did he say that in Spanish? He wracked his brain. Spanish was the easiest of the languages he'd learned in college. Why couldn't he remember a damn thing?

"*Hey.* I'm talking to you."

Still nothing. The woman was inching down the hall, her progress molasses slow. The toddler in her arms was babbling softly as if it was telling her all about its day.

He took a deep breath, shaking his head as he followed them. "Look, lady, we need to talk about the apartment. I know you discussed staying here with my friend Mason, but his offer was short term. We can't keep letting you live here while we're redoing this floor. The old landlord never should have signed a lease so late in the game."

None of the rentals had been legal by that point. The place was in bad shape—full of rats and bad wiring. Fortunately, the other tenants had been quick to find better accommodations when the extent of the problems had been pointed out to them.

The rats were long gone. It was the first problem they'd taken care of. But this girl...fuck, what was she doing now?

She had stopped halfway to the door, her arm out to touch the wall. Her arm dropped. She leaned against the wall, using it for support as she dragged herself forward. It was a familiar move. He'd done the same thing in college when he'd been too wasted to walk in a straight line to his dorm room.

And with a kid, too. Did that fucking dive bar pay her in drinks?

Really pissed now, he stalked over to her before she reached the open doorway. "Are you seriously going to pretend I'm not here?"

If she shut the fucking door in his face, he was going to break it down. Putting a hand on her arm, he gently tugged.

Her reaction was instantaneous. The woman reared back and pulled away, holding the puffy pink baby tighter to her chest. He caught a glimpse of huge brown eyes and a flushed face. She leaned against the wall again, glancing from him to the door as if weighing the distance. One step was all she could manage. She slid down the wall with the kid in her arms.

Swearing, Ethan dived. He caught them just before the kid slipped headfirst out of her mother's arms. The woman slumped, her head falling back, exposing more of her face. Cheeks red, she shivered.

What the hell? His squatter—tenant—wasn't drunk.

She was sick.

CHAPTER THREE

Ethan carried the woman and her kid inside the apartment. It was a furnished unit, but the decor was sparse with only a bed, a table, and two chairs.

The mattress had been dragged off the frame to the floor. The metal bars that should have been supporting it were stacked in pieces in the corner with a few towels and a worn bathmat thrown over it—probably for the kid's protection.

He set the kid down with one arm. It tottered around in its puffy pink suit as he laid the woman down on the mattress. He pulled her many scarves and beanie hat off.

A torrent of black hair spilled out. Her features were fine, and she had a slightly darker cast to her skin like the Cuban and Puerto Rican girls he sometimes dated. Her face was flushed and feverish. And beautiful.

Holy hell. Mason had told him she was young, but he hadn't expected her to look like jailbait. And with a kid already, too.

"Are you all right?" Ethan asked in a loud voice.

The woman's eyes narrowed to slits, then closed as her head turned to one side. Her lips moved, but no sound came out.

"Perfect," he muttered. What was he supposed to do now? Putting his fingers out, he tentatively touched her face.

Hot. Too damn hot.

"I'm Ethan," he said, a little louder. It didn't rouse her. "I'm going to look for some aspirin. You have some, right?" If she didn't, he had a bottle upstairs in his medicine cabinet.

The only response he got was a groan.

Okay, this was bad. He stood over her, disconcerted by the unevenness of her breathing. "I'm going to take your coat off," he said.

Nothing but more shallow breaths.

"Yes, Ethan. I'd appreciate some help with my many coats," he said aloud as he knelt beside her.

He opened the buttons of the inner and outer coats, then started tugging the sleeves off her arms. It was harder than it looked on TV. Despite years as an FBI agent, he'd never worked any cases that required he undress an unconscious man or woman.

Tugging gently, he slowly worked the two coats off, leaving the girl in a thin sweater. It was cut a bit low—a tip-getter if he ever saw one. He forced his eyes away from the enticing swell.

Well, he could hardly blame her for wearing something like that. She would need every bit of cash she could get with a kid that small.

Speaking of…better get that snowsuit off the baby before it roasts. He swiveled, expecting to see the little kid, but it was nowhere in sight.

Ethan sprang up, his heart sinking to his feet at the sight of the open door. *Crap.* How could he have left it open? Sprinting, he ran out to the hallway. No pink. He checked the lobby next, then the adjoining hall with the mailboxes. Nothing. He dashed back to the hallway. Could it have backtracked while he wasn't looking? Were children that age capable of climbing stairs?

He kept searching, testing doors along the way until he came upon an open one. A steep, narrow staircase disappeared into a dark void.

If that kid fell… "*No, no, no.*" He rushed to the basement entrance.

Ethan hit the switch next to the door, turning on the sickly fluorescents he should have replaced last Sunday. Weak blue-tinted light illuminated the space below. There was no pink at the bottom of the stairs. His feet pounded down the single flight, heaving a sigh of relief when he found nothing at all.

Bent over double, he forced his breathing to slow before straightening and jogging up the stairs. Where the hell was the kid? Nowhere, it seemed. *Way to go, Agent Thomas.* In less than five minutes, he'd already lost it.

Ethan bypassed the stairs, heading back to the studio apartment. Fever or not, he needed to ask the mom what the kid was called so he could start shouting its name. It would answer to its name, right?

Hustling, he pushed the door open. A little pink boot under the table caught his eye before he could put his question to the still-prone woman. Ethan knelt, biting his lip to keep from swearing.

"There you are!" Had it been there the whole time? Forgetting he shouldn't, he swore aloud. He doubled back to close the door firmly before reaching under the table to pull the toddler out.

"C'mere, kid," he growled, straightening and holding the kid at arm's length.

For a second, they stared at each other. Huge dark eyes fringed with the longest inky black lashes blinked back. Then it sneezed all over his face.

He wrinkled his nose. *There go all my efforts to stay healthy.* He'd been using hand sanitizer three times a day while avoiding sick coworkers for weeks so he wouldn't catch the many bugs that always made the rounds in his office in the wintertime.

Well, that had been pointless. Ethan wiped his cheek, examining the kid's winter suit. "How do I get this thing off?"

The kid didn't answer. Ethan hefted it sideways, searching for buttons and snaps. It took him nearly five minutes to find the zippers blended into the seams. After that, it should have been quick work to remove the outfit. It wasn't. He tugged and pulled like one those cartoon mice trying to fit an entire wheel of cheese through a mouse hole.

Once he managed to remove the pink suit, Ethan was still at a loss. He couldn't tell what sex the child was. It was wearing a little grey outfit underneath. As for its age—it was old enough to stand on its own.

The big dark eyes danced. It held its arms out. "Up."

Uh-oh. Picking the toddler up to move it was one thing, but carrying it around was another. What if the kid got used to it?

"Maybe later, kid. I gotta find your mom some aspirin." He edged away from the child as if it were radioactive.

The bathroom door was broken. Making a mental note to bring his tools down here in the morning, he then scoffed aloud. He couldn't leave the woman here on her own. As far as he could tell, she hadn't moved an inch. She was still lying in the exact position he'd left her.

Clearly, she needed a hospital—except the snow was falling past the windows at a rapid clip now. If it kept up at this rate, they would be snowed in for a couple of days, barring a miracle with the snow-plow schedule.

Plus, there had been the traffic pileup he'd passed on the way home. He could call 9-1-1, but a woman with the flu wasn't going to rate high by comparison.

Ethan couldn't rely on emergency services. The chances of an ambulance getting through to them was next to nothing. Unless aspirin could work a literal miracle, he was going to have to bring her and the kid upstairs to his place.

Fuck me. How did he get into these situations? He avoided chicks with kids like the plague. Being forced to deliver a baby a couple of years ago had made him gun shy about that sort of thing. He certainly wasn't one of those billionaires who loved to impregnate their wives. Even his partner was starting to drop ominous hints about starting a family. It made his skin crawl.

The bathroom was empty save for a few threadbare towels. There was no medicine in the cheap cabinet fixed to the wall. There didn't seem to be a shelf for that sort of thing. He checked the kitchen. There were baby gummy vitamins on the counter, but not a lot else.

Ethan checked to make sure the woman was still on the mattress before sneaking a peek in the kitchen cabinets. *I have to check for rat droppings, don't I?* He *was* her landlord.

The shelves held canned soup and some crackers. Another had bread and peanut butter. That was the only food fit for adults, and it was all from the local market's discount line. The only brand names were for the baby food. She prioritized the kid.

So should you. Ethan pulled out his cell phone, deciding to dial 9-1-

1 despite the odds. It rang and rang. After a few minutes, he gave up, slipping his cell into his pocket. He looked down, starting in surprise.

The kid was at his feet. He hadn't even heard it move. "Damn, kid. Are you some sort of ninja?"

It held its arms out again. "Up!"

The command was downright imperious. Ethan glowered. The child scowled back. Giving up, he reached down, his hand touching a wet backside. "Why didn't you just say you needed a clean diaper?" he asked.

The baby smirked.

Ethan blinked. "Aren't you too young to give me attitude?"

It responded by laughing.

"Look, you, a clean diaper is going to have to wait," he told it.

He needed to run upstairs. The sooner he got the mom's fever down, the better. He felt a moment's misgiving for leaving the baby alone, but he couldn't carry it upstairs now.

"I'll be right back," he called to the woman before wondering why he kept talking to her. She wasn't going to answer until he got that fever down.

This time, he closed the door when he exited the studio. Cursing the fact the elevators were out of order, he took the stairs two at a time until he reached his apartment.

It took him less than a minute to ransack his medicine cabinet. Aspirin—check. He pulled out the Nyquil and everything else he thought might help. On the way back down, he called his doctor friend Donovan on the off chance he was free.

Donovan didn't answer. It had been a long shot. Ethan's friend worked sixteen-hour days in some of the worst hellholes. Getting him on the phone was next to impossible. Usually, Ethan had to wait for Van to call him.

Not a problem, he thought, knowing he was lying to himself. The fever was the priority, and he remembered enough from his one semester of med school to know how to treat it.

He marched down to the studio apartment, his false bravado waning the second he reached the door. It wouldn't open.

"No freaking way." That woman had *not* locked the door on him.

He banged it with his fist twice. *"Hey*! I'm trying to help you. Open the damn door."

The nondescript white door stayed shut.

Okay, he could have put that a bit more reasonably with a softer tone. Clearly, the woman was not in her right mind at the moment. If she were processing information at all at this point, she'd registered him as a threat. Fruitlessly, he knocked on the wood again, his eyes drifting to the window.

No...I am not going to go outside to scale the fire escape. There was a record-breaking blizzard hitting the city. It would be the height of madness to go out there.

Behind the door, the baby started to cry.

Aw, shit. He turned around, trying to remember where he'd left his coat. Maybe he could still make it to his car. He kept his rock-climbing gear in the trunk.

He found the thick wool coat on the floor at the end of the hall. It had slid off the banister, landing on the dusty floor.

The buttons on his coat were giving him problems. Swearing, he tugged the lapels roughly to force it closed. He blinked at the flash of grey down the hall. The door to the studio was open a crack. The toddler's hand stuck out, waving.

What the hell? He hurried to grab the tiny hand in his much larger one.

For the second time that night, Ethan wanted to kick his own ass. The door hadn't been locked. The woman had somehow roused enough to stumble to the entrance. Perhaps she'd been trying to follow him to ask for help, but she was now on the floor, blocking the door and keeping him from opening it. In her delirium, she'd rolled away enough for the door to swing open. It must not have been latching properly. There was no way the kid had opened it herself.

Another broken thing to add to my to-do list.

The baby crawled over, pressing its little face to the gap. Ethan winced. "It's okay. I got this, kid."

Kneeling, he worked his hand in the crack, gently shooing the kid away. Pushing steadily, he managed to roll the woman's shoulders away from the door until there was enough room for him to squeeze past the threshold.

Ethan was panting by the time he was inside. The kid tugged on his fingers.

"Yeah, I know. I'm gonna get her this time. I've had enough of this shit," he added in a lower voice.

Ethan had decided to move the circus upstairs. Hopefully, he could contain this fiasco there.

CHAPTER FOUR

The aspirin was working…maybe. Ethan felt the woman's forehead as he laid her on his bed. Then he called Donovan again.

When he failed to reach his friend, he left a voicemail and followed it up with an additional, slightly desperate, email asking Donavon to call back as soon as possible. Another try at 9-1-1 was a bust as well. Like it or not, he was on his own.

Gritting his teeth, he dug out his old mercury thermometer. He put a knee on his bed to loom over her. "Hey, whatever your name is…I'm going to stick this in your mouth, okay?"

Her lids cracked open, her lips parting. They moved, but he couldn't understand the low murmur that came out.

"Err…I'm going to take that as a yes."

Ethan reached out and put his thumb on her chin, gently prying her mouth open wide enough to slip the bulbous end of the thermometer under her tongue.

One hundred and four. Fuck. That was hot enough to cook her brain, wasn't it?

"*Shit.*" He put his hands on his head. "Look, I think I need to take your clothes off, but you need to say it's okay."

She moaned.

"Can I get a clear yes or no?" He wrinkled his nose. "Consent is kind of a big thing in my line of work. There are all these seminars they make us go to..."

"*Luna.*"

He bent closer. "Luna? Is that your name."

"No."

All right. Maybe she meant the moon was full today... "Then what is your name?"

She whispered something, but he didn't catch it. Ethan lowered his head until his ear was right over her mouth.

"*Julietta.*"

"*Julietta?*" Ethan mangled it. His Spanish pronunciations had always been terrible. "Like Juliet? So, is it okay? Can I undress you?"

"Luna." Her lashes fluttered closed. She didn't say anything else.

Executive decision time. Wincing, Ethan started tugging at the sleeve of the sweater.

"I get no enjoyment from this—I swear." He rolled the bottom waistband part up until it was over the bra, a plain beige number that had seen better days.

It could have been black lace, an expensive La Perla set, and she would have looked the same to his eyes. Fucking amazing.

The slight bronze to her skin almost made her glow. Luscious curves shone against the drab beige as if they were mocking it. The full curves of her breasts made his mouth water. Unable to pull his eyes away, he followed the line of each curve over her defined arms and down to her narrowed tapered waist.

The woman wasn't perfect, though. She was a lot thinner than he would have liked. He could count each of her ribs. Something told him the anemic-model look wasn't something she was going for by choice.

Stop fucking checking her out. Ethan had seen plenty of hot girls wearing a lot less. *Hotter ones even*, he thought. Well...that was debatable. This girl was spectacular.

Ethan turned his head, undoing the waistband of her jeans by feel alone. *Good thing I've had lots of practice undoing these in the dark.*

He tugged the denim down, revealing long silky legs that went on for days. *Well, hell.* Someone up there either loved or hated him.

You forgot about her kid. Okay, hated. It was definitely hated.

The squatter— Julietta—began to shiver.

Ethan threw a sheet over her. "Uh, I'm going to go now. I know you may feel a little cold, but it's better this way. We need to get that fever down."

He closed the bedroom door behind him.

Now where was that kid?

❦

Ethan went down to the studio after securing the child in a makeshift playpen made from couch cushions. Worried about leaving the toddler alone, he hurried to grab everything he could get his hands on —diapers, wipes, bibs, and other items he didn't recognize, stuffing the supplies into a clean garbage bag.

On impulse, he decided to get the mother a change of clothes. He was surprised to find everything already packed, along with the majority of the kid's things, and piled up in the corner. They were living out of suitcases.

How many months had they been here? Even he would have been unpacked by now.

Well, you've been after her to move out. Julietta might have been apartment hunting all this time, ready to clear out, and he'd been assuming the worst, believing she hadn't been looking at all.

Ethan returned to his apartment to find his little fortification in shambles. The kid had pulled a Godzilla, managing to bust through the walls. The toddler sat on his cushion-less couch, eating a few pretzels he'd left out on a plate the night before.

"Enjoy them, kid," he said, waving a plastic jar of baby food in its direction. "That's the last junk food you're getting before it's back to this."

He risked turning his back on the child, placing the baby food and diaper-changing supplies on the coffee table as if preparing for a siege.

The setup wasn't much compared to the nurseries some of his friends had for their kids. The wealthy ones had fancy changing tables, along with machines that warmed up baby wipes and bottles.

This girl had used a piece of cardboard covered in duct tape to make a waterproof changing mat.

If it was good enough for her, it was good enough for him. He only made one small change, opting to put a towel over the cardboard. Then he called the kid over.

Naturally, it ignored him.

"Do you want a clean diaper or not?"

Ethan reached out, but it dodged his arms. "*No,*" the toddler yelled, running around him like a wide receiver trying to earn his signing bonus.

A full two minutes later, he was out of breath, sweating and panting. The kid had dodged under the dining room table before weaving around the chairs, knocking over one in the process.

He caught the chair before it hit the floor. "You have a bright future with the Patriots if you keep that up."

Taking a cue from his own speech, Ethan faked left, psyching out the kid long enough to make a grab. He wrestled the wiggling little creature onto the makeshift changing mat, hurrying to strip off the wet grey pants and full diaper before the toddler rolled off.

It was a girl.

Shit. Should he even be touching her now since he knew she was female? This was the kind of thing men found themselves in the shitter for.

It's not like you have a choice. The mom was incapacitated.

"Well, I guess you're not going to be a football player after all," he observed as he wiped her clean. "Not unless the NFL gets way more progressive by the time you grow up."

A thought occurred to him. "Hey, is *your* name Luna?"

Could that have been what the mother meant? The little girl stopped waving her arms to stare suspiciously.

"Again, I'm going to take that as a yes." Ethan sighed, working as quickly as he could to put a diaper on her.

It wasn't fast enough. With a surprisingly rapid swipe of her arm, the little girl knocked his brand-new universal remote off the table. Reacting instinctively, he knelt to pick it up. The sneaky little imp rolled and slid off the table, laughing and giggling as she ran bare-assed around his apartment.

Swearing under his breath, he dived after her. He tripped, crashing into the front of the couch and landing on his trick knee. Pain radiated up his body. Neck corded tight, he swore under his breath again before pulling himself up and hobbling after the imp.

She was going to get pee everywhere. He was glad he'd paid extra for the stain-resistant upholstery on the couch.

Okay, this is humiliating. Ethan was a fit man, an FBI agent on the fast track. He couldn't let the kid win. Plus, the furniture was brand new.

The second attempt proved worse than the first. He managed to get her down on the improvised changing table, but Luna soaked the towel before he could get the new diaper under her.

Scowling, he worked the wet cloth out from underneath her and laid her directly on the duct-taped cardboard. Luna disapproved. She screamed, a high-pitched wail worthy of a banshee.

Flinching at the ear-splitting sound, he accidentally let her roll off the mat again. By the time he got her back in position, there was baby poop all over his new cherry-wood table.

"I haven't even broken it in yet," he groused as he tugged the fresh diaper around and finally managed to get the sticky little tabs open and attached.

Her response was to kick him in the ribs. A tiny foot lifted imperiously, toes pointed like a dancer. It shouldn't have hurt, but her bony digits dug into his ribcage with surprising force. Then she kept her feet there, pushing with all her might.

"*Ow,*" he said loudly. "Cut that out!"

Luna blinked, her big brown eyes widening. Her lower lip trembled ominously, her eyes filling with crystalline tears.

"Oh hey, I'm sorry, Little Moon," he cooed, picking her up and cradling her. "I'm normally not this terrible. My godson likes me, I swear. He likes *Paw Patrol* and wrestling, too. Maybe we can watch some of that later. But I won't snap at you again, I promise..."

He pulled away to see her little face, guilt shredding his insides when she continued to cry. Ethan continued to rub her back while rocking the way he'd seen his friends do with their kids. Her crying finally turned into shuddering hiccups.

"This isn't your fault," he acknowledged, continuing to rock as he paced around the living room. "And it's not your mom's fault. She's sick, and she can't take care of you right now. We were both in the wrong place at the wrong time."

The gut-wrenching sniffles began to subside as he paused in front of double-paned glass windows. The snow was still coming down fast. He could see where the road met the curb below, but only because the snow level was a different height.

Damn. What would have happened if he'd stayed at the hotel with Jason? Julietta had barely made it to her door. Luna could be wandering the hall right now, searching for help that wouldn't arrive for days. He had no idea how serious Julietta's illness was, but she was down for the count on the eve of what promised to be one of the year's worst blizzards.

Luna was blinking heavy lids. Her rosy lips parted before she yawned hugely, her forehead pressing against his shoulder.

"I take it back. Maybe we're both in the right place," he amended, cuddling the child close until she fell asleep in his arms.

CHAPTER FIVE

Baby poop was foul stuff. Ethan wrapped a handkerchief around his mouth to clean it from the table. Thick rubber gloves completed his ensemble.

If I'd known I'd be doing this even two hours ago, I would have borrowed a gas mask from work.

At least the kid was asleep. Once she was dry, Luna had passed out in the corner of the couch, giving him a chance to attend to the mess on the table.

He wiped up as fast as he could. Fortunately, the small turd came off the wood easily—although he would hesitate to eat off the table now. He was stripping off the gloves and throwing them in the trash when the phone rang. It was his partner Jason, wanting to know how he was enjoying his new TV.

Ethan filled him in on tonight's developments, starting with Julietta passing out in the hallway.

"You're taking care of a baby?" his partner asked in disbelief. "By yourself?"

Ethan picked up a can of baby formula, then squinted at the directions. "Unless you and that gorgeous wife of yours rent a snowplow, there's not much choice about that."

"But you don't change diapers, not even for your godson."

Ethan Patrick, his namesake, was the son of Eva Stone and Sergei Damov. The rambunctious boy was three now. Thanks to his miracle of a mother, he was completely potty-trained. Ethan played with the kid whenever he saw him, but in short bursts. He'd never babysat unsupervised.

Jason was quiet for a minute. "I can't make any promises about the snowplow, but I'll see what I can do."

"Relax. I was joking. No one should be out in this weather."

"Is it that bad? You can't get the mother to a hospital? Assuming her fever is still a hundred and four."

"With any luck, it should be down by now. Let me check." Ethan moved to his bedroom.

Julietta had rolled over in his bed several times, working off the sheet as she went. She laid on her side, her glorious body perched precariously on the edge of the mattress. One more revolution and she'd land on the floor.

"Damn." He rushed over, putting a hand on her hip to keep her from rolling off the bed.

What the hell is it with these women? Why couldn't they stay put?

"Is the fever still there?" Jason asked.

"Uh…" He reached out, putting his hand on her forehead. "*Fuck.* Yeah, she's still burning up. The aspirin didn't make a dent."

"Can you get her to a hospital?"

"There's no way. I'd have to carry her there. I'd do it, too, if it weren't for the kid. But I can't manage with both."

He'd barely been able to change the imp's diaper. What if she ran off into the snowstorm?

"Are you sure?" Jason was skeptical.

"I'm telling you a car won't make it. The snowbanks must be three feet now. And they're only growing." Ethan snorted, recalling the conversation they'd had when he'd been deciding which car to buy. "I guess you were right. I should have bought the Range Rover instead of the Mustang."

"Well, you didn't. You insisted on the sexy muscle car because it was going to get you all the chicks." Ethan could hear smugness in his partner's voice. "So, you went downstairs to check the snow level?"

Unnerved by the quietness of the room, Ethan went to the living room. He'd laid the couch cushions on the floor, much like Julietta had done with the mattress downstairs. The toddler laid very still. He put his palm above her mouth, relaxing only when hot puffs warmed his hand.

Good. The kid was still breathing. "Unlike your place, this isn't a high-rise," he reminded Jason. "I can see the street level fine from my bedroom. Barring a miracle involving a gang of rogue snow plowers, these roads won't be passable for a couple of days. Assuming the snowfall stops."

He could practically hear Jason's wince across the line. "Are you sure you can manage with a toddler *and* a sick mom?"

Of course Ethan couldn't, but what could he say? He gave Luna's little form the side-eye. "Well, changing diapers is not my idea of fun, but at least I paid attention the last few times I visited Thalia and Trick at the hotel. I managed, but, honestly, dealing with mobsters and arms dealers is preferable." He sighed. "Diapers get easier with practice, right?"

Noncommittally, Jason grunted. "I wouldn't know. What about the mother?"

"Julietta," Ethan repeated, testing the name aloud again. His rusty Spanish didn't manage to get the pronunciation right. "As long as that fever breaks, I can manage both," he lied.

There wasn't anything Jason could do from across town anyway. Why worry him?

"I'll keep an eye on the weather reports. Once it improves, I'll call in the cavalry."

Ethan wrinkled his nose. "Who would that be?"

There was the sound of movement on the other end of the line. "Whoever I can find."

"Well, it would have to be someone with a snowmobile or a pack of sled dogs because no one else should be out in this weather."

Jason laughed. Ethan didn't have the heart to say he wasn't joking.

❧

Ethan held up the phone to Julietta's face.

"Turn on your flashlight and open her mouth. I want to check her glands," Donovan Carter said.

His physician friend and co-investor had finally called Ethan back. "Okay, now into her ears."

Ethan shifted the phone, replacing the cold compress on Julietta's forehead with his other hand. He'd been doing it every few minutes since hanging up with Jason, but the fever never seemed to get any lower. *Thank God Luna is still asleep.*

"Well?" he asked.

"You know diagnosis over video chat is likely to be wrong, don't you?" Donovan grumbled. "What meds do you have on hand?"

"Aspirin, ibuprofen, and some NyQuil." The cold medicine hadn't even been Ethan's. It had been left behind by a female friend who'd stayed overnight a few times during the last month at his old place. She'd religiously taken a shot every night before bed. She liked her Cosmos a bit too much as well.

That relationship hadn't lasted long.

The tapping of a keyboard brought him back to the present. "Hmm. Did you know the CDC flagged several cases of meningitis in your neighborhood?"

"*Meningitis?*" Ethan reared back. "How contagious is it?" His one semester of med school hadn't gotten that far.

"Depends on what kind. It says here the cases were viral, which is better for you, but at least one was suspected to be bacteria. That wasn't confirmed, but, with bacterial, I'd say you'd need to get that kid out of there as soon as you could."

"Not really an option, but I'll try to keep them separated from now on." Ethan checked the thermometer. It was down precisely one degree.

"Whatever you can do," Donovan replied, still shuffling papers in the background. "Do you have any face masks on hand?"

"I do actually," Ethan said with some relief. "They're for refinishing the floors."

"Use them. And don't let the mom sneeze or cough on you. Wash up often."

"How can you know which kind of meningitis it is?" Ethan asked.

"You can't. No without taking cultures. If the woman is still sick in a couple of days when the roads clear, take her in to get swabbed."

Ethan heard a door squeak open over the phone. Someone spoke French in the background. Donovan replied in a flawless Parisian accent before speaking to Ethan again. "If it's viral, it should work itself out in a week or so."

"*Ah*." Ethan put his hand on his forehead. Well, there went his snow days…unless he could convince someone to take Julietta and Luna off his hands.

The chances of that weren't high. If they had someone else, it wasn't likely they'd still be here living out of two battered suitcases and a backpack.

His low-pitched groan made his chest buzz. Some duties he couldn't shirk as much as he wished otherwise.

You became an FBI agent to help people, remember?

Ethan reminded himself he'd intended doing that by locking away criminals, not nursing strangers back to health.

"Is there anything specific I should do?" There had to be a medical protocol to treat meningitis. "What do I need to know?"

"Antibiotics would help a bacterial case, but, with viral, there's not much to do. Let her rest. Keep her hydrated. Her diet should include organic fruits and vegetables, along with high-quality protein if you can manage it. Easy on the salt."

"Err…so I guess bell peppers on frozen pizza don't count as organic?" Ethan's tastes ran more to junk food and the occasional steak and baked potato.

Donovan laughed. "Yeah, I remember what you keep in your fridge—it's never too early to get that cholesterol checked. Do the best you can on her diet and with the child. Good luck. I don't envy you."

Ethan snorted. "You're the one in the middle-of-nowhere Africa saving the world one patient at a time. This is nothing compared to that."

"I chose this path," Donovan pointed out. "These two fell into your lap. But they're lucky it was you. You'll do right by them. They couldn't be in better hands."

Ethan grunted something noncommittal. Donovan could twist the screws without even trying. Ethan was briefly ashamed for even considering pushing this chore off on anyone else.

You wouldn't have. Even if it had been an option—and with this storm, there was no chance—Ethan wasn't used to passing the buck. He had cultivated a reputation for getting things done, both in and out of the office. At work, he was a bulldog, tackling cases others wouldn't touch. He and Jason had the best closure rate in their department, mainly because they were both too stubborn to ever let a criminal go.

Work hard and play hard. He lived and breathed this motto. More importantly, Ethan considered himself a man of his word. Reminding himself that he hadn't ever agreed to take care of this unfortunate pair didn't seem to matter. Something inside him considered the promise made.

ॐ

Weakly, Juliet stirred. She could barely hold her head up. *"Luna."*

She needed to get up to feed the little girl. Luna needed her breakfast before she was dropped off at the sitter.

Why was it so hot? God, Juliet felt terrible. How was she going to make it through her shift? She couldn't afford to get sick—ever. Her wages at Tully's Bar were pathetic, but she and Luna needed every cent. Juliet couldn't afford to miss a shift.

Anxiety propelled her out of bed. Getting too sick to work was one of her greatest fears. She and Luna subsisted on a knife's edge. If Juliet misstepped, both went over the edge. She couldn't let that happen.

She started for the door, sternly telling herself all she needed was a hot shower and a little breakfast to regain her strength.

Her pep talk failed. Ahead, the space between her and the beige door stretched like that hallway scene in the *Poltergeist* movie. When her strength gave out, it was still a million miles away, and she had to take a break. She sat on the carpeted floor, wondering when the fibers had thickened and grown so plush.

"Hey." The unfamiliar voice was male and deep. "Where do you think you're going?"

Strong hands lifted her from the floor, then settled her onto a leather-covered armchair she'd never seen before.

"Where am I?" A thrill of panic shot down her spine, but it wasn't enough to galvanize her to move.

The face in front of her swam in and out of focus. She didn't recognize it. Was she in a hospital? But why did it look similar to her apartment, only bigger and more nicely furnished?

"No, it's not the hospital," the man said, answering the question she hadn't been aware she'd asked aloud.

"We're snowed in here," he continued. "I had to bring you up to my apartment. I couldn't keep an eye on you down in the studio."

His apartment? Wait, the only other person in this building was the one she'd been avoiding like the plague.

The blurry face suddenly sharpened into stark focus. Fear snaked up her spine. This was the man she'd caught glimpses of while hiding behind the cheap blinds of her only window.

Up close, the fine features and sharply defined cheekbones melded into a visage that belonged on the big screen, the star of an action movie. Except in her film, this man was the villain. He was her landlord, the one who was trying to evict her from her apartment.

There were at least two landlords, maybe three. This new group had bought the building from the previous owner—the skinny sleazebag who'd offered to knock a hundred off the rent if she slept with him. Juliet had bit back the caustic response she'd wanted to make, forcing her eyes away while insisting on paying full price.

One of the new landlords, the intimidating blond giant named Mason, had given her the first break she'd received in this country. She'd been living there for a few weeks when he'd come to tell her the building was under new management and the old leases were void.

When Mason had learned she was on her own with a toddler, he let her stay in one of the first-floor studios after everyone else had to leave.

She knew the only reason she had a roof over her head was because the tall soldier felt sorry for her, but, with Luna in tow, pride was a luxury Juliet couldn't afford. Unfortunately, Mason left town shortly after warning her the reprieve was temporary. The tenants had needed to vacate so he and his partners could finish renovating the building before spring. After that, they were going to turn management of the rentals over to an agency.

She'd been ducking the remaining landlord ever since.

The studio Mason rented her was plain and tiny compared to the house she'd grown up in, but it was clean and warm with reliable plumbing. Her haven was affordable, too, thanks to Mason's generosity with the rent—no strings attached.

But that was all over. She knew *this* landlord wanted her gone yesterday. Belatedly, she realized he was talking to her. She squinted, wondering why she was having such a hard time making out what he was saying. "So, she's fine...but you can't see her. Let me finish changing the sheets, then you can go back to bed."

"What?" Juliet squinted at the threshold, trying to make her fuzzy brain focus on her unfamiliar surroundings. Was he talking about Luna? "Where is she?"

The man drew himself up. "In the other bedroom. I found a box that works as a crib, but she's an escape artist, isn't she?" He put his hand on his chest. "By the way, I'm Ethan."

Her lips were so dry they cracked when she opened her mouth. "I want Luna. Bring Luna," she pleaded.

Ethan winced. "I'm sorry, but you can't see her right now."

The denial penetrated Juliet's lethargy like a knife. She could feel her breath freeze in her chest as icy fingers clamped around her heart.

"*What?*" She gasped, half-pulling, half-pushing to her feet. "W-why not? Where is she?"

The man tried to grab her, but she smacked his hands away. She stumbled to the door. "Luna," she called, her voice shrill.

Ethan's hands came around her waist, supporting her when she would have fallen, but she slapped them away again. She couldn't think straight. Exhaustion dragged her down like an ocean's undertow, but she fought it. Luna needed her.

Ethan frowned. "There is a more-than-decent chance you have some kind of meningitis. Exposing yourself to Luna could be extremely dangerous for her. You have to stay away for now. She's okay. I'm letting her demolish my stash of Oreos with her formula."

Oreos? Juliet never let Luna have those. Not that they ever had them—cookies were now a luxury item.

Unable to stand, even with Ethan's support, Juliet crumpled to the ground. When the room started spinning, she closed her eyes. Dear Lord, she'd never felt like this before. What was this horrible disease?

"Am I going to die?" She'd heard of meningitis, but she didn't know the details. Was it fatal?

The man crouched, effortlessly scooping her up. "It's not fatal," he said bracingly. "Not unless there's some pre-existing condition. You don't have one, do you?"

She shook her head, but immediately regretted it. The room spun, the shadows in the corners seeming to leap forward to claim her. She passed out in the landlord's arms.

CHAPTER SIX

Eighteen harrowing hours had passed since he'd brought his unexpected guests upstairs. Ethan was sleep deprived, but he was getting by. He sometimes lost sleep when working on a big case, so it wasn't a new experience for him—which was fortunate for Luna and her mom. The pair had kept him extremely busy last night.

His smallest guest had seemed to enjoy playing in the makeshift crib he'd created from his plastic laundry basket and some blankets. But after he'd made the mistake of pushing her around in it, she'd treated it like a toy and insisted on getting rides until she finally passed out around ten.

He'd settled the little girl down to sleep in his empty guest room, placing her in the laundry basket bed. The other room that doubled as his den-slash-office wasn't nearly babyproofed enough.

Ethan tried to catch some zees on his couch. That way, he'd be halfway between his guest room and his bedroom and available to both his female guests, even in sleep.

But that hadn't worked well at all.

Luna, unused to her new surroundings, had woken multiple times crying for her mother. When only Ethan appeared, she'd been damn near inconsolable. She'd sobbed her little heart out before passing out in his arms. Meanwhile, Julietta tossed and turned, feverish for hours. Her temperature had spiked twice, scaring the crap out of him.

Ethan had sponged her down with ice water both times until she'd settled into a death-like sleep somewhere around dawn. He'd crashed right after, but Luna had woken early. The sensation of being watched had roused him. Luna had been standing beside him, holding a sad little doll that had seen better days. She studied him, the assessment in her expression seeming to be far beyond her years.

"Hi," he'd said, sleep making his voice gruff.

Scowling, she'd poked him in the eye before saying 'bottle' in an imperious voice. After that, he'd been off and running, scrambling to keep up with their demands.

Ethan prided himself on being a quick study, but this was a challenge unlike any he'd faced before.

After he'd learned how to fix the milk from the powder canister, he'd been pathetically grateful when Luna had practically inhaled it and passed out again. He'd changed her while she snuffled and snored delicately. After checking on Julietta one last time, he'd showered and threw himself into housework, determined to get as much done on the apartment as he could while they were trapped by the snowstorm.

Since moving in, Ethan had made a little headway with the boxes, stacking the empty ones near the front door so he'd remember to take them to the recycling bin the next time he went out. When the toddler woke, he turned the pile of empty boxes into a jungle fort. He'd let her demolish them until she fell down too hard and started to cry. At a loss for how to make her stop, he decided to fix hotcakes, putting on a show that had impressed his overnight female guests for years.

Ethan flipped the hotcake with a flourish. He turned, disappointed when his audience of one didn't react.

"C'mon, kid, that was a great one. It almost touched the ceiling," he exaggerated.

Luna didn't look up from her milk. She continued to suck it from a straw, her little brow creased in concentration.

Ethan tried again. Luna did watch this time, but there was no noticeable reaction to his acrobatic culinary efforts.

"All right then," he grumbled good-naturedly, rolling his shoulders. He was too tired to put much more into the display in any case.

Luna simply sniffed, then kept drinking her milk. But at least she nibbled on the pieces of pancake and syrup he prepared, so he chalked it up as a victory.

At least the cabinets were in place before my guests arrived. Of all the rooms in the apartment, the kitchen was the closest to being finished —almost. He was still waiting on the new copper pans he'd ordered to replace his beat-up Teflon ones. They would hang from the wire rack over the bar-slash-island that was the centerpiece of the open kitchen space situated two steps above his sunken lounge and TV area.

He surveyed the room with a critical eye, resigned to the lack of progress.

If only I could get the new flooring down. That would mark the end of the major renovations. The remaining stuff was purely cosmetic— painting and other finishing touches. But laying down the hardwood with Luna around might prove impossible—unless he could try to make a game of it.

Optimistically, Ethan laid out some of the boards along each wall, stacking them at the edges of the room as quietly as possible while Luna finished lunch. Then he went to check on Julietta. She was awake, but she didn't react when he entered the room with a meal tray. The woman sat on his bed. She was wrapped in a blanket, staring blankly at the flatscreen. It was off.

"I don't have a television," she said as he set the tray over her lap. The confusion in her voice was concerning.

"Um, no you don't. This one's mine. You remember where you are, right?"

Fathomless dark eyes stared blankly before the light of recognition dawned. Her lips parted, fear flitting across her features for a second before she got control over herself. Then her expression blanked.

"Luna is fine. She's still eating. You should, too." He gestured to the stack of pancakes.

He watched her struggle with that, a fine line appearing between her brows. "I told you her name?" she rasped.

"Uh, yeah. I know yours now, too. It's Julietta. Am I saying that right?"

"No!" There was tightness in her voice, and she tried to sit up but collapsed back wearily. "It's Jul—Julie."

"*Oh,*" he said. "Okay." Something about that didn't smell right, but he wasn't going to argue with the woman about her name.

She tried the fork again, eating in bites smaller than Luna.

"We should leave as soon as I finish," she continued in a raspy voice. "I need to get back to work."

He bit his tongue to keep from answering. The girl could barely lift the fork.

"Err...I think you should finish this plate, then we'll talk about what to do," he hedged, running his eyes over her as she struggled to cut the second pancake. Should he do it for her or would that be a step too far?

"Here, let me," he said decisively. He took the knife and fork, cutting the rounds swiftly before she could react.

The poor thing was as weak as a kitten. *A really hot kitten.* Even unwashed with stringy hair and no makeup, his houseguest was disconcertingly attractive. Julietta, or Julie as she insisted on being called, checked all his boxes and then some.

Her skin was a light cocoa color with a complexion so rich it seemed to radiate like honey in sunlight despite her illness. With dark eyes and luscious lips, she reminded him of those Mexican soap stars he pretended not to watch at the gym's televisions—the ones with long dark hair and legs for days.

Not to mention a killer rack. Okay, he had to stop that. This was someone in need. He was lending a helping hand for a brief time. Once Julie was back on her feet, he would be able to wash his hands of her and Luna with a clear conscience. The last thing he needed was to get involved with a single mom. Plus, there was something a little off about her...

Ethan couldn't put his finger on what it was that bothered him. Maybe it was living out of a suitcase or the lack of calls and texts on the beat-up secondhand cell phone he'd found. He'd taken the liberty of looking through the contacts last night in an effort to notify her friends and family. The only people in her address list were the staff at Tully's and a local two-star daycare. No one else.

He told himself he was being too suspicious. It was one of the hazards of the job. Julie was new in town. Not everyone had family.

She'd make friends soon enough. No doubt having a kid put a damper on her social life.

Julie continued lifting the fork as if it weighed a ton. "Is it still snowing?"

Damn, it hurt to hear her speak. Her throat must feel like raw meat.

"Yes," he confirmed. "Tully's is closed for the duration of the storm. None of their business numbers are picking up, but even if it were open, you still need a few more days to rebuild your strength. The plows aren't scheduled for this neighborhood today."

Half the city was shut down. The blizzard had hit them hard. The news was filled with dire proclamations of the blizzard of the century, the way they always did up until the next storm hit. But travel advisories were in effect for the greater metro area. Ethan suspected he wouldn't be able to move his car until the plows cleared the impassable snowbanks in the surrounding streets.

He tossed the little burner phone on the bed. "In case you need to call anyone."

Julie snatched up the phone, pressing it to her chest. Deciding to give her a few minutes of privacy, he went to check on Luna. The little one was still occupied with her food, so he ran to the linen closet in the hall, pulling out clean sheets for his bed.

Julie had called someone in the intervening period. She looked up guiltily as he entered the room, pulling the phone closer to her face. Pretending not to notice, he bustled around, putting the sheets on the chair before pulling out some of his clothes for later. He'd wash up in the guest room when he got the chance.

Julie's hushed tones were hard to pick up, but it was obvious she had called her boss. A minute later, she hung up and called a woman, touching base with her babysitter. Not her boyfriend or a family member... Didn't she have anyone to help her? Was there no one she could count on?

Leave it alone, Ethan. This wasn't his problem. All he was obligated to do was get them up and running again.

Julie hung up the phone, looking despondent.

Don't ask. Don't ask. You don't need to get more involved... Ethan cleared his throat. "Is everything okay?

"Oh, I suppose." She grimaced. "You were right. I'm not missing work because there is no work. Tully's is closed until further notice. Old Tully is in the hospital with whatever I had. The rest of the staff is in and out. No one is going out in this weather. The bartender, Mike, told me to check back in a few days."

"Sorry," he replied. It had been a long time since he'd depended on hourly wages. His paycheck from Uncle Sam wasn't anything to write home about, but it was steady and came with decent benefits.

"Um, thank you for everything you've done." She hesitated, clearing her throat, touching it as if it hurt.

"But?" He knew there was one.

"I should go back downstairs now. You don't need us in your way. Luna is too much to handle on your own. She gets in everything." Blushing, she looked down at her soiled clothes. "Besides, I need a shower."

He raised an eyebrow. "Do you think you can stand long enough for that?"

Ethan doubted it.

"Of course." The faux bravado lasted about as long as it took her to push the tray away and stand. She swayed on her feet.

"Here," he said, helping her to the chair instead. "Since you're up, I can change the sheets fast, but you should rest after that. And don't worry about Luna. We're becoming friends," he said, suddenly determined to prove her wrong.

Yes, the toddler had been a handful, but compared to some of his friend's children, she was a relatively easy kid. Granted, last night had been crazy, but that was understandable under the circumstance. With a little prep work, they'd get through this blizzard fine. He simply had to lay down some ground rules.

Julie worried her lip. He closed his eyes briefly and turned away, surprised at the rush of heat. The woman was next to an invalid for Pete's sake. The fact she could do this to him was a testament to her pulling power. *Crap.* He was going to have to tread carefully for the next couple of days.

Ethan finished changing the sheets, gesturing for the woman to stand. He threw the clean top sheet over her before guiding her to the bed, carefully avoiding contact with her skin.

"So I won't have to wash my hands before touching Luna," he explained, well aware he was going to wash them regardless. Donovan had been clear on that point. He would wash every time he moved between them.

Julie nodded. With a soft goodbye, he left the room, telling himself it was because the toddler had been on her own long enough.

He closed the door, shaking his head at his behavior. The reaction not to touch Julie had been instinctive, but he didn't dwell on it. If there was anything he'd learned on the job, it was that little white lies made the world go round.

CHAPTER SEVEN

Juliet dragged herself to the window, kneeling on the leather chair as she tried to measure the height of the snowbanks on the street below. With a sinking feeling, she realized the snow was almost level with the post office mailbox across the street. The distance from the door of the building to the street looked so short, but, with snow that deep, it would have taken a snowmobile to cross it. Not that she had one…anymore.

How long would the street be impassible? According to Ethan, more snow was forecast for this evening. It might last the whole night, and the snowplows were nowhere in sight.

She pulled the clammy sheet tighter around her shoulders. *Driving would be impossible, too,* she thought, then snorted lightly. Juliet didn't even have a car. She hadn't driven anywhere since she left Mexico.

Grimacing, she tried to eat. How badly she had underestimated and misjudged everything shook her. Life in the United States was so much harder than anticipated. The prices of needed items had been a huge shock. Actually, scratch that. The prices were nothing compared to what she used to spend on clothes and shoes as a teen. In the old days, she would drop more on a weekend shopping trip than she'd earned in the last six months here.

By comparison, a box of diapers was cheap—but then household necessities had always been bought by the housekeepers her family employed. Juliet had never learned the economy of scale.

Everything was different now. Leaving had been a spur-of-the-moment decision. Her fight-or-flight instincts had kicked in, and she'd flown. There had been no time to think, let alone plan. She'd grabbed the necessities she and Luna needed, pretending they were going shopping.

Juliet had driven to the local mall, but only to use her bank cards to withdraw all the cash she could. Then she dumped the lot in the trash. They would be too easy to trace. She'd held onto her ID a little longer, hoping to use the picture to create another identification. The best she'd been able to do was remove a few extra letters from her first name. But, in any case, the Mexican identification was useless the moment she crossed the border. Without a forged visa to use with them, it did her no good in the United States.

Without proper documentation, she'd been forced to do whatever work she could find. It hadn't been easy with Luna, but Juliet was smart and willing to work harder than the next guy. Being paid under the table meant earning slave wages. It had been terrifying getting that first wad of crumpled bills and realizing how little it was. If she hadn't pawned her jewelry, she wouldn't have been able to pay for that first illegal sublet in Texas.

The door opening shook her out of her reverie. Blinking, she slid down the seat to see her landlord.

His broad shoulders almost filled the doorway. He was carrying a tray with a sandwich and a bowl of soup. When he saw she was awake, he grinned broadly, making her freeze. He was shockingly beautiful when he smiled.

"Hey," he said. "I brought you lunch, but Luna finally went down for a nap. I thought you might like to take a shower while I can help."

Eyes widening, she could feel her face heat. "Um…"

His lips parted. "I mean…while I can be on hand in case you need help. I'm not sure you can stand the whole time. You're still very weak."

"I'm sure I can. I don't need help," she replied. With ill-judged bravado, she stood and took a few steps.

The room spun. Ethan's arm shot out to support her. He helped her to the side of the bed, easily balancing the heavy-looking wood tray in his other hand.

"Maybe I'll sit in the shower," she amended, grateful he did not appear to be one of those men who said, '*I told you so*'.

"Why don't I draw you a bath instead?" he offered. "I have a brand-spanking new whirlpool tub I haven't used yet."

He hadn't? How long had he been living here? "Don't you want to be the one to break it in?"

His expression blanked. Clearing his throat, he shook his head. "No worries. You can do that for me. I'll go get the water started."

He crossed the room, disappearing into the bathroom. The water began to run and he came back, taking her arm to guide her into the marble-tiled room. The European-style bathroom had a separate toilet and sink behind another door off to one side. She hadn't gone much beyond it because she couldn't figure out the space-age lighting panel.

Ethan pressed a few buttons, and overhead lights flooded the room. The polished tiles were done in swirling light brown tones flecked with gold. The accents were a rich caramel. Compared to her recent accommodations, it was glamorous, but, unlike her parent's home, it managed to be warm as well as luxurious.

Ethan fussed with the tub controls, turning the water tap off. "You don't want to boil, particularly since you keep running a temperature."

Tossing a few towels on a bench next to the tub, he turned to face her. "Do you need help undressing?"

His delivery was matter of fact. He didn't seem the least bit embarrassed, but Juliet flushed wildly.

"I can manage if I sit down," she said weakly.

Ethan maneuvered her to a small bench next to the tub before hesitating. "I was going to talk to you about the studio you've been using..."

Panic flitted across her expression, and he rushed to hold up his hands. "I don't mean you have to move out. Not yet. But without speaking to the other owners, I think we might be able to work something out for a longer stay—that is, if I can get in there and do some of the upgrades we have planned. If I can finish them quickly, you can sublet for a few more months, at least until we turn the rentals over to the management company."

Oh. Of course he and his partners didn't want to be bothered with finding tenants or doing day-to-day repairs. After the renovation was done, a management company would takeover. Mason had mentioned this. She'd forgotten.

"That's so kind of you…" Juliet stared at the floor. "I'm afraid I don't have any other place to go just yet."

He gave her a slightly exasperated smile. "I don't expect you to apartment hunt in a blizzard. You can stay here during the work. My guest room is almost ready. I have some furniture—Luna is small and doesn't need much, but I was going to go out and pick up a real bed for the guest room as soon as the streets are drivable."

She fiddled with the grubby T-shirt, her chin tight. "I can't impose any more than I already have."

"You've been no trouble. Well, except for scaring the crap out of me when you were out of your mind with fever," he added, softening the words with a smile. "Other than that, you've been no bother. I've barely heard a peep from you."

"I took your bed." She winced, twisting the hem of the shirt.

"The pull-out couch isn't that bad. Believe me, I've slept in worse places. In my line of work, it's a hazard…"

She frowned, wondering what he did for a living. Investing in this place would have cost him a small fortune. Although, for some reason, he didn't strike her as a man who would be content working in an office.

"I'm making some serious headway on my paperwork thanks to the blizzard," he elaborated, immediately contradicting her.

So he does have a white-collar job.

Now she was picturing him in a suit, maybe at a law firm. Guilt and frustration swamped, fighting for supremacy.

Ethan bent at the waist to test the water temperature in the tub, swirling it around with a long-fingered hand. He straightened. "Even if the office is open, I can take Friday off. Barring any hidden problems, the studio is small enough for me to handle the renovations on my own. It should take a few days at the most. You and Luna can hole up here until it's habitable again."

Her lips parted. After a moment's hesitation, she finally said, "Thank you. I accept, but I still want to pay rent."

Juliet tried to sound grateful, but the words came out of her mouth with a jagged edge, as if they had been ripped from her core. She hated depending on others, and it showed.

Ethan's mouth pulled down. "I think you should be saving for a deposit on a new place."

He braced himself, as if waiting for the inevitable plea to stay in the studio at the old rent after renovations, but she kept her lips firmly shut. Juliet wasn't in a position to let pride govern her behavior. She owed Luna that much...but she had never begged for anything in her life. Pride was all she had left.

Her host stared for a moment before nodding. "You're in luck. I finished redoing the bathroom a few days ago—it has a steam shower in addition to the whirlpool bath."

He pressed a button next to the water tap, and the water in tub began to bubble and swirl.

"It works!" Ethan grinned unexpectedly. The expression warmed his face, transfiguring it from merely attractive to dazzling. Confused at her reaction, she gaped, blinking stupidly.

"Wasn't it supposed to?" she asked when he continued to watch her expectantly. Her fuzzy mind wasn't connecting the dots fast enough. That and being this close to someone so physically attractive was tying her tongue in knots.

"Yes, but I did the work myself, so there was still room for doubt," he answered, self-deprecation making him impossibly more handsome.

He gestured to the door. "There's even some heat lamps for after. I'll hit the switch on my way out."

"Thank you," she said, wondering how many times she would tell him that before this was over.

Not trusting herself to stop staring, she kept her eyes downcast, waiting until the door closed behind him before starting to undress.

CHAPTER EIGHT

Ethan was almost sorry Luna had fallen asleep. Taking care of her would have kept his mind off what was going on in the bathroom. X-rated images flashed through his mind—caramel-colored limbs with water streaming over them…

He coughed, shifting around his sudden arousal. *Damn. Right when I need a cold shower, the bathroom is busy.*

Determined to get his mind out of the gutter, he flipped through the notes from his newest case file. It was ironic he should have to be dealing with the Komarov clan again.

Despite working in the white-collar division, Ethan had been aware of the Russian crime family since he moved to Boston. He'd made a study of the local syndicates, expecting one of his cases would involve them sooner or later. Only his first brush with the family had come from a more personal avenue…

His partner Jason's wife was a wealthy hotel heiress. It was through her that Ethan had ended up rubbing shoulders with a slew of billionaires. Most were bachelors, or at least they had been when he'd met them. One, Calen MacLachlan, had met Maia, a girl on the run from the Komarov crew. He'd ended up marrying her, but Timur Komarov had still gone after her, determined to silence her for the crime she'd witnessed him committing. In the end, Maia had been okay. Her personal safety had been guaranteed by Anton Komarov himself, or so Calen had been assured by an intermediary.

Ethan thumbed the card with the scrawled note, promising Maia would never be bothered again. He was almost sure it had been written by Viktor, the six-and-a half-foot bodyguard who had been charged with keeping Timur in line.

Now that the Komarov's heir was rusticating in eastern Europe, Viktor's profile had been substantially raised. Rumor had it he had been handed a hell of a lot of responsibility in the last year, which surprised most of Ethan's coworkers. They had only ever seen him in pictures—a giant bull of a man with massive hands who could choke the life out of the Hulk. Most people dismissed someone that big as stupid. But Ethan had met the man in the flesh in the aftermath of the Timur debacle, and he'd soon realized that Viktor's size and silence was an effective mask for a razor-sharp mind.

That one could take over the Komarovs if he put his mind to it... But if Ethan was right, the deceptively threatening man also had an equally well-honed conscience. He lifted the note his office had anonymously received last week, addressed to him and Jason.

9, the Lorano, Friday the 20th, midnight.

After a little legwork, Jason had discovered the *Lorano* was a boat out of Croatia. It was due at the docks week after next. It wasn't a known smuggling vessel, but that meant nothing. What or why someone wanted them to take a look was a mystery.

It could be nine alligators or nine weapons of mass destruction. He snorted. Jason had said it was more likely nine boxes of Cubans or something innocuous. His partner couldn't credit that they might get actionable intel from an anonymous tip.

Ethan wasn't convinced. His eyes narrowed on the peculiar slant on the *L* of the second note. The writing didn't look the same, but the office handwriting expert had agreed with his assessment. A concerted effort had been made to disguise the writing, but the emphasis on both notes was similar. Not enough for a definitive answer, however.

Jason had laughed out loud when Ethan had suggested the new note came from Viktor, but his partner trusted Ethan's hunches enough to agree to investigate the possibility regardless.

Ethan dived back into his files, determined to find a connection. They needed a viable lead to convince the upper brass to let them proceed. Thirty minutes later, he raised his head, belatedly wondering how Julie was faring. He'd expected her to call out to him if she needed help after her bath, but there had been nothing.

He went to the bathroom door to listen. No splashing sounds. No sound at all. *Crap.* He knocked. "You didn't fall asleep in there, did you?"

There was no answer. He knocked louder, but there was still no response.

Ah, hell.

Ethan cracked open the door, then raised his voice. "Are you all right in there?"

He strained his ear. She hadn't even shifted the water in response. *It's your apartment, and she might have fallen asleep in the tub.* Ethan had every right to enter and check on her.

It was harder than he would have imagined to push the door open. *Too many mandatory sensitivity-training seminars...*

The pearlescent tiles were a little shinier than usual, and the mirror was fogged. Julie lay in the tub, her head resting on the far wall.

"Hey," he said loudly, concerned when she didn't move.

Sighing, Julie shifted, sliding a few inches lower in the water. Cursing under his breath, he stepped forward. He didn't own any fancy bubble bath or those things that made the water change color. There was nothing to prevent him from seeing Julie in all her glory, the only thing between her naked body and him was a few inches of soapy water.

Moving fast, Ethan grabbed the nearest towel, scooping the woman out of the tub with one hand while simultaneously tossing the towel between them.

Her eyes flew open as he set her on her feet, her gloriously naked body inadvertently pressed against his chest. She blinked, still dazed, but her focus sharpened as she woke and realized where she was.

"You fell asleep," he informed her tersely, his tone sharper than he'd intended.

Julie hiked the towel up, covering herself up to the neck. It was far too late for that, however. He'd already seen everything, and damn if it wasn't going to take him a long time to forget it.

He cleared his throat, setting her gently on the bench.

The color on her cheeks deepened to a dusky rose. "I'm sorry," she said, staring bemusedly, her eyes wide and fixed on his face.

Ethan's pulse throbbed. He could feel the heat between them like a tangible thing. It thickened the air. He was suddenly tense, actively fighting his own impulse to grab her and carry her to the bedroom.

He cleared his throat. "I'll let you get dressed now." He rushed out of the room as if his pants were on fire.

&

The following morning, Juliet sat up groggily, shaking her head to clear the fog from her brain. As awareness returned, so did her embarrassment from the night before.

Heat flooded her cheeks as she recalled the moment when she realized she was in Ethan's arms with only a cotton towel to shield her nudity. And that wasn't the worst part. No, that had been her response. For a brief moment, she'd been ready to drop the cloth and press against him. Thank goodness, she'd been too slow and lethargic to do anything about her sudden case of rampant lust.

She was going to have to be incredibly careful. Ethan was being kind to her and Luna the past few days, but she didn't know him. They had been railroaded into an enforced intimacy by the blizzard and her illness. It was easy to get confused under the circumstances.

Ashamed of her moment of weakness, she decided to try to get dressed. Last night before she passed out a second time, Ethan had mentioned the snowplows might come today. Her boss at Tully's hadn't called her back. She wasn't sure if the bar had reopened or not. If it had, she had to make the effort.

Don't let the plows come until tomorrow. It would be a small reprieve that might enable her to regroup and regain her strength.

Ethan's apartment was warm, much more so than the studio downstairs. Juliet had always kept the thermostat on her apartment low to save on the heating bill, but Ethan's apartment was extremely comfortable. She slipped on a tank top she'd assumed she wouldn't be able to wear until spring. Pairing it with a worn pair of yoga pants, she walked out into the living room with slow, uncertain steps.

Juliet stopped dead in her tracks. Ethan was with Luna in the kitchen, feeding her tiny bites of pancake while humming an old rock tune she recognized but couldn't name.

And I thought I was feeling shaky before. Ethan's back was to her. He was wearing low-slung jeans so worn and form-fitting she could see the outline of his rear end in perfect relief. He was also naked from the waist up.

Ethan turned around when she took another step, even though she was sure she hadn't made a sound. He grinned, grabbing the t-shirt slung over the top of one of the dining chairs.

"Just changing into something I can ruin before I tackle the floors," he said. Ethan threw the shirt over his head, pulling it over a six-pack of abs so defined she could have scrubbed her clothes clean on them.

Ruined? He was a work of art. Her mind flashed back to the one time she had seen Alvaro without a shirt. He'd been attending one of her sister Daniella's many pool parties. She'd been terribly impressed with his flat stomach and slim wiry arms. Compared to Ethan, Alvaro could have been an underweight youth. *This* was what a man should look like.

Ethan cocked his head, no doubt studying her stupefied expression. "Are you okay?"

"I'm fine," she answered, her voice distant. He was wearing a shirt now. Why was she still seeing his abs in her head?

"Do you need to sit?"

"Uh..." Juliet felt lightheaded, but she wasn't sure she could blame it on her illness. Nevertheless, she shuffled to the couch, disconcerted when Ethan hurried to help her.

It would be so much better if he didn't touch her.

"Your English is quite good," Ethan observed, studying her as she tried to affect a casual air. It was difficult with him standing over her. "How long have you been living in the States?"

"Not long."

"Really? I would have guessed years and years. Your grasp of slang and colloquial English is excellent."

She cleared her throat, surprised to still find it a bit painful. "Well,

I did attend school here for a while," she admitted before blanching. Regret was immediate. Telling him anything true was a mistake.

"Where?"

"A school in Florida," she improvised. "It was a brief exchange program."

His smile could melt the snow. "What was it called?"

"Um. Mezo-American Art and Archeology," she said, naming a real course she had taken once upon a time at Harvard.

"I meant the school."

"Oh, uh, it was Florida State." That was an exceptionally large school, wasn't it? Was Julie Alvarez a common-enough name? He wouldn't bother to check, would he?

I knew I should have called myself Maria.

"Can I move into the guest room with Luna today?" she asked hopefully.

He winced. "It may still be too soon. My friend, Donovan—he's a doctor—said it would be a full week before you were well. It might be best to wait another few days. The good news is Luna isn't showing any symptoms. I think it's safe enough for you two to be in the same room as long as you don't touch her."

"*Oh.*" She couldn't touch the baby? Her chest felt hollow. It made sense, but she couldn't help feeling suddenly unmoored. Everything she had done, she'd done for Luna. Juliet cast her eyes down, not wanting him to see her disappointment. His touch startled her. Ethan put a finger under her chin, nudging her a tiny bit so she would meet his eyes.

"It won't be for long. I promise." He straightened. "Luna is half-asleep, so I'm going to try to put her down for another quick nap. Don't worry about anything this morning except breakfast."

Nodding weakly, she watched him swing Luna up in his broad muscled arms. The little girl babbled and yawned. He disappeared down the hallway with her, the tight denim doing magical things to his backside.

Despite her despondency, she couldn't help but notice...

It was a hell of a view.

CHAPTER NINE

Most of the day passed in a blur. Juliet managed to eat breakfast, but she was so tired afterward she had to lie down again. She made it to Ethan's bedroom on her own, too tired to feel guilty she was still taking his space. The rest of the day was made up of snatches of consciousness, with Ethan poking his head in to update her and ask the occasional question. Did Luna have any allergies? Would she eat blueberries? Was he supposed to try taking her to the toilet or should he stick to the diapers?

She answered the questions as best she could, repeating what the doctor at the free clinic had told her about Luna's diet. Two more days passed in a similar fashion. She got stronger, but she was still a far cry from healthy. The snowplows came, but it made little difference because the snow kept falling.

On the third morning, Ethan knocked, coming into the bedroom as she sat up.

"Julietta?"

Her eyes widened as she took in his appearance. He wasn't dressed for renovation work. Instead, he was wearing grey slacks paired with a dark blue shirt that set off the color of his eyes. But she couldn't process how handsome he looked. Her attention was fixed on the shiny gold badge hanging around his neck.

Ethan was a police officer. Tendrils of icy cold shot down her spine, pooling in her gut.

"It's Julie," she reminded in an absent whisper, her eyes never leaving the shining shield.

"Sorry. Morning, Julie," he apologized, hesitating before coming inside.

If he'd been looking at her, he would have instantly read her shock and dismay, but he was scanning an open file folder in his hands. "I was going to keep working on your studio today, but I got called in unexpectedly—a surprise raid. I'm going to run Luna over to her sitter again. Martha said she didn't mind keeping her until this evening when I can pick her up again on my way home from work."

Juliet didn't reply. Her tongue seemed fixed, stuck to the roof of her mouth. Eventually, the silence grew awkward.

"Is everything okay?" he asked, pinning her down with those deep blue eyes.

"I need to call the sitter myself. I, uh, usually clean her place to get a discount. Also, I should text work again. I'm feeling much better. I need to pick up a shift tonight if I can," she said hoarsely.

"Absolutely not." Ethan scowled. "It's too soon. Your shift manager is down with the same illness by the way. The big boss—Max something?—he is still thinking about reopening. If he does, though, it will be with a skeleton crew. There's more snow forecasted tonight, but not as much as the last few. Only the die-hard alcoholics will be at Tully's if they open."

"That's half of our clientele," she protested weakly.

He laughed before glancing at his watch. "Call your boss if you feel you have to, but tell him you need another couple of days."

"I need to work, Ethan," she said. His name felt strange on her lips. For so long, she'd thought of him as her own personal bogeyman—the Landlord with a capital L.

"And you will. But you need to rest a little longer." After he walked over to the bedside table, he knelt to open one of the drawers. He pulled out a lockbox with a push-button pad on the top.

"Excuse me," he said, setting it on the dresser to open it, taking care to cover it with his bulk so she couldn't see the combination.

When he turned around again, he was slipping a massive grey gun into a shoulder holster she hadn't even noticed him wearing.

Juliet staggered to the bed. Blackness swamped her vision as she let herself fall on the plush mattress.

Ethan knelt in front of her before she could blink. His smile was wry. "I knew it was too soon for you to be out of bed. The doctor said it would be at least a week before you began to recover. You need more time."

The gun was inches away from her thigh now. Helpless to stop herself, she let out a strangled whimper. His face soft in sympathy, Ethan leaned toward her, reaching out to put his hand on her forehead.

Involuntarily, she reared back. His face cleared in understanding. "Is my service piece bothering you?"

His hand covered the gun, and he shifted before rising to stand. "I apologize, but it's part of the job."

"O-okay." Blinking, she tried to appear calm, although she was screaming inside. Swallowing, she gestured at the gun and badge. "When you said the storm gave you a chance to catch up on your case-load, I thought you meant regular paperwork like an accountant or lawyer."

He was one of the landlords of the building. To her, that had meant he was a businessman, someone in the finance industry. That would have explained how he could afford to pay for his share. But he was wearing a badge... Cops didn't make much money, did they?

"A *lawyer?*" Ethan's face curdled. "Please, never say that word to me."

The expression on her face froze. "You don't like lawyers?"

"I like them fine—as long as they stay out of my cases. No, I come from a long line of men who are either in law enforcement or the military. My dad was career army, but I tried it and it wasn't for me. I have to get to work, but don't worry about my service piece."

He gestured to the weapon at his side. "Unless it's on me, it stays in that box. That gun safe would be impossible for Luna to open. My gun will be locked up tight whenever you two are here unless I'm coming from or going to work. It's only going to be for a few days."

Juliet took a deep breath, then gave him a bracing smile. "Yes, of course. And thank you for considering my feelings. I will feel a lot better if I know your weapon is locked up," she said, trying to excuse her reaction as a normal apprehension for guns.

His grin was dazzling. Thankfully, it was gone before it could do any lasting damage. "Good. I have to run or I'm going to be late. You need to get your strength back so you can take care of Luna. I've only had her for a few days, and I can barely keep up. And don't rush to be up and around. You still have some healing to do."

"I know," she acknowledged, waving.

Juliet waited until he was gone to burst into tears. *It's okay, it's okay. You didn't tell him your real name.*

Ethan never needed to know she was a wanted woman.

"Oh no," Juliet breathed aloud in consternation, turning her head to examine the studio apartment she called home.

The floor was in shreds, jagged pieces of linoleum sticking straight up in the air. The effort was only half-done. Most of it needed to be pulled up.

When Ethan had said he was starting the renovation on her studio yesterday, she thought he meant slapping on a few coats of paint and perhaps refinishing the cabinets. She'd come down the steps, stopping at every landing to rest for a few minutes, to see if there was a way to live down here while he did the work.

It was impossible now. She had no idea he'd been planning to rip up the entire floor. Despondent, she dragged herself upstairs. What was she going to do? This was her worst nightmare.

No, it isn't. There's a far worse one.

A wave of panic threatened to knock her to her knees. *Breathe. You can get through this*, she told herself. But she couldn't make herself believe the lie.

Living with a cop, even for a few days, was too much for her. If he found out who she really was—that she had an arrest warrant issued for her in her native country of Mexico—he'd turn her over to the authorities. He wouldn't have a choice. Cops swore oaths to uphold the law.

Calm down. Ethan didn't know anything about her. She'd left all traces of her old identity behind when she escaped across the border. Ethan only knew her as Julie, the poor waitress who'd rented a crappy basement apartment in his new investment.

Except he knows your real name. Juliet dug her fingernails into the soft part of her palms. That didn't matter, or it wouldn't soon. Once she was better, she was going to do as Ethan had asked—she was going to find a new place to live. He'd forget about her as soon as she moved out. She just had to get through the next few days without tipping him off.

You can do that, she thought. If he got curious about her, she had a backstory ready. Juliet knew it by heart. She should—she'd practiced it often enough.

And, so far, I've hardly used it at all. She snorted aloud as she remembered how hard she worked on her elaborately crafted history. The reality was very few people had asked about her background. All they cared about—sometimes—was the phony green card that had cost her over a thousand dollars. In the circles Juliet now found herself in, people were more concerned with what she could do for them than where she came from.

Except Ethan was a cop. He was naturally curious. And in her weakened state, she hadn't been as careful as she normally was. She'd told him part of the truth before she could catch herself—that she'd studied in the states and her real name.

Just stop there. Don't volunteer anything else. Ethan didn't need to know her time here had been for law school or that she came from a moneyed background.

Why did Ethan have to be so kind? In all her time in Boston, she hadn't met anyone like him. Most people wouldn't cross the street to spit on her here. Well, some of the men would do that and more if she let them. But she had no intention of letting anyone get close to her.

However, Ethan was making that difficult. He kept surprising her over and over again. Most men wouldn't help a sick woman, especially not when they came with a toddler in tow. But this one had opened his home to her. True, he hadn't seemed thrilled in the beginning. She had a vague recollection of him swearing up a storm every other minute during her fever.

But as soon as she was out of danger, he'd calmed down and had acted like a gracious host. It wouldn't have been out of bounds to call him downright enthusiastic, charming even. And he was so sweet to Luna...

A vision of him playing with the toddler, telling her a nonsense story about a bear named Jason and his best friend, a skunk named Liam, nearly made Juliet tear up. He'd fed the little girl, carried her, and soothed her when she cried. And he never complained. Not even when Luna spilled juice all over the new couch.

You're forgetting the most pertinent detail. Ethan was a cop. The thought kept sliding around her fuzzy mind as if she were trying to block it out and forget. But that was the last thing she could do.

Sighing, she let herself back into the top-floor apartment, examining the front rooms fully for the first time. The clear light of winter lit the room in a pale gold. A green-and-black marble countertop sparkled from the kitchen island in front of a huge two-door refrigerator. Her stomach rumbled. That had to be a sign of recovery. During the first few days of her illness, she couldn't even think about food.

Juliet opened the door to reveal well-stocked shelves. If he hadn't been called into a raid, Ethan would have made her breakfast alongside his. Ravenous, she took a piece of cheese from a drawer, popping it in her mouth. It wasn't enough, but she wasn't up to cooking yet.

How long had it been since she'd been able to do nothing like this? For the better part of this year, she'd been moving at a breakneck pace, scrambling to do whatever she needed to do to keep herself and Luna housed and fed.

After tea and toast, she took stock of her surroundings. Though it still needed a lot of work, the apartment was going to be beautiful when it was finished. With two large bedrooms and another spare room being used as an office, it was the biggest apartment she'd set foot in since leaving Mexico. The sunken living room opened onto the kitchen with the main bedroom she was using with its big en-suite bathroom. There was even a gas fireplace in the bedroom instead of a television for snowy winter nights. The widescreen TV had a place of honor in the living room.

Determined to make herself useful, Juliet started cleaning. Ethan wasn't a messy man, but there was a lot scattered around—tools and materials he was using in the ongoing renovation of this place and possibly hers. Most of it had been placed high enough up to stay out of Luna's reach, but the little girl was a bit of an acrobat in addition to being an escape artist. With a little effort, she might reach some of those tools and sharp-looking pieces of flooring.

Carefully, she organized the objects on high shelves, leaving them out in the open where Ethan could still easily find them. Then she went into his office. His papers were all over the desk. Not wanting to disrupt his work, she pushed the haphazard piles into neat stacks.

An ornate paperweight was carelessly tossed between piles. Picking it up, she read the letters engraved on it—FBI Medal for Meritorious Achievement. It was followed by Ethan's name. *Santo cielo.* He wasn't a normal police officer. Ethan was an FBI agent.

Sick to her stomach, Juliet sat down in the leather office chair behind the desk. Was this better or worse than being a run-of-the-mill cop?

Worse, definitely worse.

Though she had spent time in Boston during her school days, she didn't know much about the FBI in this country. She had been studying corporate and international law. Television shows and movies glorified cops and FBI agents, but the newspapers reported on crooked policeman all the time.

It's supposed to be better here, she reminded herself. Though corruption was real, it wasn't institutionalized the way it was back home. In fact, she might be able to find someone who could help her. Someday.

What if she showed Ethan the video?

Stop that. Stop it right there. Despite his kindness, she didn't know anything about the man. She couldn't take the chance he would be on her side. Too much was at stake. Confiding in anyone, especially an FBI agent, was too big a risk.

Exhausted after her small efforts at organizing, she went to the bedroom to rest, but her brain was buzzing and she couldn't settle down to sleep. Today had been too much of a shock.

Dear Lord, what's going to happen tonight?

CHAPTER TEN

"Going home to the little woman?" Jason asked, leaning back in his chair with his hands behind his head.

Ethan dropped the finished stack of reports in his outgoing mail-box. "Bite your tongue."

His partner snorted. "Well, a woman is waiting for you, right? A pretty one if I don't miss my guess."

He scowled. "How do you figure that? Furthermore, why do you care? Aren't you supposed to be a happily married man?"

Jason smirked. "I am. But I know this girl is attractive or you wouldn't be playing the white knight to this extent."

Ethan rolled his shoulders, stretching before tossing his notes into his messenger bag. "Why? Am I incapable of helping someone in need unless they're smoking hot?"

"Oooh. So she's not plain old hot? She's *smoking*. This gets better and better."

Ethan threw his pen at his partner, who caught it neatly. "Of course you would help a mother in need," Jason said generously. "However, I seriously doubt you would move her in with you if she didn't make your downstairs bits stand and take notice..."

"Nice." Ethan sniffed disdainfully. "Except the moving-in part is temporary. She goes right back to the studio apartment once I finish putting down the bamboo flooring. This weekend at the latest."

Jason stood, shutting off his desktop as he rose. "Well, if she lasts a little longer than that, you might think about bringing her to the Caislean for dinner some night. I'm sure a working mom would appreciate a night out at a five-star restaurant. You can even bring the kid. Maggie would enjoy meeting them."

They headed to the elevators. "Trust me, you don't want me to do that," Ethan said. "Women get ideas when you put them around babies. I thought you were determined to keep that gorgeous wife of yours in the honeymoon phase."

Jason shrugged. "I'm not a newlywed anymore. It might be time to start talking about expanding our twosome to three—for starters. I'm determined to field a baseball team by the time Maggie and I are through."

Ethan groaned aloud. "Good God, don't you start with that. I mean it, Jason. First Patrick and now you going full-bore marriage and family. I refuse to be the last man standing."

His partner's snicker was not comforting. *Damn it.* Mason and Donovan needed to move back here ASAP. He was surrounded.

❧

The smell of cooking food permeated the hallway. Instantly starving, Ethan threw open the door, calling out Julie's name in a loud stage whisper. Luna dozed against him, completely tuckered out from the full day of play at her babysitter's. His free hand held his suitcase and a few surprises Jason had pulled out of his trunk in the parking lot after work.

"What is that?" he called, looking for Julie. "It smells great."

The oven buzzer was his only answer. Juggling the toddler, he checked the new oven, pleased the timer had shut off the heating elements. If Julie were taking a nap, then at least she wouldn't have burned down the apartment.

After setting Luna down for a pre-dinner nap, he found the woman sleeping in his bed. She was wearing one of his many FBI T-shirts—and nothing else.

His cock stirred at the sight of her shapely legs. *Whoa. Down, boy.* Now was not the time and this was not the woman for that kind of thing. Moving quietly, he stowed his gun in the lockbox, deciding to transfer it to the bottom drawer of his office desk. Julie would sleep easier if it were farther away from her.

Unfortunately, even when she was out of sight, his hard-on stubbornly stayed where it was. It was as if her image were burned into his brain.

Fuck. The bad weather had to let up soon. Ethan needed to hit a few of his favorite bars, the ones where it was easy to find a quick hookup. Except that wasn't going to happen. The forecast called for frigid temperatures for the next few nights, which would make the roads icy. Only the most desperate of women would be out on the prowl for a little strange this week.

A noise made him glance up. A sleep-tousled Julie stood in the doorway of his office, still in only his t-shirt.

With her drowsy expression and disheveled hair, she looked as if she'd just been fucked. Or at least that was what he imagined she would look like, flushed with deep pink full lips.

Hell, did the woman bite them in her sleep?

Just like that, he was burning again. *She's flushed because she's running a temperature,* he chastised himself.

Awkwardly, Julie waved.

"Hi. Sorry about this." She gestured to the T-shirt. "I was behind on laundry. Since you have a set of machines up here, I took advantage to get caught up. I hope you don't mind."

"Of course not." He glanced down at himself, then sat abruptly in his chair to hide his obvious erection. "Luna's asleep. How are you feeling?"

"Better. I took the clothes you left in the drier and folded them. I was going to put them away in the drawers, but then I decided I should ask for permission first. I left them folded on top of your dresser in the bedroom."

Her blush told him some of his underwear had been included in that load. "That's fine. I don't keep anything sensitive in the drawers."

His extra-large box of condoms was stashed in the bedside table. He didn't know whether she had peeked in there, but he wasn't going to be embarrassed about those. Ethan was young, virile. The sooner his houseguest learned that, the better.

She needed to learn a few other things, too. For example, wearing a man's shirt and nothing else was asking for trouble.

His stare must have made Julie realize that fact. Flushing a deeper red, she excused herself and practically ran to the bedroom. She returned in a few minutes wearing her own clothes.

He met her in the living room. "I see you did a little child-proofing."

"Yes...sorry."

Why was she always apologizing to him?

"Don't be. It was a good idea. Something I should have thought of myself. Did you talk to Luna today? I told her sitter to call you."

"Yes, thank you." She gestured to the stuffed bear he'd dropped on the counter. "Is that yours?" She sounded amused.

He laughed. "It's for Luna from my partner's wife. Maggie—that's Jason's wife—also sent over a few new outfits. They're in the bag on the couch."

Her expression grew tight. "She didn't have to get her anything. Really, you've done too much already."

He walked around the kitchen island to the fridge for a beer. "A few new clothes and toys can't hurt. And trust me, Maggie loves any excuse to shop."

"She's too generous," Julie said, examining the contents of the bag. He'd checked inside—there were onesies and a cute little pajama outfit as well as two dresses with matching winter tights. At the bottom of the bag was another pack of diapers and wipes.

She handled each item, studying it pensively before putting it back in the bag. Ethan cocked his head at her downcast expression. "You don't like taking help, do you?"

A corner of her mouth twisted up. "Am I that easy to read?"

"To me you are."

Her expression grew even more troubled, but he only caught a glimpse before she turned away and busied herself at the oven. "I hope you like casserole—I saw you had plenty of cheese and tuna. If not, I can make another one of the frozen pizzas."

"Whatever it is it smells great. And sorry about the frozen pizzas. I know they can get monotonous. But we could have ordered take-out now that the roads are a bit better. You should be resting."

"It was no trouble. Besides, I feel much better today. As for the pizzas, I like them, but I thought you might appreciate something different. Tuna noodle is Luna's favorite. Well, when she's eating. She's very picky about her food. I also made rolls to go with it."

She gestured to a basket covered with a kitchen towel. He lifted the towel, revealing golden-brown dinner rolls. Not known for his patience, he immediately gobbled one up.

"Holy crap. These are amazing." He grabbed two more.

"Leave room for the main course," she said with a laugh, pulling out the glass baking dish from the oven and peeling back the foil covering. Shell pasta was smothered in bubbling cheddar and Monterey Jack cheese.

His stomach growled aloud. "So, it's basically mac and cheese with tuna? That sounds amazing."

"I also grilled some of your frozen asparagus," she added with a quirk of her lip.

He started to set the table. "Oh, that was something the grocer threw in. I guess I can have some of that, too."

Smiling, she carried the casserole to the table, but by the time she set it down, she was wilting again.

Ethan hurried to pull the chair out for her. "Thank you for making dinner, but I would rather have frozen pizza than have you overextend yourself. You need to regain your strength. Sit and eat."

"I was going to dine later," she said, holding the chair for support. "I might go lie down again."

"No. You're up. Sit," he insisted, rising to guide her to the seat across from his. He ushered her into the chair despite her protests.

"Are you sure you wouldn't prefer to eat alone?"

"I eat alone all the time. I'll be glad for the company."

Even eating with Luna had been kind of nice, but the little girl frequently napped for a few hours after getting home.

Juliet smiled weakly. "I don't want to impose..."

Scooping a heaping helping of noodles on his plate, he sat with a grin. "Don't worry about it. So, Julietta, tell me about yourself."

She dropped her fork. "What? I'm sorry. It's Julie, not Julietta."

Ethan noted her sudden agitation before taking a bite. He swallowed, letting his eyes roll back into his head in ecstasy. "Damn, that's good."

For such a simple dish, it was divine. "Your name—you said it was Julietta when you were sick that first night. You also told me Luna's name."

She ducked her head. "Oh, it's Julie. But I was named after an aunt, Julietta, so I was sometimes called that. I don't use it now. Everyone at the bar calls me Julie."

Ethan served himself a heap of casserole, wondering why she wasn't meeting his eyes. "So Julietta is a family name? It's pretty."

"I prefer Julie." Picking up her fork again, she began to eat.

"Julie it is then." He waved his fork. "Why did you move to Boston?"

"After I finished school in Mexico, I was promised a job by a small law firm here as a paralegal, but the office closed up shortly after I arrived. I had to scramble to find other work."

"And your parents? Where are they?"

Her eyes grew distant. "They're gone. Over a year now."

"I'm sorry." That explained why they hadn't been around to help. "Can I ask how they died?"

She tensed, her grip strangling that fork. "It was a car accident."

He paused to take a sip. "I'm prying, aren't I? I'm sorry. You can tell me to stop."

"It's all right." But it wasn't. She was holding her fork, but she wasn't using it. His stubborn curiosity must have made her lose her appetite. *Do I try to make her feel better or go for broke?*

"What about Luna's father?" he asked, kicking himself for his damnable curiosity.

"Oh...well, he's not in the picture."

Determined to keep talking despite the foot in his mouth, he said, "I figured that part out, but maybe your ex could contribute. Have you tried suing for child support? I know a few people who did that— women I met on the job. It does work."

Her expression firmed. "Child support isn't a possibility. And I don't want anything from my ex. He's not who I thought he was."

Was it pride or fear talking? The way she lived—the two battered suitcases and backpack. It was the hallmark of a woman on the run. Had Luna's father been a bad guy?

He wanted to question her further, but Julie looked so uncomfortable he decided to let it go for the moment. She wasn't a subject in an interrogation room. He could afford to wait, to establish some trust.

Instead of talking, he helped himself to more of the casserole. By the time he was done, half the large platter was empty.

Throughout his meal, Julie watched him with wide eyes. "I guess you were hungry."

"Actually, I grabbed a slice on the way home. But this was too good to pass up."

Julie laughed, picking up one of his untouched asparagus spears with her fork. She bit it, then gave him a coy smile. "I don't know how you stay in shape. If I ate like you, I'd have to be wheeled around in a hand truck."

"So you noticed my fine figure?" He flexed under his shirt, tossing her a flirtatious grin.

Her smile dampened. "I noticed you weren't five hundred pounds, which I would be if I ate like you with any regularity."

Ethan downed the last of his beer.

"I have the right genes, I guess. I inherited a fast metabolism." His daily workouts didn't hurt either.

Julie finished her meal, then rose and began to clean up.

"Let me do that," he said, rising. "You're still weak."

"I'm much better now that I've eaten. Please go enjoy one of your sports shows. This is no trouble."

He took the plate from her. "Not a chance."

"I can do the dishes at least," she insisted.

"That's what I have a dishwasher for." He opened the appliance door, then started loading it.

Julie craned her neck to see inside. "I've never lived in a place with one. How does it work?"

Ethan explained where to load what and how to run the washing cycles. When they were done, she stepped away and started wiping down the counters and wrapping the leftovers up. They worked together with an odd synchronization that felt oddly familiar.

"Would you mind if I kept child-proofing?" she asked afterward. "There are a few more things I meant to store out of reach. I can return everything to its place once the studio is ready."

"All right." Ethan was about to offer to help when he remembered. He checked his watch. "Damn. I forgot the guest room furniture is on its way. The delivery is due any minute."

"There's a furniture store that delivers this late?"

"It's only a little after six."

She glanced at the darkened windows. "Oh, I think I've lost track of time being inside all day. It gets dark so early, and it feels much later."

He agreed with a murmur. "If you don't mind, I'm going to call the delivery company to see how far out they are."

"No problem." After excusing herself, she began to bustle around the background while Ethan made his call.

It was fortuitous timing. The delivery van had just turned onto his street. He went downstairs. Feeling a little bad the elevator was still out, he helped them carry the bedroom end tables inside while the men handled the bed and frame.

By the time they were done hauling everything to the top floor, he needed another beer.

I wonder if Julie could drink one with me, he thought as he tossed fresh sheets onto the bed. If she didn't like beer, he had a few bottles of wine stashed somewhere in the closet. He hadn't been able to get her antibiotics, but the meningitis appeared to be clearing up without them, confirming it had been viral in origin. It also meant she could have a drink with him. If Luna was still asleep, he'd ask.

He went in search of his houseguest, finding her on the stepladder in the hallway in front of the linen closet

"Do you need any help?"

Julie turned to face him with a start. She lost her balance, falling forward. If he hadn't been there to catch her, she would have face-planted on the carpet.

Ethan twisted her in his arms, so she was facing up. Her face was the picture of embarrassment.

"I'm sorry," she said, her arm wrapping around his neck for

support. The move brought them closer until her breasts grazed his chest.

Fuck.

"We have to stop meeting like this," he said before giving into the impulse that had been riding him since he first got a good look at her. He kissed her. *Hard.*

CHAPTER ELEVEN

Juliet felt Ethan's lips on hers. Her response was visceral, immediate, and completely out of her control. If she hadn't been lying in his arms, she would have swooned.

Her hands tightened on his head, and she pulled him closer. *Why does he have to taste so damn good?*

Even at the height of her infatuation with Alvaro, there hadn't been a moment where she'd felt like this—as if her insides were melting into a puddle of liquid silver. More like mercury, something toxic. Pushing at Ethan, she broke the kiss. But she wasn't able to get any farther.

"I can't stand up," she whispered, staring up into his dark eyes. Her legs felt like gelatin.

"Is that a bad thing?" His grin was downright devilish.

"Um…" Fear and heat flooded her body, a potent and completely enervating combination.

Ethan's demeanor changed, the teasing light in his eyes dying. Contrite, he set her on her feet, but when she didn't immediately walk away, he thought better of it and scooped her up. He carried her to the living room and set her on the couch with a sigh before stepping around the coffee table in an obvious effort to put some space between them.

Despite the fact she'd been the one to push him away, she felt rejected.

You're being stupid.

The last thing she needed was to build up a fantasy around this man. He was FBI for saint's sake.

Now he was watching her, but she couldn't tell what he was thinking. Was he regretting kissing her?

Of course he was. She'd acted like he had the plague. Then there was the fact she was living as a guest in his home.

"I shouldn't have done that," he began, his face stiff. "I don't want you to think I'm expecting anything from you. It just happened."

"No," she said, standing with a hand up to stop him. "I—I understand. And you're very..." She held up her hands in an unconscious gesture, mimicking the breadth of his stunning biceps. "But I've never gotten involved with someone in circumstances like these."

"Like I said, I took advantage." Ethan grimaced.

"No. It's not because I'm in your debt...it's more because we are so unequal."

He blinked at the too-fine distinction. "I mean I'm only a waitress," she added lamely.

Her comedown in society had been meteoric, but instead of streaking higher in the heavens, she'd crashed to the ground like a fallen star.

This man was good and kind. She could feel it in her bones. What would he say if he knew what she'd been accused of back home?

"I've dated quite a few waitresses actually, but not one who is a guest in my home," Ethan said, chagrined. "Please forget this happened. I know how to keep my hands to myself. I promise you don't have to worry about this."

Acutely uncomfortable, she twisted her hands together. Tears stung her eyes. She hated crying. It was proof of her frailty. Ever since she'd left home, she'd changed, grown more vulnerable. Every day, she lived in fear of exposure. It had worn down her natural confidence and faith in herself.

Those weren't the reasons she had to resist Ethan. She was reacting to his protectiveness. Juliet wanted to throw herself at him, to find shelter in his strong arms. She knew better than to trust those impulses. The desire to lean on someone, to confess her fears, and to accept help were what had gotten her into this mess in the first place.

Ethan watched her face with an increasingly stricken expression.

"I'm sorry," she said in a low voice. "I'm being silly. You were right. I'm tired."

His Adam's apple bobbed. "Why don't you go lie down?"

"Good idea," she murmured, escaping as fast as she could manage.

⚜

"What did you say?" Juliet gripped the bar so tightly her knuckles hurt.

Mike didn't bother to look at her. He kept washing and stacking glasses as if he hadn't just shattered her entire world.

"I said I kept your job open as long as I could, but I had to hire someone else."

How could he say that? "I only missed one night. You barely reopened!"

"We opened two nights ago," he corrected, his voice hard. "You missed two whole nights. We were swamped. I did what I had to do. And Al did a great job, so I've decided to keep him on and let you go."

They had reopened two nights ago? Why hadn't he texted her?

"You were swamped? You probably had four customers the whole night." The weather had been terrible the night before last. Then she remembered something. "*Al?* Do you mean your best friend Al?"

The chubby guy came in to sponge free beers on Mike's shifts.

"He lost his job, and he needs a new one." Mike shrugged, wiping the counter. "One was available here."

"Except my job wasn't available! I was out sick. Tully himself hired me." The owner had personally picked her. Sure, he'd leered at her at the time, but since he kept his hands to himself during the interview, she'd taken the job and hadn't regretted it. The only people who pawed her here were the customers. Even Mike left her alone. His steady girlfriend would have kneecapped him if he cheated.

Mike glared at her through slitted eyes. "Tully won't be back for a long time. He's old, and that illness took a lot out of him. His son Kevin told me to take care of things here, so that's what I'm doing."

The sinking feeling deepened to a spiral. Kevin, the owner's son, was a busy man. He worked at a bank out of state, or so Tully had said. Kevin hadn't visited once in her time working there. If he did come now, it would be to help his father. He wouldn't care what Mike was doing, not as long as the bar kept running.

"Tully hired me because I bring in the male customers. Al isn't likely to help with that," she pointed out, pressing a hand to her queasy stomach.

Mike flattened his hands on the bar. "I've said what needs to be said. If you don't want me to call INS, I would leave now."

Juliet's head drew back. "I have a green card," she whispered, stung.

"And if I call ICE, are they going to agree?" Mike's face twisted sourly. "Not that it matters these days. You know they just round people up and toss them in cells. It all gets sorted out later."

Forcing herself to breathe slowly, she parted her lips. "I need this job."

He smacked his lips, waving the towel. "You're going to get another one in no time. Wear a low-cut shirt and a push-up bra. Al *needs* this." He walked over to the cash register, opening it and pulling out a wad of cash.

"Take it. It's more than we owe you for last week."

Shivering, Juliet swallowed, blinking rapidly. She reached over and snatched the cash, turning on her heel and throwing open the main doors before she started to cry.

The frigid winter air cooled her burning cheeks. She scrubbed her face with both hands, wiping her tears away before they froze to her skin.

What am I going to do now?

CHAPTER TWELVE

I'm getting closer to the Russians. I can feel it. Ethan waved to the elevator repairman as he jogged up the stairs of his building. It had been a frustrating day at the office but at least he'd gotten out of there in time to meet the repair van.

Ethan had spent the day pitching in, writing reports on the collars from the last raid. He managed to steal an hour for himself, trying to dig up more data to justify a warrant for the *Lorano*.

It hadn't been enough. The boat was due in a little over a week now. His boss, Robert Angel aka the Angel, had let it be known Ethan needed something soon if he wanted a green light for any kind of organized sting. He was running out of time.

I need to pull the crew's background. Maybe he would get lucky and one had been in the kind of trouble he could use.

At least the elevator would be up and running soon. The many delivery men they were going to need to finish up the work would thank him for that. Of course, running up the stairs helped him to work off some of the tension that lingered at the end of the office. He should keep taking them, even if they did fix the lift. Plus, Luna enjoyed the bouncing.

It had become a habit for Ethan to swing by the babysitter to pick Luna up on his way home from work. As long as he didn't have a raid or drew a surveillance detail, he could keep that up. That would let Julie go into Tully's a few hours before she would normally be able to.

Although that simply lets her rack up more hours. It wouldn't get her out of work any earlier. She intended to stay until closing—well after he was asleep. Ethan didn't like that. If it weren't for Luna and the need to keep her on a decent schedule, he would pick Julie up at the end of her shift. Tully's wasn't far, but Ethan had seen too many crime scenes involving women to be comfortable with even a block. The bar would have to be in the building for him to rest easy...and maybe not even then.

As was her habit, Luna passed out on the trip up the stairs. Maybe the bouncing also helped knock her out? He would have to ask Julie.

Ethan opened the door, calling out before remembering Julie was at work. Luna slept through the bustle. Only the loudest of shouts would wake her. She was a sound sleeper—a detail he was grateful for.

He went to his room, intending to put his service piece away, before he remembered the lockbox was now in his office. Ethan was backtracking when he heard a sniffle.

He found Julie on the floor next to his bed. Her head was resting against the mattress, fresh tear tracks running down her face.

"*Hey.*" Ethan sat on his haunches next to her, pulling her into his arms before he could think better of it.

"What's wrong?" he asked, pressing her face to his chest and rubbing her back.

She let out a little hiccup and turned, presumably to back out of his embrace, but, halfway through, she gave up and collapsed against him. She spoke, a series of garbled, out-of-breath words.

"Sorry, I didn't catch any of that."

Julie pressed a crumpled tissue to her face. "I lost my job. Or rather, it was given to someone else who didn't miss two days of work."

He scowled. "Tully didn't hold it open for you?"

How could the old man do that?

"It wasn't him." She sniffled. "Mike, the bartender, is in charge. He gave the job to his friend Al."

His frown deepened. "That sounds fishy."

She shrugged. "His friend needed the job. Tully won't be running things for a while. He's pretty old. By the time he comes back in—*if* he comes back—weeks will have passed. Maybe months. I can't afford to wait that long. I need to work now."

He winced. "Do you want me to make some calls? I can speak to Tully myself."

She drew away a little, hesitating. "No, it's okay. I'll find a new job. I'm just feeling sorry for myself."

Julie pulled farther away, wrapping her arms around her chest. Ethan closed the distance, putting an arm around her. "You don't have to worry about the rent. You and Luna can stay here until you get back on your feet."

The words were hanging between them before he could even think about what he'd said. But once they were out, he didn't take them back. Ethan was suddenly certain they should stay. Their little trio had been making it work, surprisingly enough.

"Oh, no. We can't." Julie twisted to stare at him.

She was awfully close. Her eyes were a bit swollen and her nose was red, but it was her mouth that did him in. He couldn't stop staring at her full pink lips. Just like that, he was on fire. Shifting, he hoped she wouldn't notice the sudden, and, in this case, inappropriate erection.

Don't you dare kiss her. Julie needed help, not a guy who wanted to strip her down and fuck her brains out. His cock was not going to fix her life as an unemployed single mother. She would pack up and leave if he wasn't careful. There had to be no strings to this offer. Ethan needed to make her think she was doing him a favor.

"I was thinking of emailing my partners about our situation," he told her. "Mason was supposed to be back last month, but he's tied up in California and Donovan can't take leave from his latest assignment."

He didn't know if he'd explained about his friend being a part of *Doctors Without Borders*, so he stopped and did it now. "Anyway," he said after he finished, "I'm on my own here, holding down the fort, but work is about to get busy—at least it is if all goes well and I get the warrant I need."

Julie had stopped crying, but her brow was still creased. "I hope you get what you need for your work, but we've imposed on you long enough and—"

Ethan held up a hand. "I was thinking you might be able to pitch in," he explained. "Mason was meant to pick up the slack, but, since I'm on my own, I was thinking you might be able to help—not that you have to do any of the heavy lifting or anything. Most of the major renovations are done. We always planned on bringing in specialists, craftsmen, and electricians for the trickier work. We were going to wait until all the floors were done, but that plan is out the window now. If we have any prayer of staying on track for a spring opening, we have to get moving. The crews will have to work around what isn't done. Someone needs to be here to let the guys in, possibly coordinate them and keep them on track."

Her brown eyes were wide. "And you want me to do that?"

"I *need* you to." He laughed. "At this point, you know this place as well as anyone else. I trust you. You're smart and speak both English and Spanish. I think the latter would be a huge help with the work-men, which are a mixed crew."

"I don't want to take charity," she rasped, but she was weakening. He could tell.

"It's not. Like I said, I've been left high and dry by my best mates and co-investors. Hiring you would be a cheap solution for us. I can get you up to speed on what you need to know. The rest we can work out as we go along. And since the studio downstairs still isn't ready, it makes more sense for you to stay up here."

"That's the part I feel bad about," she said, stating the obvious. "We've invaded your personal space. I found one of Luna's toys wedged behind the refrigerator today. I have no idea how she got it stuck in there."

He snorted. "I found her doll on top of the middle of my desk. She would have had to climb into the office chair to reach. She's quite agile for her age. But I didn't mind."

Ethan lifted one shoulder, nudging her. "C'mon, the timing is fortuitous. It will give you time to find something else—a better job than slinging drinks at night. Didn't you say you came to the city for a job as a law clerk? Now you'll be able to find something like that."

Julie bit her lip, still indecisive, so he pulled out the big guns.

"With an office job, you'd be able to stay with Luna every night instead of depending on after-hours babysitters. And you'd be able to afford a better daycare."

Her lips parted, and she took a shaky breath. "I don't know anything about construction."

"I don't know much myself. I have some books and watched some videos." He left out the part about doing renovations on his dad's house as a teen. Compared to the task of getting an entire apartment building ready, it was apples and oranges.

Julie stared off into space. He could almost see the wheels in her mind turning.

Her pink lips parted. "Did you hear about the woman who built a whole house for her family? She learned everything she needed to know by watching YouTube videos."

Ethan grinned. His Juliet had taken the bait.

CHAPTER THIRTEEN

"I got it." Ethan waved the paper, still hot from the printer, in his partner's face.

Jason wrinkled his nose, snatching the paper. "What's this then?"

"It's what we need to get a team approved for the Lorano."

Jason squinted at the rap sheet Ethan had handed him. "Who am I looking at?" he said past the pencil in his mouth. He flipped to the second sheet of mostly misdemeanor crimes.

"This is our new best friend—Ilia Kuznetsov."

Jason put the pencil down. "I take it this guy is part of the Lorano's crew?"

"The first mate." Ethan leaned down, pointing out the most relevant crime. "A known smuggler."

His partner squinted at the line. "This says exotic animals. Any judge we go to will want more. Even the boss will tell us to hand it over to fish and game."

"No, I don't think so."

Jason leaned closer. "What do you know that I don't?"

Ethan sat in his chair, putting his feet up on his desk. "I know Earl Harris—a friendly judge who owes me a favor. But we'll need to pitch it to the Angel just right," he said, referring to their supervisor.

"You think this and an anonymous tip are enough for a warrant?" Jason asked.

"We've acted on less," Ethan pointed out.

"Other agents in the department have acted on less," his partner corrected, narrowing his eyes. "But you don't usually take risks like this."

Ethan sniffed, surveying the busy office. Jimenez and Walsh, the two agents at the neighboring desks, were by the coffee machine with intense expressions. They were no doubt hashing out their tactics on how to deal with the douchebags in the DA's office now that their op was wrapping up. *Fucking lawyers.*

"I'm going with my gut on this one."

"Yeah, I know. And it's not like you."

"High risk, high reward?" Ethan shrugged.

Jason's pulled his mouth into a pucker, smacking his teeth. "You're not the ambitious sort."

"Of course I am," Ethan protested. "Otherwise, I wouldn't have joined the bureau."

His partner leaned back in his chair. "Nah. You came here because it suited you better than the army, but you still needed the adrenaline. You're not gunning for a higher office. You want to stay in the field as long as you can, but you're too much of a pit bull to leave a case unsolved. If you're not careful, you're going to get yourself promoted to a desk—which you'll give up soon after out of boredom. But you're not stupid and you want a nice life after retirement, thus the dabbling in real estate."

"It's hardly dabbling when you buy a whole apartment building." Ethan blinked, wondering if the rest were true. He didn't think about promotions, just finishing his next case. Cleaning up the streets and the boardrooms was an added benefit. So was the occasional fistfight.

"The *Lorano* is our ticket to cracking the Komarov crew. I can feel it."

"You *feel* it?" Jason snorted. "There are so many jokes there, I can't even." Then he sobered. "I hope you're right about the Russian. If Viktor turned informant, it would change everything."

It was Ethan's turn to tap the brakes. "Let's not count our chickens yet. First, we get on that boat and find out what's there. We'll go from there."

Jason sighed. "Fine. It's your rodeo. I just hope we don't end up all dressed up with nowhere to go on Saturday night."

"We know where to go," Ethan said, waving the rap sheet again.

The pen flew at him. He caught it neatly before it hit his face.

"That's not what I meant, and you know it."

Ethan tossed the pen back. "Then choose your metaphors better."

❧

A few days later, Judge Harris approved the warrant. Ethan and Jason were leading the raid at the docks tomorrow night.

They had been getting ready all day, poring over plans and coordinating with the rest of their team. Ethan was in the mood to celebrate so when Jason invited him and Julie over to the hotel, promising they wouldn't need a babysitter, he accepted on their behalf. He was sure he could talk Julie into a night out on the town.

He wanted her to meet his friends.

Once home, he danced up the first flight of steps, making Luna laugh. He stopped to strip off her little winter suit so she wouldn't roast with the change of outdoor to indoor temperatures. The activity kept her awake and alert, so he took her to the second floor instead of the top. He could hear a lot of movement there, and he found Julie talking to an electrician while a second lay in a tangled pile of wires.

He took a moment to appreciate the picture she made. Julie wasn't smiling or anything, simply talking in Spanish, using her hands for emphasis. Ethan watched as the man nodded respectfully, responding to an innate authority he hadn't suspected his houseguest possessed until now.

Was it his imagination or was she standing a little straighter, too? She looked taller today, but as his eyes ran down her form in assessment, he immediately got distracted.

Damn. It should have been illegal for that woman to wear denim. The way the cloth hugged her curves always made his IQ nosedive. It was the way her narrow waist flared, stretching the material over an ass he wanted to take a bite out of. And Ethan wasn't even an ass man.

He'd always been a breast guy. But he didn't dare look at those for everyone's sake.... Suffice to say, confidence suited Julie.

She felt his eyes on her a beat later.

"Hey, Mommy, we're home," he called. He bounced a smiling Luna to make her giggle.

Tiny hands reached for Julie. She excused herself from the men, giving a final set of instructions in a clear and assured tone. He said goodbye instead of getting a rundown from them himself—one they showed signs of wanting to give him. But letting them think Julie was in charge was to his advantage.

"It's nice having someone to run interference," he observed as he herded his guest and her mini-me into the now-working elevator. "That could come in handy down the line. Me and the guys haven't discussed it, but it would be useful to have a go-between—someone to run interference between us and the tenants. We were counting on the property management company to take care of their needs, but if the neighbors discover we live onsite, things could get complicated."

He pictured late-night knocks asking for help with a plumbing problem. What if he had a morning meeting? Or worse, what if he was up late with a woman?

His overactive imagination sent a flash of creamy brown skin to his brain, front and center. He avoided looking directly at Julie as he opened the door to his apartment. He also didn't offer her a full-time job. It was still early days.

Instead, he coaxed her into telling him about her day. As predicted, Julie was thriving in her new role. She'd watched dozens of online home improvement videos, and she'd spent a chunk of the day reading power tool technical manuals in between coordinating with the electrical crew.

"I think I can take over on the floor situation in the studio," she said after summarizing what the workmen had accomplished. "It's a lot easier than I thought it would be. You bought the kind that snaps together, so it's mostly a matter of measuring."

Wait. Did that mean she wanted to move out of his apartment? "You don't have to do that," he said quickly. "I'll get to it this weekend. Or next week, tops."

"But I should help, right? I mean, I learned how a toilet works today!" She waved her arms enthusiastically while Luna crawled to her doll and began to gnaw on its head.

Julie knelt to remove one of the yarn hair strands before the little girl choked on it. "I mean, I knew in theory how a toilet worked, but I never looked in the tank. I think I can fix most by myself now."

He laughed. "I've never heard anyone be so enthusiastic about a toilet before. But I want you to forget about work for tonight—especially the floor downstairs. Do you have a dress by chance?"

Julie blinked. "Yes, why?"

CHAPTER FOURTEEN

Oh, this is wrong. Juliet grabbed on to Ethan's arm, wondering what the hell was going on. Why were they at this fancy hotel? And why was the staff treating Ethan like he was some sort of VIP? They all seemed to know his name.

"I thought we were meeting your partner at his place for drinks," she said, turning every which way to take in the dark mahogany paneling at the reception desk and the tasteful chandeliers overhead. Her heels clicked on the marble floor, the different colored white-and-gold stones forming a sunburst pattern in the center.

"We are," Ethan assured her as he guided them into the interior of an opulent-looking restaurant. "He lives here. For the moment, anyway. Jason keeps saying he and the wife are searching for the perfect condo, but he's been saying that for over a year. Personally, I think they're going to be here until they start dropping kids and need more room than the suite they live in. It would take something like that to give this place up."

Juliet's mouth had dropped open at the beginning of his explanation. "How can your partner afford it?"

She'd never been to this hotel, but she'd been enough like them in her life to know this place was astronomically expensive. Yeah, Jason and Ethan could afford a night or two in this place. They had nice government jobs that came with expense accounts, but *living* here was something else entirely.

"I've told you about Mags, haven't I?" Ethan asked. He put his hand on Juliet's back to guide her to the back of the nearly full restaurant. The small touch made her already-nervous body overheat.

"Maggie and her brothers own this hotel and quite a few others," he explained. "Well, they have a number of investors, too—their friends for the most part. Jason texted that some were in town. I might get to see my godson, so they moved the party to one of the private rooms back here."

Juliet swallowed, then nodded as agreeably as she could. She had no idea Ethan had friends like these. With every step, she grew more lightheaded until she was clutching his arm. When he glanced at her questioningly, she smiled weakly, forcing herself to ease her grip.

He doesn't need to know that staying at a place like this was once normal for me.

Juliet glanced down at her black dress, adjusting the waistline self-consciously. It was one of the items from her old wardrobe she'd held onto because it was simple and utilitarian. Or, at least, that was what she kept telling herself whenever she was short on cash and considered selling it. This was the first time she'd worn it since moving to Boston.

Ethan pushed open the door, and Juliet was hit by a wall of sound —loud and boisterous conversation overwhelmed the conservative quiet of the main dining room. She hesitated at the threshold, wishing she had Luna in her arms to use as a shield when a group of very well-dressed men and women turned to stare at them.

What the fu—? Wow, this was an intimidating group. Everyone was young, fit, and obviously wealthy. It was hands down the most exclusive gathering she'd ever seen, and, once upon a time, she'd spent a semester rubbing elbows with the intellectual elite at Harvard.

Ethan gave her the tiniest of pushes, hoisting Luna up higher in his arms as a blond man broke away to come say hello.

"Hey, you must be Juliet," he said, taking her hand and pumping it. "I'm Jason."

Not again. "It's Julie," she corrected with a smile that felt stiff and painful.

"Of course. Sorry, Julie," he said, reaching out and plucking Luna out of Ethan's arms. "And this must be the little moon. Hey there, kid."

Jason turned to Ethan. "Eva Stone texted they're on their way."

"Good," Ethan said, wrapping a casual arm around Juliet's waist to propel her forward again. "Eva is an old friend and my godson's mother, so you'll be able to meet Ethan Patrick."

Another surprise. "Is he named after you?" she asked.

A very pretty brunette rose to greet them as they reached the table. "He sure is, and let me tell you the exciting story behind that. Hi, I'm Maggie. You must be Julie." She held out her hand and shook, then turned to the toddler. "And this must be Luna."

She nudged her husband, then held up her arms. "Gimme!"

Smiling broadly, Maggie took the baby. A whirl of introductions followed.

"You'll be lucky to get that kid back." Jason laughed when there was a pause in the greetings. "It's not enough Maggie's brother just had one. She's kind of baby crazy at the moment."

Laughing, Juliet sat next to Ethan who was beside a tiny pixie of a woman who introduced herself as Maia. The table was set for a dozen people with elegant china and real silver flatware, but that didn't stop them from setting up two highchairs for Luna and presumably for Ethan's godson. Maggie's nephew was only a few months old, so he was upstairs napping with a nurse to watch over him.

Ethan joked around with his partner as a slew of waiters came in and out with trays of hors d'oeuvres and fresh bottles of both white and red wine. After a few rather liberally poured glasses, Juliet relaxed in a way she hadn't been able to for years, enjoying casual conversation with their friendly hosts and their extended circle of friends.

The meal was devastatingly good. Foie gras was served with a fig compote on sweet malt bread. That was followed by a parmesan risotto made with cheese from Italy. It was topped with slices of rare duck, braised in a sauce the chef must have made a deal with the devil to learn how to make. Dessert was something chocolate she couldn't pronounce, but it made her toes curl in her shoes.

Occasionally, she would look at Ethan seated next to her, who was laughing and joking around with genuine good humor. Half the time, he had his arms draped over the back of her chair. If he noticed she'd stopped talking to her neighbors, he would turn to her, deftly asking her something innocuous that would draw her back into the conversation.

It felt good and slightly surreal, as if she were having a glimpse of a life she might have had if she'd been born in another time and place.

The fact everyone was treating her as if she were Ethan's girlfriend didn't penetrate right away. By the time she realized they were eyeing her with a special type of scrutiny under their friendly welcome, she was too comfortable. The edges of her ever-present anxiety were pleasantly blurred by the delicious wine that had accompanied each course.

Juliet should have been panicking, but she was content to sit there and pretend it were true. It was only for one night. What could be the harm?

Somewhere near the end of the meal, Maggie stood, rushing to greet the couple who came in. "You're late," she called.

A petite blonde had walked in, flanked by a big dark-haired man carrying a sturdy-looking little boy.

Ethan stood, too. "My godson is here," he said with an undeniable air of excitement. He took the little boy from his parents, swinging him up in the air until the boy shouted with glee.

Sergei and Eva, the parents, joined them at the table as the waiters hurried to serve them dinner so they could catch up. Ethan horsed around with the little boy for an entire ten minutes. Then he settled his namesake in the highchair next to Luna, but the boy started screaming the house down. A compromise was reached, and both children were put on the floor on a blanket to play together.

They made such an adorable picture, a slew of cameras was whipped out. Apparently used to the attention, the little boy decided to put on a show. He took Luna with both hands, grabbing her and kissing her cheek with a loud smacking noise.

A chorus of 'awws' from the adults greeted the gesture, but Ethan scowled, going over to pluck Luna from the floor as she started to cry.

Ethan picked up his godson, too, holding one child in each arm while he scolded the boy. "Hey, little buddy, there's this thing called consent. You better learn it now. No kissy-kissy unless the girls say it's okay."

Ethan handed the boy to his father, shaking his finger as he came around the table with Luna in his arms. "He gets that from you. You better teach him not to do shit like that."

The big Russian laughed, saying something in his native tongue. To her surprise, Ethan answered in kind.

"What did he say?" Juliet asked, bewildered.

Ethan laughed. "He said that's what godfathers are for."

He sat next to her, soothing Luna with a hand on her back, rubbing in little circles. Juliet tried to take her, but Luna buried her face in Ethan's neck, hiccupping softly.

"I had no idea you spoke Russian," she marveled.

"And you speak French," he pointed out.

She blinked. "I do?"

Ethan twisted to face her. "You did a few minutes ago," he said with a laugh.

"Oh," she said, belatedly remembering a quick aside she'd had with Eva, who had been speaking about their most recent trip to Paris. "I spent a little time in France before my quinceañera," she said, fudging the date.

In reality, she and her mother had spent most of her seventeenth year in Europe. Again, that was something Ethan did not need to know.

"*Estas bien, mi linda,*" she soothed the still-fussy Luna, pressing a kiss to the girl's soft cheek. Continuing to lean in, she whispered words of encouragement and love. Ethan turned his shoulder until the three were a private little knot, a separate and inviolable trio.

After a minute, he raised his head and announced Luna had had enough. He nodded at Jason as he stood. "That goes for you, too. We have a big day tomorrow."

"Aw, ten more minutes, Mom," Jason protested. His wife laughed, but she poked him until he stood and excused himself, too.

"Go on ahead. I'll be up soon!" She waved airily, making a production of pouring another wine glass. Jason scowled, and she laughed. "What? *I* don't have a career-changing raid tomorrow."

"A what?" Juliet asked, brow creasing.

"Nothing, never mind," Ethan said, managing to toss her coat over her shoulders with one hand while holding Luna in the other. They were out the door before she could ask anything else.

CHAPTER FIFTEEN

Julie was incredibly quiet on the ride up the elevator. She had lapsed into silence on the drive home and was now holding Luna like a shield, occasionally rocking the sleeping toddler instead of conversing.

Not ready to call it a night, he talked about a safe subject, his godson, until they were safely in his apartment.

"Don't worry," he said. "I have complete faith that Eva, Ethan Patrick's mother, will straighten him out. That kid will grow up right —that woman is a total boss. Even Sergei bows down to her authority."

He said the last in a decent imitation of Cartman from South Park, but all he got was a lip twitch.

"What's on your mind?" he asked finally.

"Oh, I was realizing why you're so good with Luna. You were great with Ethan Patrick," she said. "I'm surprised you aren't married with kids of your own already."

He shrugged, aware any truthful answer might tread on dangerous territory. "I guess I haven't met the right person yet."

Julie peeked from under her impossibly thick lashes. "Did you want to have kids with Peyton?"

Ethan glanced at her sharply. "Who mentioned Peyton?"

"I don't remember. I think it was Maggie. She got a text from her at some point during the second course. She mentioned Peyton was on her honeymoon."

He nodded, trying to read her face.

"Peyton is Maggie's best friend," he offered after a short silence.

Julie continued to watch him expectantly. His shoulders dropped. "All right. Peyton is someone I had a thing for, but we never dated. She was taken, even if it was only in her head at first. Eventually, it wasn't. She just married Maggie's oldest brother Liam—him and this other guy named Matthias."

Julie's lips parted. "She married *two* men?"

"Yup." Ethan grinned carelessly. "It was fun to flirt with her, but I can't say I'm pining. I think I'm looking for someone a little more traditional than that."

"Oh," Julie said, a little breathlessly. "I can see why."

The room was warmer than it should have been, probably because they were standing a lot closer than was strictly necessary. Julie seemed to feel the tension in the air that even the mention of Peyton hadn't been able to dampen. Flushing, she looked away.

"I should put her down," she said, heading in the direction of the spare bedroom.

"I'll help." Helplessly, he followed, even though she didn't need help. Luna's diaper had been changed before the car ride home. The little one was out for the night.

Julie flipped on the hallway light, then nudged the bedroom door open. Stopping short, she gasped.

"Where did this come from?" Julie stepped into the room, circling the crib he'd ordered online.

"Ikea," he replied. "I assembled it this morning before you got up. I guess you didn't see it earlier."

She pivoted to face him, tears shimmering in the dim light. "No, I was busy with the workmen. Oh, Ethan, thank you, but you didn't have to do this. It was nice pretending tonight, but we're only here temporarily."

Pretending? There was no pretense in what they had done tonight.

Instinct kept him from saying that aloud. For some reason, Julie still needed to act as if there was nothing going on between them.

"Even if you all move on soon, Luna's going to need a proper crib," he said, choosing his words carefully. "Don't worry. She won't outgrow this one for a while."

To prove his point, he nudged her, taking the little girl from her arms. He laid her on the bed, covering her in a blanket he'd ordered for his bed that had arrived in the wrong size. The narrow twin flannel made a decent toddler blanket, provided he folded it in half.

"There," he said, tucking in the excess flannel into the sides between the mattress and the wood. "Now, she's all set."

He put an arm around Julie, admiring the picture and the peace the sight of a sleeping toddler inspired. It made her tense. He was going to let go, but, after a beat, she relaxed into him, melting against his chest.

"What did you mean when you said it was fun to pretend?"

Her eyes had drifted closed. "With your friends tonight—the way they looked at us."

"How?" he prodded.

Her lashes were so long he'd never be able to read her eyes from this position. "Like we were a family."

Those words should have acted like a bucket of ice water. It was saying something that he felt hotter, as if his abdomen had melted.

"It doesn't have to be pretend."

He leaned closer until his lips were touching hers.

The instant he kissed her for the second time, he *knew*. Their first kiss had been a spur-of-the-moment thing—insanely hot, but ultimately not life-changing. This was different. This woman had been living in his space, breathing the same air, and sleeping in his bed *without him* for weeks.

He was going to change that tonight.

"I'm not supposed to kiss you again until you say yes," he muttered in between hot, openmouthed kisses. He pulled away to check her reaction.

Her eyes were clouded with desire, but there was the tiniest pucker between her brows. "Wh—" she began, but he'd already covered her mouth with his again.

Another blistering kiss. This one shredded his self-control. Pulling her into the hallway before he did something indecent in front of the sleeping toddler, he lifted her into his arms.

He felt like cheering when her long legs wrapped around his waist, but his mouth was busy. *Very* busy.

Pressing her hard against the wall, he nudged the door to Luna's room until it almost closed, then he carried Julie down the hall to the threshold of his room. But he didn't move inside. Not yet.

"Ethan," she moaned. It was music to his ears. But it wasn't the definitive *yes* he wanted.

He pulled away. "As I was explaining to my namesake tonight, the verbal consent part is important." He moved his mouth to her neck, licking and biting gently.

God. She tasted like caramelized sugar. Who actually tasted as good as they looked? *Who?*

"*Yes, yes,*" Julie panted, burying her hands in his hair as she pressed her breasts against him.

Thank the fucking stars. Ethan hauled her closer, pulling her legs tightly against his cloth-covered crotch. He kicked open the door to his room a little too hard. He paused at the threshold but the bang hadn't woken Luna, so he carried Julie inside and closed the door.

He laid Julie on the bed, but he didn't give her a chance to change her mind. He was on her the next second, stretching his hard body over her lush curves. It felt amazing, and they weren't even naked yet. He decided to take care of that as soon as possible.

Ethan stripped out of his shirt, hazily aware he'd tugged too hard and lost a button. His pants were next. He was down to his boxers when he realized Julie was staring up, her mouth open.

There was enough light coming through the windows for him to see her bemused expression.

"What's wrong?" he whispered, wondering with dismay if she had changed her mind. But she simply reached out, touching the top ridge of his six-pack with tentative fingers.

After that, her little black dress stayed on for roughly six seconds. Moving faster than he thought possible, he tugged it over her head, revealing paradise.

It didn't matter she was wearing a basic cotton bra and panties. She could have been wearing La Perla and it wouldn't have enhanced the view in any way.

Creamy light brown curves gleamed like candy. Her breasts spilled over the top of the bra as she took a shaky breath. His hands covered the glorious mounds, kneading them briefly over the fabric before slipping under the tight band to palm her nipples.

Julie gasped, moving up. Her legs parted involuntarily as he rubbed the tight buds for a second before undoing the bra and tossing it away. The panties joined it in short order.

Feeling like a glutton, Ethan moved down her body. The taste of sugar filled his mouth as he kissed and licked her skin, lingering on places he'd been fantasizing about since that first night. It had been so wrong to desire such a vulnerable woman, but the heavens had smiled at him for that act of selflessness. Ethan was being rewarded now.

He drew the skin of her inner thigh into his mouth hard enough to leave a mark before moving his attention to the heated flesh between her legs.

Julie was breathing fast, but he didn't gentle his touch. Instead, he pulled her thighs toward him as he loomed over her pussy, an unmistakable sign he was about to feast.

He bent his head, taking a long, slow lick. He lapped her from top to bottom before reversing the circuit. When he swirled the tip of his tongue over her clit, she cried out.

"You taste better than the dessert we had tonight," he said, blowing over her burning folds before going back for more.

Julie giggled, but it was cut off as she gasped, squirming.

He settled over her slick velvet, working it with all the skill he'd learned from years of playing the field. But it wasn't like before. Doing this to other women had simply been a means to an end.

Tonight, every sound and shudder Julie made was a personal victory. He could have come from that moan alone.

Julie's legs thrashed, and she tightened around his tongue. Holding her legs down, he waited for the tell-tale pulse of her orgasm, letting her ride it out before rearing up until his cock probed the pink vee at her core. He let the tip caress her clit before circling back down to flirt with the tight ring at the entrance of her sheath.

"Please," Julie begged, urging him on with her legs. Her fingers shook as she pressed against him, rubbing those fabulous creamy tits against his chest.

His plan to tease Julie and bring her to climax again before he fucked her flew out the window. In the next heartbeat, his cock was throbbing, pushing inside her.

It was more difficult than he would have guessed. She was so tight he had to push hard to breach her entrance, yet she still didn't give. Breathing hard, he flexed his hips, pressing his hard-on deep until she yielded, going soft around him as he drove home into her honeyed warmth.

"Fuck," he groaned as he slid home. It must have been a *really* long time for her.

Ethan raised his head to ask if he'd hurt her, but her mouth touched his as her hips undulated beneath him with a restless, almost-frenzied motion.

That was all it took. His vision swamped out and instinct took over until he was bucking, withdrawing and surging in a rhythm older than time itself.

Sensation blurred as he gave himself over to that primal drive. Ethan was little more than an animal, a creature of testosterone and hunger whose only desire was to claim their mate. Mid-surge, he stopped to bite down on the juicy under-curve of Julie's breast until she cried out. It was a touch too hard to be truly playful, but he couldn't stop himself. It was as if he were imprinting himself on her very skin.

He threw his head back, lost in the pulsing pleasure. Underneath him, Julie tightened, surging up to meet him with a cry. She clamped down around him, taking her with him as she splintered in a second climax.

Ethan let go with a strangled shout, pouring every bit of himself into her before collapsing on top of her. It took him a full minute to raise his head. He kissed her still-panting mouth.

"Sorry," he breathed, apologizing for crushing her. He rolled to the side, pulling her tightly against him.

"Ethan," Julie whispered when she caught her breath.

"What?" he murmured, drowsy now.

"Never apologize for *that*."

He fell asleep laughing.

CHAPTER SIXTEEN

Juliet stirred early the next morning, instinctively sensing she was alone in bed.

Her sleep-addled brain roused swiftly as she remembered the night before. The memories were like a warm wave, spreading from her tingling and slightly bruised lips, down her body to the tips of her toes.

Even her breasts felt swollen under the sheet, the tips hard and aching. And that was nothing compared to the ache between her legs. She was prepared to linger, replaying the night's events when she realized she was not alone.

Ethan sat in the chair by the bed. Juliet scrambled up abruptly, pulling the sheet higher against her bare breasts.

"Hi."

"Hey." His voice was flat, and he didn't smile. Juliet swallowed suddenly, unable to shake the presentiment of disaster. *Something is wrong.*

Ethan's serious demeanor continued to chill her despite the warmth of the bed.

Mierda. You shouldn't have slept with him. He regretted getting intimate with her. And why should he have been happy about it? She was a parasite, a needy single mother dependent on his largess, and he'd come to senses.

"Ethan," she began, but he held up a hand.

"I woke up early. Too keyed up about the raid later, I guess."

"*Oh.*" Was his issue related to that? "Is it dangerous?"

She hadn't even considered he might be worried, and how selfish was that? To her mind, Ethan was superhuman, so solid and strong it seemed as if nothing could touch him. And that was stupid. She, of all people, should know better.

He shrugged, dismissing her fears. "Not really. We plan everything down to the last detail. It's as safe as crossing the street for us."

"But something might still go wrong," she persisted. His manner was kindling her anxiety. What if something happened to him?

"Forget about that for now. I have to talk to you about something."

Oh, God. He was going to ask her to leave. Bracing herself, Juliet tightened her grip on the sheets and waited.

Ethan passed a hand over his face. "I, uh, I woke up early."

"You said that already."

He cleared his throat. "Yeah. Anyway, I was going to wake you, too, because I felt bad about passing out after only one time. It's been a long week and what we did—well, it was…intense."

"For me, too," she said, wondering where he was going with this.

After a beat, Ethan continued. "Then I realized you couldn't go again, not for a while. You need time to recover, right?"

"Uh, maybe." She was sore, but why was he so concerned? And why was he watching her as if she'd just kicked a puppy?

Ethan leaned back in the chair. "Look at the sheets."

She glanced down, confused. "What?"

His face hardened. "I said, look at the damn sheets, *Julietta.*"

He might as well have slapped her. Stricken, Juliet glanced down, finally seeing the blood.

Ethan stood, crossing his arms over his broad chest. "If you were a virgin last night, then who is Luna's mother?"

CHAPTER SEVENTEEN

He knew before she opened her mouth that Julie was about to lie. It was all over her face.

Fuck. This was not how he'd thought this morning was going to go.

"Who is Luna's mother?" he ground out again. It felt as if his throat was closing in on itself. It was so hard to get the words out. "Because I know for a fact it *can't* be you."

She stared, her mouth opening and closing a few times beneath panicked brown eyes.

"I am her mother...now."

It was almost a whisper, harsh and ragged, as if he'd torn the confession from her. But he couldn't stop. This was too fucking big. "Please tell me you didn't take that baby from her birth mother."

"No!" Julie closed her eyes, shaking her head with a jerk. "And I never said I gave birth to her."

Unbelievable. "You know that's what I thought. You let everyone believe she was yours."

Ethan scrubbed his face with his hands, pacing back and forth a few steps in front of the bed. "It was a lie of omission, but it was still a *lie*—well, I need the fucking truth cause I'm a goddamned agent of the FBI. You know I cannot let this go. Who gave birth to Luna and why is it just the two of you now?"

Julie bunched the covers, pressing them to her stomach as if it were hurting. "I...she...Luna is my sister Daniela's baby. Daniela is gone now. Dead."

It was terribly tragic information, but all Ethan could feel was relief. Julie was Luna's aunt. He could breathe again. But they weren't out of the woods yet.

"And Luna's father?" he asked.

Julie's head snapped up. She stared him square in the eyes. "My sister's husband is also dead."

"I'm sorry," he said, completely softening. "When did they die?"

"Over a year ago."

Over a year ago? Fucking hell. The gnawing pit in his stomach was back, but for a whole other reason. "That was when your parents died."

She breathed through her nose audibly before nodding.

He swallowed hard. "The same day?"

Another nod.

Fuck, fuck, fuck. "They didn't die in a car accident, did they?"

Julie shuddered, her face crumpling.

Ethan was on the bed like a shot. He wrapped his arms around her, pulling her against his chest as she started to cry. Feeling like an asshole, he rubbed her back, pressing her against him hard enough to meld their bodies.

"I'm sorry. But, after last night, I had to find out what was going on."

It took a long while, but then she nodded. "I know. I should have said something, but I never tell anyone about my family. I—I just didn't think. Last night wasn't supposed to happen and..."

"And you didn't think I'd be able to tell it was your first time," he finished.

He felt her shoulders move in the tiniest of shrugs. Ethan's mind was turning, but it didn't take a genius to figure out the rest of the story.

Julie was highly educated. She spoke French like a Parisian and had been very much at home at the Caislean, a five-star hotel for dinner. Julie came from money—money he strongly suspected had some blood on it.

"They were gunned down, weren't they?" he asked. "That's why you don't like guns."

She tensed in his arms. "Yes," she whispered.

He waited another long moment. "Cartel?"

Julie hesitated, but then she nodded before shivering violently. "I know the guns weren't like yours. They had been shot many times. There were too many bullets for a handgun."

Automatic weapons. That didn't necessarily mean cartel violence, not these days, but it was the most obvious explanation.

"We were having a small party," she said with a tiny hiccup. "It was for Luna's christening. I...I hid with her in a closet until the noises stopped."

Son of a bitch. The gut punches kept coming. Taking a deep breath, he rubbed her back. "Can I ask one more thing?"

Her face was buried in his chest. *"What?"* The word was barely intelligible.

"Is it legal?

"Is what legal?

"Having custody of Luna. Is it a formal arrangement?"

"Not exactly," she said, peeking up. "I didn't file any paperwork, but there was no time. I had to leave. It...it wasn't safe."

"You didn't have more family down in Mexico you could have gone to?" he asked, aware the answer didn't matter. If Julie had been scared enough to run with a baby, then nowhere in Mexico would have been safe.

Julie spoke haltingly, as if she were thinking about it. "I have some cousins somewhere, but we never visited. My parents were different from them. They liked money and lived well. They had a million friends, some of whom I called aunt or uncle, but that was just our way. They weren't blood. I know both sets of grandparents are dead."

Another mixed blessing. There was no family member with a stronger claim to Luna. That was good. They were going to get through this.

Ethan eased Julie back down on the pillow, covering her body with his. "I need you to do something for me."

Confusion clouded her expression. "What?"

"I need you to forgive me for what I just did to you."

Her lips parted.

"I know I hurt you," he elaborated before she found her tongue. "Hell, I hurt you last night even though I didn't realize it until this morning. But I had to ask."

"I know." Her face cleared a bit. "And it didn't hurt."

The stains on the sheets spoke to her lie, but it was a little white one. As long as he gave her time to recover, it wouldn't matter.

He shifted positions, lying on his side and pulling her into him until they were spooning. Caressing her arm, he breathed in the scent of her hair. She had used his shampoo, but it smelled different on her. Better.

"I don't want to, but I have to go soon. This is really bad timing, but I won't be reachable today."

"Because of the raid?"

"Yes," he confirmed. "But don't worry about anything. We can talk some more when I get back. We'll figure everything out."

She turned toward him. "What things?"

"Stuff—like how to make sure everything is aboveboard with you keeping Luna." He rubbed her backside, unable to help himself. "That's an issue that needs to be addressed. I'm sure there are more, but we'll deal with all that later."

In the distance, the toddler in question started to cry. Ethan glanced at his watch. "I have time to get her up and make her first bottle. Why don't you stay here and take your time getting up? I'll pass her off to you when I need to leave."

Julie sniffed and nodded.

He left her alone to collect herself, feeling a mix of relief and concern.

This is way too much emotion before nine, he thought as he lifted Luna from her new crib. Impulsively, he cuddled her to him, letting her warm little body soothe his ragged soul.

He held her close until she wiggled away.

"Everything is going to be okay now. The worst is over," he said.

But Ethan wasn't stupid. He'd opened Pandora's box last night when he took Julie to bed.

"Time to get ready, Little Moon." He set the baby on the changing table. The transition to a new diaper happened in record time.

"I may be getting better at this," he conceded before dressing Luna in one of the cozy outfits Maggie had bought. Then he stood her on top of the table, assessing his work critically.

She stared back, a contest of wills. Hers was stronger. Ethan broke and laughed, shaking his head before sobering.

"I know it's been only you and your mom for a while now," he told her in a low voice. "But I want you to know you have me now, too."

Luna blinked. "Up," she said imperiously, holding up her arms.

"Yes, Your Highness. Consider it done," he said, slinging her up and carrying her to the kitchen.

CHAPTER EIGHTEEN

The *Lorano* was late.

Ethan could tell the team was getting restless, but there was nothing he could do about it now. The only thing was to stay in position until the damn thing docked.

"At least it's not a large freighter. Can you imagine if we had to wait for them to unload a bunch of these?" Jason asked, waving around at the empty shipping container they set up as a surveillance command center. According to the manifest, the Lorano would offload a bunch of crates, but no full-sized shipping containers.

Ethan grunted in response, his mind back in his apartment. He couldn't stop rehashing the morning's events in his head.

He'd texted Julie an update to say he'd be in late. Ethan didn't ask her to stay up and wait for him, but he hoped she would.

"Hey, what's up?" His partner scowled. "This op is not a complete wash yet. The ship will be here soon."

"Yeah, I know. It's not that."

"If not the *Lorano*, what crawled up your butt and died?"

Ethan turned off the mic on his comm, signaling Jason to do the same. The team was maintaining radio silence, and he and Jason would hear them if they broke it. But the other guys didn't need to listen to him discuss what an asshole he was.

"I slept with Julie last night."

Jason nodded. "Well, I can't say I'm surprised. I think we all saw that one coming after last night. Props for finally landing that plane by the way."

Smirking, his partner paused. "Julie is way above your pay-grade. She's like a Mexican Maggie. Not that I think you did it all on your own. Dinner with your awesome partner must have convinced her you weren't a total deviant."

"Julie looks nothing like your wife," he said with a sniff. Maggie was pretty and all, but Julie was next-level sexy. He was probably biased, though.

Jason dismissed that. "I'm only referring to the general hotness level. I have no shame in admitting I damn near tripped going over to say hi to her."

He was exaggerating, but only slightly. Despite being happily married, his partner had been close to drooling, though he'd hid it well. Most of the men in the room had done a double take when Julie took off her coat.

"All respect to my gorgeous wife—who I love more than anything," his partner continued, "but after a slew of sevens and the occasional eight, you somehow pulled a ten and a half. Seriously, the girl is *stacked*. Julie looks like a character on a Mexican soap opera who begins as the ingenue, but is about to break out of that into the bad-girl role."

"Enough." Ethan groaned because his partner was right. "You need to shut your piehole now."

Jason snickered. "I don't see what your problem is. You're into her. She's into you. Plus, she's smart and great with kids. Or is that the problem? Are you getting cold feet over getting mixed up with a single mom?"

"In a roundabout way, that is kind of the problem," Ethan admitted, picturing Julie's face when he had accused her of kidnapping.

A pen flew toward him, hitting him on the neck. "Seriously? That kind of shit is beneath you."

Ethan picked up the pen, then threw it back.

"It's complicated." He rubbed the spot where the pen had hit even though it wasn't bothering him. "Julie was a virgin until last night."

Jason screwed his face up until the corners of his lips were next to his ears. "Hold up, how the hell does that work?"

Ethan sighed. "She's not Luna's birth mother. She's her aunt. Her sister, Luna's real mom, is dead—along with the rest of her family."

"Oh, fuck. That's some heavy shit." Jason twisted in his chair. He waved his hand in a vague motion. "And you figured it out when you slid into home. That is…"

"Heavy shit?" Ethan finished.

Jason nodded, widening his eyes for emphasis. "Exactly."

"Yeah, except I didn't figure it out until this morning when I saw the state of the sheets. I did the math after that."

His partner tsked in sympathy. "A virgin. I thought they cancelled those."

"What about Maggie?" Jason's wife had been inexperienced when he'd met her, too.

"Well, see, Mags being one makes sense. She had two older brothers constantly policing her every move before she met me. It's rare to find one in the wild." His mouth pulled down. "Poor kid."

"Do you mean Julietta or Luna?"

"Both." Jason checked the cams before turning back to him. "Hey, man, stop looking like you did something wrong by sleeping with her. You're both consenting adults. She's been living with you for weeks. It's not your fault. You didn't know she was a virgin. She was not precisely forthcoming about her status."

"That's true," Ethan agreed, then winced. "Although, I'm not sure that excuses the fact I basically accused her of kidnapping her own niece this morning. Looking back, Julie never lied outright, but she left a hell of a lot out whenever she talked about her past."

"You mean the one where she grew up with scads of cash?"

Ethan raised his head. "You picked up on that, too?"

Jason fluttered his lashes. "I think we all did. After a few glasses of wine—which she held very well, by the way—she slipped up on the details. The woman is well-traveled, speaks French like a native, and knows how to use a fish knife."

"I thought only Sergei noticed that." Ethan had almost missed it, but he'd been talking with the Russian when Sergei had cocked his head at Julie's hands, raising an imperious eyebrow in question. He'd gestured to Julie after she picked up the knife and started to use it with unconscious grace. Most of the others at the table hadn't bothered with one—if they even knew what one was. He certainly hadn't before sharing all those formal dinners at the Caislean.

"So..." Jason began more cautiously. "Given the circumstances, how much are we betting Julie is not her real name?"

Ethan considered that. "I'm almost sure it's Julietta," he said, pronouncing it the Hispanic way as if the *J* was an *H*. "I don't think she meant to share it. But she was so ill that first night, her defenses were down."

"Her family might have called her Julie," Jason pointed out. "It could be a nickname. Especially if they spent time in Europe or here in the States."

He thought it over, but that didn't feel right. Whenever he used the name, her insistence on being called something else had been emphatic. Even being called Juliet had been too close for her comfort. Each time, she had reacted with dismay.

"Or they didn't call her that, and she had to cover after telling me the real one. It's possible she never meant to go by Julie at all," he mused. "For all I know, the folks at Tully's called her something else entirely."

Jason scratched his head. "You think she's gone that far to hide her identity?"

"I don't know. It depends on whether she thinks the trouble she's hiding from is going to follow her. And don't bother telling me I need to figure that shit out. I already know I do. I just need to work out a way to get answers without making a total hash of it like I did this morning."

His partner stood, checking the weapon at his side.

"Good, but we're going to have to get your love life straightened out later." He gestured to the screen where the *Lorano* was being tied to the dock. "Our ship has come in."

CHAPTER NINETEEN

"What do you mean there's nothing?" Jason hissed, ready to tear someone's head off.

Rivera, the strike team's second, inclined his head to avoid being overheard by the *Lorano's* crew, whom they'd lined up on their stomachs on the dock, close together like a tin of sardines.

Everything had gone as planned. The team had let the *Lorano* dock. They'd held their position until the ship was unloaded. Once the bulk of the crates had been offloaded, they surrounded the vessel and boarded it.

There hadn't been much action. The majority of the crew had given up without a fight, bemused at suddenly being swarmed by an armed group wearing navy windbreakers emblazoned with FBI in yellow letters.

"I mean there's nothing," Agent Rivera said, his tone perilously close to smug. "We've opened most of the crates on the dock, and it's all regular goods—electronics and machine parts. No contraband."

A few feet away, one of the Lorano's crew had the temerity to smirk, despite being splayed on the rough wooden planks of the dock like yesterday's catch.

Ethan narrowed his eyes at the men before walking farther away, forcing Jason and Rivera to follow him.

"No. These assholes are hiding something. Get some thermal cameras down here," he ordered once he judged they were out of earshot. "Whatever we're searching for, it's still on the fucking ship."

Rivera flicked him a look. "For your sake, I hope you're right. You still owe me twenty bucks. It would be a damn shame if you got put on unpaid leave for this shit-show."

Jason surreptitiously flipped off the other agent as he stalked away. "When did Rivera become such an asshole?"

"He's getting a divorce," Ethan said, dismissing their colleague's behavior. "The poor fucker is sleeping on his partner's couch."

"Well, that sucks for him, but that ass has a selective damn memory. You paid him back last month. Remind me never to borrow any cash from him when I forget my wallet."

"Yeah... Look, I'm going to do another circuit of the vessel."

"You sure?" Jason wouldn't admit it in front of Rivera, but it was obvious he was thinking they'd been set up for shits and giggles, too.

"The *Lorano* is a smuggling vessel, and I'm going to prove it." Ethan climbed back over the deck railing with determined steps.

He ignored the rest of the milling search team, including the fact Agent Walsh was sneaking a fucking cigarette on the cramped boat's bridge. Locating the steps down to the hold, he took them slowly, mulling over the situation.

The *Lorano* was small for a cargo vessel. It had one large central hold in the front of the ship, with the engines in the back. The remaining bit was a warren of twisting metal tunnels and small rooms for the crew—plenty of places to hide a small stash of guns or drugs.

Ethan went cabin by cabin, making a mental map. He'd gone over the crew space twice before realizing it was too narrow given the width of the ship.

Just like the f'ing Millennium Falcon, this place has smugglers compartments. And they were deep in the ship, far enough from the hull to mask them from surveillance tools like the IR cameras and thermal imaging.

Oh my fucking God, this is exactly like Star Wars, he thought when he realized where the secret compartment was. The hidden space was under his feet.

He was on his walkie the next minute. "Jason, get your ass over here. I need some help getting this shit open."

It took both to find the seal to the top of the compartment. Ethan felt his well-used muscles protesting when they lifted the heavy steel partition off the top.

He and Jason gazed down into the dark hole in dismay. Eight pairs of terrified eyes stared back at them.

"Well, fuck me," Jason muttered. The *Lorano* hadn't smuggled nine boxes of guns or kilograms of heroin into the country. Their contraband was humans.

CHAPTER TWENTY

Ethan studied the huddle of women shivering in the open air, glancing around them fearfully.

Of course it was an all-female group. The oldest appeared to be about twenty-three or four. The rest were younger.

Fuck. There weren't enough blankets to go around, more proof this was the last thing they had been expecting. He took off his wind-breaker, handing it to the nearest girl at the edge of the cluster—the one who looked about fourteen fucking years old.

She put it on without meeting his eyes, as if she were afraid to make contact. Beside him, Jason also took off his jacket.

"Are the ambulances on their way?" Ethan asked. "We need these women checked out." God knew what had happened to them on the trip.

"Yeah, they're on their way," Jason confirmed. "Ten minutes out, tops.

"We haven't found any other girls," Rivera said, coming back to give him an update. The agent's bad attitude had disappeared the minute they brought the girls abovedeck. "I think this is it."

"Keep searching," Ethan ordered in a low aside. "There's one missing."

The note had been clear. The *Lorano* had been carrying *nine* women, not eight.

Rivera nodded before disappearing into the crowd. More agents had been called in, as well as local PD, for backup. Somewhere in the crowd, INS agents waited. The social services people were on their way, too.

"It's possible they started out with nine," Jason said in an undertone, voicing the hard fact Ethan had been trying not to think about. "They might have lost one on the way."

An image of Julie floating in the cold depths of the ocean flashed through his mind before he could shut it down.

"Let's go with the best-case scenario," he ground out. The ninth girl could still be alive. Perhaps she had gotten sick and had been separated from the others to avoid spreading disease.

Or she'd been taken out of the hold for someone's amusement...

Ethan stared hard at the line of men still on the floor. The smug bastard who'd laughed—he was going to pay for that now.

Ethan thought fast. They would take one girl out at a time. Even if these shitheads hadn't cared for the girl's comfort, they would have cared about their own. Most of the cabins were doubles or triples, but one of the berths had a single bed...

"Hey, we found the last girl!"

Ethan followed the shout, leaving the rest of the victims in Jason's care. He was back on the boat in a flash.

One of the team, Smith, pointed down the hall.

"She ran past me. I think she was loose when the ship docked."

Ethan grunted, waving the guy past. "Hello?" he called in Russian, taking a chance. The boat may have been Croatian, but he got that note from Viktor, he was sure of it now.

He could see her now, a little slip of a thing wearing a thin white shirt and jeans that hung off her. She was huddled in the corner of one of the sleeping quarters as if she were trying to hide.

"Hey there. I'm with the FBI," he murmured softly, holstering his weapon.

That was a mistake. It should have been safe. The entire boat had been cleared, but some of those damn smuggling holds were craftily hidden. And, apparently, some were large enough for a full-grown man.

He felt a rush of air on his back right before a pair of fat wide arms clamped around him.

Reacting instantly, Ethan threw himself backward, slamming his attacker against the wall. There was a loud crack as the attacker's head slammed into the metal. Ethan shook the man off, but the shit took hold of the strap holding his shield on the way down.

Ethan's air cut off abruptly. Grunting, he tried to slip the strap over his head, but he ended up breaking it. Taking in a burning lungful of air, he felt his shield clatter to the floor just as Ethan swung his leg up. A strong kick to the guy's head, and he was done.

"*Shit.*" Ethan coughed, rubbing his neck. Bleary-eyed, he looked around as two of his men ran to him.

"Where'd she go?" one asked.

Ethan rubbed his neck and pivoted. The girl was gone. In the fight, she had somehow squeezed past him.

He stumbled past the agents, leaving them to deal with the fallen man while he called out hoarsely in Russian. When there was no answer, he tried Czech, French, and finally Spanish for the hell of it.

The girl had managed to make it outside. He made it to the door leading to the deck when he spotted her at the railing.

Ethan hailed her, raising his hand. She turned around, her eyes wide and alarmingly empty. It didn't matter what language he spoke. The look in her eye was wild. She was beyond understanding anyone.

He approached her slowly, his hands up. He murmured words in a soft voice, hoping his tone would register and she would realize he wasn't a threat. More agents joined them at the side of the boat, but he signaled them to stop.

He was only two steps from being able to grab her when she climbed over the railing and jumped over the side.

"*Fuck.*" There was no time to strip down. Ethan flipped the safety on his gun before taking it off. He slipped off his sidearm, then handed it to the nearest agent.

Ethan hit the water seconds later, stroking hard to where the poor girl thrashed in an uncoordinated effort to stop from sinking.

How fucking scared did she have to be to jump into the water when she didn't know how to swim? Ethan had never been a life-guard, but he had seen a few water rescues in movies. Reaching the girl, he overpowered her, tipping her head back and holding her arms so she couldn't take him down with her.

Her continued struggles made the swim back hellish, but Ethan somehow managed to get them around the stern through sheer brute strength.

He didn't have to shout for help. As soon as he was close enough, multiple arms reached out to haul them out of the water.

The next few minutes were a blur. A woman who ID'd herself as social services came over to whisk the girl away. Someone tossed a blanket over him and he bitched them out, yelling to save them for the girls.

"They're all set," Jason assured him, emerging from the mess of law enforcement that had taken over the dock. "The ambulances pulled up right after you went back aboard."

"And the ship's crew?" Ethan asked, wiping his face with a towel.

"We're about to load them up in that pair of paddy wagons over there." His partner gestured in the other direction, but Ethan was busy glaring daggers at the crew.

He knew it might cost him big, but it didn't matter. Ethan was soaking wet and a hairbreadth from a full-blown Hulk out. He stepped over the crewman who had laughed in the beginning—and then he kept going.

"Oops," he said as he stomped on the asshole's balls. The man cried out, but Ethan pivoted, grinding his heel before returning to his part-ner's side.

Jason tried hard not to laugh. "Feeling better now?"

"No, but it will do," he said with a sniff.

His partner shook his head. "Why don't you head on home before you freeze your dick off?"

Ethan grunted. They were nowhere near done. "I'm fine. The rage is more than enough to keep me warm. Besides, I need to be on hand in case the girls start talking."

Since the ninth girl hadn't responded to Russian, it was still a toss-up if that was where they came from, but he had a better chance of making himself understood than the other agents.

But his partner wasn't having it. "Don't worry about them. We'll muddle through until we can get some translators down here."

Jason indicated Ethan's soaking-wet clothes. "Meanwhile, you've got to wash all that shit off. The water in Boston Harbor is not as polluted as some places, but why take the chance? You want to have kids someday, right?"

Ethan hesitated, glancing down. He didn't see any obvious muck. "I'm sure it's fine. It's not like I have any open wounds."

"Well, let's see if you're still singing the same tune tomorrow. Besides, it's freezing. Go home before you catch pneumonia. I don't want to do all the paperwork for this shitshow on my own."

Jason clapped him on the back. "It's okay. I got this. Go home. Take a hot shower and talk to your girl. Your night is just getting started."

Shit. Ethan hated it when Jason was right.

"Thanks, man," he said, waving to the rest of the team as he headed to the parking lot.

CHAPTER TWENTY-ONE

Ethan's skin was starting to itch under his clean sweatshirt. He'd changed into his gym clothes in the dock parking lot to avoid spreading Boston Harbor's many germs all over the interior of his car.

As an extra precaution, he used the car cover he kept in the trunk to drape over the driver's seat. He was going to have to toss the whole thing in his heavy-duty washing machine.

Exhausted, he let himself into his place, leaving his shoes and socks outside the door so he wouldn't get any crap on the new hardwood. Luna could walk, but she still spent an inordinate amount of time crawling around or playing on the floor.

"Julie, can you take this for me?" he called, hefting the car cover so it wouldn't drag on the floor. There was no answer, so he repeated himself a little louder.

She must be asleep.

It was a little late, almost half-past ten, but Ethan was surprised Julie hadn't waited up for him. If he'd been her, he would have been waiting on pins and needles. Shoving a sudden disquiet away, Ethan dropped the cover and wet clothes on top of the washing machine in the laundry room, taking the time to wash his hands and arms before going to search for Julie.

His bed was empty. She'd made it up, tucking the down cover

under the mattress the way hotels did. Even the pillows had been straightened with military precision.

He scanned the room, wondering why that bothered him so much. His apartment was too quiet. *She's not with Luna.*

Her stuff was gone. A quick search revealed all Julie's clothes were missing, along with the beat-up suitcases and backpack that had once held them. The empty spot where they used to sit in the closet screamed.

The pain didn't truly hit him until he went into Luna's room. The crib was empty except for a small assortment of toys, whatever she hadn't been able to fit in the suitcases or that backpack she used to carry.

He tried to console himself with the fact Julie hadn't let her pride get in the way when she left him. She had taken all the warm winter clothes Maggie and his friends had bought for Luna. But she still had to travel light, so the toys had been left behind.

He ran to the kitchen. The coffee pot was still warm. She had left, but very recently.

Icy fingers spread up from his gut to his chest.

He didn't know where to go. Ethan formed a vague idea of trying Tully's before discarding it. She wouldn't go there. No, she had taken off again.

He was too far from a subway stop, so he had to start with the nearest bus stops.

Deciding not to think too hard, he ran back down the stairs, palming his keys. He hit the parking lot at a run, skidding to a stop at the Mustang's driver's side door, dropping his keys in the process.

If he hadn't bent to pick them up, he might have missed the bobbing light coming from one of the first-floor windows. It was coming from the studio Julie used to live in.

Ever so slowly, he walked back inside. Suddenly, he was at the door of the studio with absolutely no memory of how he'd gotten there.

Ethan pushed the door open.

He saw the suitcases and backpack first. They were stacked by the door. Julie was crouched in the corner with a flashlight on the floor next to her, pointed at the wall.

Luna sat on the floor in her winter suit. She yawned sleepily, watching whatever her mother was doing with little interest.

He didn't say a word. Reaching for the switch, he flipped it, flooding the room with light.

Julie started, whirling around so swiftly she fell on her backside. A screwdriver landed on the floor. She had been using it to remove the old-fashioned grill that covered the heating duct.

"You need a Phillips-head to get that open," he informed her. She was using the wrong kind.

Julie scrambled to her feet. "*Ethan*. I didn't think you were coming home until later. Your text said…"

She trailed off, cringing as he picked up one of the suitcases. It was full.

And just like that, she'd accomplished what the crew of the *Lorano* hadn't managed. He lost it, seeing red.

"No," he said. "Get Luna and go back upstairs."

Shifting her weight, Julie gazed longingly past him at the door. "But, Ethan…"

"*No*," he repeated in a hiss. "You are not running off with that baby in the middle of the fucking night!"

By the time he was done, he was yelling. He could feel the cords in his neck standing out in stark relief.

Luna started to cry. Her wide eyes eviscerated him when she opened her little mouth to wail. Swallowing his anger with effort, he bent to pick her up before Julie could, cuddling and soothing the little girl with incoherent murmurs.

He couldn't speak. If he did, he would regret what came out for the rest of his life.

Julie was crying, too. The tears were choking her, but she still tried. "W-we can't stay."

Ethan wanted to break something. The only thing keeping him in check was the tiny sniffling toddler in his arms. Luna was depending on him to get a hold of the situation.

"We are not going to talk about this tonight," he managed to say. "Right now, we are going upstairs. I'm putting Luna to bed, then I'm taking a hot shower. You and I will discuss this in the morning."

"But—"

"I said... *tomorrow!*" He picked up the suitcases in his free hand before marching to the elevator. After a beat, Julie followed, holding that fucking backpack in her hands.

On the elevator, Julie cried the entire way up. Once they were back in his place, he set Luna in her crib. The toddler must have been emotionally wrung out, too, because she closed her eyes and went to sleep as soon as her head hit the mattress.

He tossed the suitcase into the closet. Julie sat on the couch, wiping her eyes with the heel of her hand. She stopped when she saw him under the lights. "Oh my God! What happened to you?"

Puzzled, Ethan froze as she rushed over, putting cold fingers on his neck. He stepped into the hall where he'd hung a full-length mirror so he could do spot checks on his appearance on those rare days he had a meeting or a presentation.

There was an angry red stripe burned in the side of his neck from when that guy had surprised him by pulling on his badge.

"It's nothing."

And it wasn't. The fucker could have taken his head off if Ethan hadn't reacted so quickly, but he hadn't been truly hurt until he came home.

"But you're injured." Her hand clutched his arm.

"You're going to pretend to care about that?" he spat, shaking her hand off. "You were about to run off into the night—with no note or explanation."

Her eyes sparkled with fresh tears, and she curled her hand against her chest. She bit her lip. "I...I left an explanation on your desk."

Ethan stared for a long moment, his emotions a churning storm. Explanations aside, there was something he didn't understand.

"I don't get it. You could have been long gone. Why the hell did you wait until this hour of the night to leave?

She looked down. "I wanted to make sure you came home from the raid. I needed to know you were safe before..."

Before she left, tearing his heart out of his chest.

Ethan scrubbed his face with his hands. How the hell had this happened? He'd simply been doing a good deed, helping out a mom and her kid who were in a bind. And now he had discovered he was in love with her—with *them*—in the worst possible way.

"Why?"

The words hung in the air, taking up more room than one syllable should.

Julie shuddered, closing her eyes briefly. "It was what you said about making Luna mine legally. If we file papers to legitimize our relationship, he might find us."

He.

Ethan chose his next words carefully. "Do you think this person would follow you here?"

Julie wrapped her arms around herself. "I don't know. I hope not."

He waited a little longer, biting his tongue as tears began to stream down her cheeks.

"Oh, Ethan, I was so stupid. I thought he was going to save me from my family—that he was so much better than them. I couldn't have been more wrong."

"Who is this man?"

"Alvaro," she whispered, shivering. "He was my fiancé."

O-kay. This was going be a long fucking night. But then Ethan reached out and touched her hand. "Hell, you're colder than I am, and I took a dunk in the damn harbor tonight."

She looked up, startled. "Did you fall off the boat?"

"Technically, I jumped." Ethan stripped off his sweatshirt, herding Julie into his bedroom and through it to the bathroom.

"Strip," he ordered, turning on the overhead heat lamps.

Quizzically, she raised an eyebrow.

"This isn't about sex. You're shivering like you're in shock. Strip. We're taking a hot shower and going to bed. Luna is out for the night. Everything else can wait until morning."

"Oh, I'm fine," she said, but she fumbled with her coat with unsteady hands, dropping it to the ground.

"Here, let me help," he said, reaching for her shirt. He undressed her as fast as he could, denying himself the pleasure of a slow reveal. Then he turned on the double shower head, adjusting them so they both got a steady stream.

Ethan rarely gave much thought to his own morality. He simply checked the box for law-abiding citizen and moved on. But after undressing Julie and soaping her down without trying anything sexual, he was convinced sainthood was on the table.

He was polishing his halo when Julie decided to help him lather up. Ethan should have stopped her, but it felt too good.

Julie rubbed the washcloth across his chest, circling to wash his back. She washed his legs, too, but he twisted to take the washcloth from her before she could do the front. He scrubbed himself rapidly while she hovered behind him. Eventually, he felt her cheek press against his back.

"I didn't want to leave," she confessed. "If I could have anything, I would pick staying here with you."

He didn't miss the underlying message. Julie was still at the edge, debating whether she should leave.

"You can't run forever."

"I don't know how to stop."

He turned around to face her. "Start by taking stock. Weigh what you gain and what you will lose by leaving."

Yes, she could keep running. Julie was smart, and she worked hard. If she had to, she could start over and succeed. It would help if she picked a friendlier city than Boston next time. Perhaps she'd be better off.

Maybe somewhere down the line, she'd decide the only thing chasing her was a phantom. Maybe she'd find some nice computer programmer or something equally lame to someday tie the knot and have two or three kids of their own.

"Fuck that," he muttered aloud before he could stop himself. He reached for her, not questioning it when she almost flew into his arms, her wet creamy skin slapping against his chest. Her mouth opened to his under the streaming water.

Sainthood was off the table.

CHAPTER TWENTY-TWO

Juliet didn't care that she had been prepared to leave this man only a few hours ago with no plans to look back. All she cared about now was pressing closer against him so hard she was squeezing the air out of her lungs.

Ethan kissed her, his tongue invading her mouth, possessing it as he guided her head this way and that. She drank him in, feeling more and more detached until she was flying.

His hands stroked over the globes of her ass before going around her thighs. He hauled her up, urging her legs around his waist. Juliet wrapped her arms around his neck, gasping when his cock parted her folds, driving in her with one long, hard stroke.

There was no pain this time. All Juliet felt was a slick burning heat. Panting, she used her thigh and ass muscles to wiggle up and down on his steel, hungrier for him now that he was buried inside her. It didn't matter that she wasn't used to this. Her appetite for Ethan had been building for weeks. She'd tried not to watch him, the way he moved and how his long, muscled form looked at rest. Even the way he smelled—more mint than musk. If she took a bite of him, her mouth would come away tingling with peppermint.

Ethan pressed her back against the cool shower tiles, using the additional support to wrestle back control. Hips pistoning, he fucked her against the wall, his driving strokes not making any allowances for her relative lack of experience.

Not that it mattered. In his arms, her body had a mind of its own. Her sheath fluttered and flexed, trying to keep him inside or absorb him. She didn't know which.

He didn't waste any time. When the end came, it was quick. Ethan ground against her, reverently working the head of his cock over a magical tight spot deep inside her. Crying out, she clamped against him as he came with a shout.

Her mind was quiet when Ethan set her down on her feet. Exhausted, she leaned against him as he rinsed them off and toweled them dry.

They were in bed, covered in his thick down comforter, before he spoke again.

"Your real name is Julietta." It was a statement of fact.

"I thought it was better to go by something else, just in case. I prefer Juliet. It's what my mom and dad used to call me, but it's too close to the real one."

He pulled her close, settling her lax body against his hard one. "I like Juliet. That's going to be my name for you."

She stirred, twisting toward him. "But you might forget. Isn't it better to always use Julie?"

Ethan tightened one arm around her waist.

"I won't forget." He flicked a hand at the windows. "Out there, you're Julie. In here, your mine—you're my Juliet."

Ethan woke at dawn. He should have been tired. Yesterday had been grueling, but he was pumped and flooded with purpose.

He dressed before checking on Luna, resolving to buy a baby monitor at the earliest opportunity. Juliet hadn't said so aloud, but, in his mind, she agreed to stay when she'd given herself to him in the shower. Now he needed to convince her the decision was already made.

Grabbing his phone, he texted Jason, thanking him again for wrapping everything up last night and informing his partner he wasn't

going to be in today. It was Sunday. The brass at work would understand if they didn't hit the piles of paperwork waiting for them until
Monday.

Then he went to his office, intending to toss out Juliet's note
without reading it. Whatever she'd had to say no longer mattered
because she wasn't leaving.

But it wasn't a note. There was a small USB drive on his ink
blotter.

The model was familiar. He checked his desk, confirming one of
his stashes of new thumb drives was missing. Though it was verboten
to use them to copy FBI case files, there was an overabundance of
related manuals, case studies, and tech sheets he shuttled back and
forth to the office.

Fishing out his laptop from the bottom drawer, he plugged in the
drive and hit play on the movie file he found there.

At first, the only thing on the screen was white lace. He pursed his
lips, deciding they were curtains. His guess was confirmed when they
were pulled aside, revealing the view through an upper-story window.

The angle was bad and the view obstructed, but Ethan was able to
make out the wide expanse of a spacious lawn and part of a driveway.

Three men argued next to the hood of a black SUV. As he watched
two push the third man to his knees, another man appeared on the
screen. He was well-formed, not tall but lean with obvious strength.
And he was in uniform.

Alvaro. He knew it without being told.

Ethan didn't recognize the uniform, but he would have bet his life
savings it was a Mexican cop's. He couldn't see a shield or any insignia
to denote rank, but he didn't need them. This guy was high up. It was
all in his bearing, in the way he held himself.

Alvaro's lips moved, and a gun appeared in his hand. The blast of
the bullet sounded tiny and distant. The gasp of the person holding
the camera was much louder...and remarkably familiar.

Juliet had taken the video.

On screen, the image whirled as the camera fell to the floor. Ethan
caught a glimpse of dark hair flying past the white paint of an uniden-
tified ceiling. Then the video ended.

Ethan took a deep breath. *No wonder she ran...*

Alvaro was a murderer. After everything Ethan had seen on the job, he wasn't surprised. No, what had blindsided him was the fact Alvaro was a cop. A memory came back—the way Juliet had reacted to Ethan's gun. Or had it been to his shield?

Both. It had been both.

Well, fuck.

CHAPTER TWENTY-THREE

Groaning, Ethan sat back in the chair. Juliet must have freaked when she found out he was an FBI agent.

I was so stupid. I thought he was going to save me from my family—that he was so much better than them. That was what she'd said. And here he was with his own shiny badge, a representative of the same rule of law Alvaro was perverting.

Humorless mirth bubbled up, and Ethan laughed sardonically.

"Laughter is not the reaction I was expecting."

Juliet stood in the dooryard. She wore one of his shirts again. An inappropriate surge of lust distracted him.

All of her stuff is still in the suitcase, his brain helpfully reminded him. The wave of desire retreated, although it didn't go far.

"I was replaying the moment when you saw my badge and gun. I severely underestimated how terrified you must have been."

She twisted the front of the shirt she wore in her hands. "You have no idea."

He rose and took her hand, leading her out to the living room so they could sit on the couch. She curled up, clutching one of the pillows Maggie had insisted he order when she had picked out the couch for him.

"When I realized you were a police officer, or rather an FBI agent,

I thought I was going to pass out. It felt as if I'd made the same mistake—only ten times worse."

"Alvaro, your former fiancé, is the trigger man in the video, right? He's in law enforcement."

Juliet nodded. "I know you're not anything like him. Not now. But, in the beginning, I was scared."

Understandable under the circumstances. "I'm going to make some coffee," he said, getting to his feet. "Then you're going to start at the beginning. I want you to tell me about your family."

Her sharp intake of breath betrayed her anxiety, but he didn't call attention to it. The best thing he could do was act matter of fact, as if there were no other option but to tell him everything.

Ethan waited until the mug of coffee was ready. He handed it to her. She added cream, took a sip, and grimaced.

"More sugar?" he asked.

She added it gratefully, mixing in extra cream as well. Then she put the mug down, appearing to forget about it as he studied her.

Juliet lifted her hand, pushing her hair behind her ear.

"I, uh, I didn't know what my father did," she began. "He wasn't a cartel lieutenant or anything like that. He was a lawyer with a degree in finance. All I knew was that we always had money. We owned multiple homes, and my parents drove the newest model car."

She shrugged. "Dad was successful. People always wanted to speak with him or were badgering him for appointments. Actually, both my parents had hangers-on. My mom was a starlet."

Ethan took a premature sip of his black coffee, burning his tongue. "Starlet? She was an actress?"

"Yeah." Juliet reached for the mug, but she just wrapped her fingers around it instead of picking it up. "I was born in Los Angeles. My mom was doing a Spanish-speaking soap opera there at the time. My older sister Daniela was born in London during one of Mom's theater runs. But our primary home was in Mexico because my dad's work was there."

Ethan held his breath. "So, you're a US citizen?"

She nodded. "Dual. So was my sister. My mom insisted on getting our American passports. She wanted to be able to fly to L.A. or Miami at will to do commercials or plays. Or to go shopping in New York. We did that a lot."

He leaned back on the couch. "Do you know that's what I thought our biggest problem was likely to be? I thought you were undocumented."

"Does it matter when I can't live under my own name?"

She had a point. "What about Luna?"

Juliet shook her head. "No. My sister Daniela...she wasn't a planner. Luna was born in Mexico."

Okay, that wasn't the best news. He passed a hand over his face. "We'll worry about that later. When did you realize your dad was a cartel lawyer? Or did he use the law degree for something else?"

"It took a long while. I had finished college a few months earlier." She raised her hands in a helpless gesture. "It wasn't like he spent his days getting low-level dealers out of jail. But he was always in meetings. He used his legal expertise to broker deals that somehow ended with lots of dirty money being cleaned."

"Ah." A money launderer with a law degree. If he were as smart and capable as his daughter, then the man must have been extraordinarily successful indeed.

"What about Alvaro?"

The question hung in the air. Juliet's eyes were distressingly blank for a long while she gazed into the past.

"Juliet," he prodded.

She gave herself a shake. "When I said I thought Alvaro was going to save me from my family, I didn't mean literally. They were never a danger to me. But I had discovered my father's real profession. From that moment on, I was on a crusade. I wanted my father to cut ties with his employers or retire."

She hung her head. "I was foolishly idealistic, crammed full of ideas and morals...only some of which were mine." Blinking rapidly, she gave him a sad smile. "I thought I could convince my father to do something else. But whenever I tried, he would look at me with this resigned superior look. However, I didn't let up. I even threatened to tell my mother, thinking I could get her on my side."

"Let me guess," Ethan broke in. "She already knew, and she was on board with it."

"Yes. Both were accustomed to a certain lifestyle." She rubbed her temples. "My older sister was a carbon copy of my mom in looks and attitude. Daniela didn't go to school abroad like I did. Instead, she married a musician at nineteen, divorced at twenty, and partied for the next six or seven years until she married a second time—to a much older man with even older money."

He wanted to push her on the subject of her ex, but she came back around to it herself. "My sister liked to throw extravagant parties. I met Alvaro at one."

Ethan made a noncommittal noise.

"I should have wondered more about what he was doing there, but I confess I didn't think about that. At first, I didn't know who he was, but it didn't take long to find out. The local papers were starting to cover him, you see. They painted Alvaro as a crusader. And a lot of people went to my sister's parties."

She picked up the cup of coffee. "We didn't get together right away. I was finishing college abroad, then I started law school."

He had chosen the wrong moment to sip his drink because her words made him spit it back out. Hastily, he stood and got a paper towel to wipe his mouth and chin. "A lawyer? You're a lawyer?"

A small shrug. "I know you don't like them. If it's any consolation, I didn't finish."

"I like them fine," he lied.

She laughed before subsiding. "You're a good liar, but you forget I have receipts."

He suppressed a groan, wishing he hadn't been quite so honest about his feelings toward those in the legal profession.

"I'm more than willing to make an exception for you even if you decide to go back to law school," he said magnanimously.

"Thanks. Although, I'm not sure I'm going to do that. When I left, I was studying contract and international law, like my father wanted. I told myself that didn't mean anything—I wasn't going to follow in his footsteps."

"Of course you weren't. You would never do that." Ethan was sure.

She smiled. "I know. After my first year, I told my father I was going to switch to environmental law."

"How did he react?"

"He said *great, pay for it yourself.*" She sighed. "Unless I switched back, of course."

"Which you refused to do," he guessed.

"I dropped out, then took a job as a waitress at a local café instead."

"Good for you."

"Or not," she said flatly. "You see, that's where I got to know Alvaro better. He found out I was working there, so he started coming in to eat. He was a regular at lunchtime."

Ethan grunted. "And how did your family react to your new job?"

"My father was furious, especially when I moved into this crappy studio apartment. My mother was the same. A daughter who worked was bad for her image. My sister was amused. She said a menial job would force me to grow up really fast."

"But Alvaro wasn't like that, was he?" Ethan didn't need to be told how easy it would have been for a predator like Alvaro to cast himself in the role of hero. "I'd bet he was supportive. He probably repeatedly told you how much he admired you for not taking their money."

She snorted lightly. "And I fell for it. I believed everything he said. When he started to paint us as allies—as if it were us against the world of corruption—I was filled with self-righteous vindication. This was despite the fact I still saw my family. I used to go over for dinner two or three times a month. In my mind, it was justified, as if being a good example would sway them somehow. Like I said, I was stupidly idealistic."

Ethan didn't want to know the answer to his next question, but he needed all the facts. "When did things become romantic?"

Her brow furrowed. "It took a lot longer than you would think."

"I'm actually trying really hard to avoid thinking about it."

"*Oh.*" Juliet flushed. "I simply meant his courtship was slow—so slow I was convinced he wasn't interested—until he finally kissed me almost six months after he started coming by the café."

Ethan pictured the Alvaro from the video kissing *his* Juliet. Then he pictured himself breaking both of the man's arms, and he felt better.

"I had no idea he was involved in the drug trade, either. He had this image, you see. He was part of the new uncorruptibles that were going to take down the cartels and corruption in our town. He made quite a name for himself as a crime fighter. There was even talk of Alvaro running for mayor. It was something he took seriously, too. He had money, respect, and could command an audience. A career in politics seemed like the next natural step."

Juliet picked at the pillow's cover. "It was all a set up. Alvaro was using me. Word had gotten around that I was refusing to take my family's money. Not everyone knew where that money came from, but it didn't matter. I was a story he could exploit. As long as I was on his arm, Alvaro could point to me as proof of his incorruptibility when, in reality, he was part of the drug trade."

"How did you put it together?" he asked quietly.

Juliet looked up, startled. "I...I didn't."

He frowned as she laughed humorlessly. "I really didn't. I was oblivious up until the moment Alvaro killed that man."

"Do you know who he was?"

She nodded. "I read his name online—on the web page of the local newspaper. It was Sagrado Juarez... He was supposed to be one of the men who gunned down my family."

"*Fuck.*"

"My sentiments exactly."

"So, you were in the dark until Luna's christening?"

"I wasn't even sure I was going to go. My sister hadn't included me in her pregnancy. I mean, we used to fight, but, after Alvaro and I got engaged, she barely spoke to me. However, there was a new baby. I wanted to at least be there for her, even if it was uncomfortable. That...and my mother said she'd never speak to me again if I didn't go. And then, after the church service, Daniela and I got into a huge fight."

Juliet covered her eyes with both hands. "I can still hear the things she said...the poison." There were tears on her cheeks when she raised her head. "I don't want to repeat the comments, but the fight is why I ran upstairs instead of partaking in the party. I stayed up there long enough for the nanny to come up with the baby. She put Luna down for a nap, then went downstairs to her quarters. I stayed to watch Luna sleep. Outside, the party was winding down."

"Did you see any of the shooters?"

"No. Like I said before, I took Luna from her crib and hid. The baby slept through the whole thing. When it was over, there were six people dead—including my parents, sister, and her husband."

"Who were the other two?"

"One was a guest—another lawyer who worked with my dad sometimes. The other was a valet hired to park cars for the day."

This was where things got murky for him. "What happened afterward?"

"The police came. I went downstairs with them, where I saw the bodies. But then Alvaro swept in and took charge, making sure I didn't have to identify the bodies at the morgue."

Fat lot of good that did. She'd still seen the victims at the scene.

"How long after that was the video shot?"

"Not long...there had been no suspects. All I was told was the shooting was retaliation of some kind, but no one was arrested." She broke off, peering up from under her lashes. "I was living at Alvaro's by then. He told me that my studio apartment wasn't secure enough, not when I had Luna with me. So I moved into his house at the edge of town. It was very private. According to him, it was also more secure."

I'll bet. "And then he shot the suspect."

"That was several weeks later."

He tried to pitch his voice to sound casual. "So how long did you live with him?"

Ethan didn't fool her. "Almost a month."

"And you never slept with him?"

She shook her head. "After my family was gunned down, he generously gave me time to myself to recover. Luna and I had our own suite. I was touched by his consideration, although other things started to get my attention."

"What kind of things?"

She ran her teeth over her lip. When she spoke, it was as if she were peering through a veil he couldn't see.

"It took me a long time to realize what was really going on in my family. Once I did, it was all around me. Afterward, I couldn't help but see the signs. It was in the company Alvaro kept—the phone conversations he didn't want me to hear. One night, his men came and roused him, but they weren't in uniform. He didn't want me to see them. Instead, he shooed them away as soon as he saw I was awake. After that, I decided I wasn't going to fly blind or be a trusting idiot. I went online, then bought a bug and a nanny cam disguised as a bear."

He hadn't expected that. Ethan snapped his fingers. "The vent downstairs."

"It's where I hid the bear, but you already saw what it recorded."

"And the bug in his office?"

"It didn't catch enough to be incriminating in the legal sense—at least, I don't think so—but it was enough to convince me that he knew all about the drug trade because he was on the inside."

The skin around her eyes tightened. "Ethan, there is a warrant for my arrest back home—for the death of Sagrado Juarez—the man who was supposed to be part of the group that killed my family. But I don't even know if he had anything to do with it."

"My guess is he did." Ethan could easily put the rest together. "Alvaro probably hired outside shooters, then got rid of them to cover it up. He was cleaning up after himself."

"I think so. And the crusade that followed took down the higher-ups of the cartel my father worked for."

Ah-ha. "It was a hostile takeover."

Juliet collapsed against the couch. She didn't answer, but she didn't have to.

Ethan rubbed his chin. "So Alvaro killed your family, then found a patsy or several to answer for it. But why did he kill that guy when he knew you were in the house?"

"Oh, I wasn't supposed to be there. Luna had a doctor's appointment that got rescheduled. I didn't mention the change to him. I believed he was going to be out, too. My plan was to go through his office while I could. I never got the chance. Instead, I left with Luna the next day."

He grunted. "The timing of that would have told him everything he needed to know. I mean, who the hell kills someone in their driveway?"

"Someone ruthless and without a conscience who is used to abso-lute power?" Juliet shivered. "Ethan, you have to leave my past there. Please leave Alvaro alone."

Okay, no more rhetorical questions. Not when Juliet had an unfortunate habit of answering them. But he had to be honest with her.

"Burying your head in the sand is not going to make your problems go away. When you ran off, Alvaro decided to pin that man's death on you, killing two birds with one stone," he said. "But it's also true this may be the end of it."

Juliet shot him a look of patent disbelief.

He reached over to take her hand. "I understand how scared of Alvaro you are. After watching that video, I don't blame you. But he's in a precarious position, too. He has a lot of power in your hometown, but leaving to chase after you would endanger that. Alvaro needs to be there to make sure none of the competition encroaches on his territory or his underlings get ideas about a coup."

It would have been stupid of the man to risk coming here, but sending a lackey to do his dirty work would have been smart... expected even. Especially if Alvaro thought Juliet witnessed the murder.

Imagine if he knew she had it on video...

Ethan didn't want to think about that scenario. And he wasn't going to mention it.

Juliet opened her mouth to respond, but Luna marched into the living room on her own tiny feet. She gave him and Juliet a downright dirty look before holding her arms out. "Up."

Laughing, he stood and picked her up. "How did you get out of your crib?"

Juliet stood, too. "I warned you she's an escape artist."

Resigned to getting the rest of the story later, he looked down at Luna.

"Her real name is Delilah. My sister named her after one of the character's Mother played, and because it sounded like her own name, Daniela."

"Really?" He glanced down at the toddler. She stared back, then bopped him in the face with her doll with all her strength while making smooching noises.

Ethan tried not to laugh, but he failed. "No, she's not a Delilah."

Juliet almost smiled. "I like Luna, too."

CHAPTER TWENTY-FOUR

A lot had changed in a few days. Under normal circumstances, Ethan would have been taking a victory lap around the office today. Instead, he was ducking all compliments and pretending to plow through the reports to avoid talking. The only place he wanted to be was at home with his family.

And that was how he thought of Juliet and Luna now. There was no point in denying it. Ethan was in love with Juliet. He wanted her more than he wanted his next breath. He also loved her daughter. It didn't matter that Luna wasn't her biological child. Juliet was her mom, and he...

Ethan hesitated. It was easy to do and say the right things when Juliet was in front of him, but verbally committing to be someone's dad was something else.

"What are you thinking about so hard?" Jason sat in the neighboring chair, taking a sip from his mug.

"Fatherhood."

Jason coughed, spraying Ethan with a light dusting of hazelnut coffee.

"Whoa," he said once he'd stopped choking. "That'll teach me to ask you loaded questions while drinking anything."

"Teach *you*?" Ethan wrinkled his nose as he searched for a napkin.

Finding a crumpled tissue in his top desk drawer, he wiped his face. "I'm the one wearing eau de artificial flavoring here."

Recovering, Jason laughed like a ghoul. "Well, well. I guess someone has been thinking about the commitments he made when he ordered his live-in lover not to leave him. I guess that explains why you look so constipated."

Ethan tossed the soiled napkin in Jason's face. He had filled his partner in on last night's drama on the way to work. Jason had been sympathetic when he learned exactly what kind of trouble Juliet was in—up to a point.

Jason understood Juliet's position, and her desire to not want to dig up trouble by looking into her past, but he also wanted to know all about Alvaro and he wanted to know yesterday. Ethan agreed with him, so they had been tag-teaming researching the bastard all morning. One would run a search while the other knocked out the paperwork the big brass needed on the raid.

His partner leaned in. "Hey, I sweet-talked Rivera into picking up some of the slack. He's feeling a little bad for being such an ass lately."

"What brought about this change of heart?"

Jason sucked in a breath through his teeth. "His divorce is final."

"Ouch." Ethan had never met Rivera's wife, but he knew the relationship had been a stormy one. The whole office did. Rivera had wanted to make it work, though, so it dragged on. But now it seemed the poor guy had finally thrown in the towel. "Well, hopefully, it'll improve his sour-ass disposition."

"It can't hurt. Especially once he starts hitting the bars again and finally gets laid more than once a year." Jason saw Ethan's expression and shrugged. "He used to clean up before the ill-conceived marriage."

Ethan made a face. "I don't need to know this shit. But I am grateful for the assist."

"Yeah. By the way, social services and a few non-profits have stepped up to help with the girls we found. The one who took a swan dive off the boat is okay, too. They were worried about the effects of hypothermia because she was in pretty bad shape already, but she's recovering nicely."

"Good." Most of his concern had been reserved for his situation, but those girls had claim to it, too. He couldn't forget that.

Jason turned to his computer, then typed for a few minutes. "Hey, check this out."

Ethan spun in his chair, then nudged Jason's out of the way with his own when he saw the screen.

It was a news account on the page of a major Mexican newspaper, reporting the death of a high-profile cartel lawyer and his family at a child's christening.

Ethan read over the disturbing details in a flash. Juliet's parents had been relatively young when they died. Both had been in their mid-fifties. Her sister had been twenty-nine, more than a decade and a half younger than her husband. The gory pictures that accompanied the story didn't feature their bodies, only the other two victims.

That must have been Alvaro pulling strings behind the scene. He would have still been playing the white knight for Juliet at the time of publication. Using his influence to make sure pictures of her dead family weren't plastered all over the papers would have been play number one in the evil mastermind handbook.

"I want to see this asshole," he growled.

Jason banged Ethan's chair, pushing him a few inches to the left. "I thought you would never ask."

Jason punched a few keys, then a photo popped up. Ethan narrowed his eyes at the aviator-clad man. Alvaro was in his early thirties—whipcord lean and wiry with black hair greased back with too much pomade. In the photo, Alvaro directed uniformed officers.

"He looks like a poser in those glasses," Ethan grumbled. Aside from the obvious he's-a-villain thing, Ethan was realizing it was difficult to find something to criticize about the man.

"Oh? I thought they kind of looked like yours." Jason smirked. He caught Ethan's glare. "All right, all right. Alvaro looks smelly. You can almost see the stink fumes coming off him. And he's too skinny, practically anemic."

Ethan nodded approvingly. "I don't know about the stink fumes, but he is too skinny, isn't he?"

Jason stifled a laugh. "I also found most of his service record. Wouldn't you know it? He's squeaky clean—the local papers paint him as a hero, part of the small group battling the cartels and government corruption."

"That confirms what Juliet said about him. Nothing else on the guy? Does he have a family?

"Well, not a wife obviously." Jason wrinkled his nose. "I'll keep digging. In the meantime, we should put an alert on Alvaro with the border patrol. If he enters the country, we want to know."

It was a good idea. "Agreed."

His partner drummed his fingers on the table. "On second thought, the brass at BPD still owes me for that mess with Maggie and Detective Dawson. We should have them run the alert, so it can't be traced back to us."

"Even better," Ethan said, waving him on.

Just then, Bullock, another agent, came up behind them. "Hey," he said, leaning over to peer at the screen. Both the article and the photo of Alvaro were still up. "Is this related to the Russians you bagged last night?"

"No, this is prep for another case."

Bullock's head drew back. "Shouldn't you wrap up this case before you move on to the next?"

"See, Bullock, that's why you're going to be busting two-bit identity thieves long after Ethan moves up to the big leagues."

Ethan smiled as Bullock scowled. "Hey, that identity theft case is big. The ring I'm tracking has stolen tens of thousands of stolen social security numbers."

He stalked off, and Jason grinned. Bullock was notoriously easy to rile. "We better get our damn reports in, or the Angel won't care how many girls we saved last night."

Ethan nodded and got to work, setting aside the issue of Juliet's ex for the time being. He spent hours on his report, including the background info on both the agents and the girls the rest of the team and the social workers had gathered. Occasionally, he would text Juliet. With Luna off at daycare, she had insisted on resuming her position as his renovation's supervisor. Ethan had gone along with it. The less time she had to think about things, the better. Predictably, Juliet had thrown herself back into the work with zeal and a determination that put his to shame.

Sometime in the mid-afternoon, he decided to go to the hospital to check on the girl who had taken a swan dive into the harbor. He was putting on his coat when Jason appeared from God knew where with Rivera and Jimenez flanking him.

Jason gave him a courtly bow before getting down on one knee. He held up a piece of paper the way a man presented his sword to swear fealty.

Ethan, used to his partner's antics, took the paper absently, his mind already on the traffic. "What's this?"

"You have another invitation, milord."

"What the f—" Ethan lifted the paper. The handwriting was the same as the first.

Meet me at the Whole in the Wall
   Wednesday ten o'clock.
   We need to talk.

The informant wanted a face-to-face talk. "What the fuck is the Whole in the Wall?"

Jason hopped to his feet. "Glad you asked. It's what passes for a dive bar in Newton. Apparently, it gets its name by virtue of the fact it's right next to a Whole Foods."

Rivera snorted. "Wednesday night is amateur beat poetry night."

"*What?*" Ethan smirked. "I wouldn't have figured our man for a…poet."

Jason laughed "It's still a long shot that it's Viktor. I mean, the location alone says it's not."

"That or he wants to meet someplace his crew would never spot him."

His partner grinned. "Viktor would stick out like a sore thumb in that place. Ten bucks says it's anyone but him."

"Fifty." Ethan stuck out his hand, and they shook on it.

CHAPTER TWENTY-FIVE

"Holy shit, baby, that feels so good."

It was nine o'clock on Wednesday night, and the last thing Ethan wanted to do was get in his car and drive to Newton. Of course, that may have had something to do with the fact he was on his new couch, balls deep in the woman he loved as she rode him like a stallion.

Ethan grabbed a fistful of her hair, inhaling her unique scent of caramel and flowers while her snug sheath caressed and squeezed him tight.

They were both bare from the waist up. He loved the all-access pass to her creamy skin, especially sucking her nipples into his mouth as he fucked her.

She moaned after he drew hard on a tightly furled bud, sending corresponding vibrations down to his shaft.

Fuck. This felt too good to be normal. Pleasure this intense had to be illegal. It should have been necessary to break into a bank to get remotely close to this sensation.

Putting a hand on the back of her head, Ethan pulled her close, taking her mouth as she drove him crazy, flexing and twisting until he had to stop kissing her to catch his breath.

"Ride me harder, baby," he hissed, flexing his hips to meet her halfway.

"You're in me so deep like this," Juliet panted, her hips breaking rhythm as he flexed, making sure he hit her G-spot on the down-stroke. She threw back her head and cried out, giving him permission to let go.

The supernova blindsided him. Choking back a shout, he wrapped his arms around her and let go. His hot seed shot into her waiting womb with a last wrench as she ground against him.

"I want every Wednesday to be like this," he said when he could breathe again.

Juliet giggled. "Tuesday wasn't bad, either." She pressed her face into his neck, still breathing fast. "And Monday in the shower was pretty nice, too."

He laughed, pulling her close against him. "I don't want to leave. I just want to stay and do that two or three more times. Maybe four."

He could feel her smile against his skin. "As if Luna would let that happen."

She had a point. Ethan glanced over her head at the camera-enabled baby monitor he'd set up on the coffee table behind them.

"Is she still asleep?" Juliet was a drowsy weight on his chest.

"Yeah, don't worry." In the short time he'd been in her life, the toddler's schedule had changed, adapting to the new one he'd imposed on her. She now slept through the night, dropping off after dinner. She woke bright and early the second he nudged her. Then he got her ready for daycare, giving Juliet time to wake up slowly. She was a deep sleeper, and it always took her a little longer to get going in the morning.

He dropped the toddler off at daycare every day on his way to work.

For now, the regime was working out. Ethan could count on some private time with Juliet every night—although, for good measure, he'd added a motion detector at the threshold of Luna's door. Just in case…

"If the new pattern holds, she'll be out until morning and you can do something for me," Ethan said, stroking Juliet's hair.

She lifted her head, clearly curious about his serious tone. "What's that?"

"Take a long bubble bath and relax for a change."

Juliet had come a long way. She was no longer the walking ball of tension he'd first met after her illness, but she was still pushing herself too much.

"You deserve a break. And I'll feel better about having to work tonight if I can picture you relaxing in the tub. On second thought, don't. The image of you naked in the tub makes me want to blow off my meeting."

Putting her hand on his cheek, she kissed him. "I know you can't do that."

Juliet didn't know the reason for his late-night rendezvous. He felt a little bad about not telling her, but the danger should be minimal tonight. Probably. Almost certainly.

He wondered how Jason handled this with his partner. Technically, every day on the job was dangerous. He wasn't worried about tonight, but he'd never faced this situation before, even with the girl-friends who had lasted longer than a few months. It wasn't even because there was a child in the mix now, either. He felt more for Juliet than he had any other woman in his past. His life was no longer his own.

Fuck, is this what responsibility feels like?

Juliet tugged at his arm, lifting his watch up to check the time. "You need to jump in the shower if you're going to make your meeting."

"That's right." Reluctantly, he let go of her so she could climb off him. "I would ask you to join me, but I would definitely be late then."

"What if I promise to keep my hands to myself?" she breathed, trailing her fingers down his chest as he stood.

Ethan pictured Viktor waiting through a single-beat poet trying to rhyme '*Scanlon*' with '*fake tan*'.

He backed away, his arms up. "Can't do it, sorry."

He jogged to the bathroom. "You have no idea how much," he called behind him.

It wasn't beat poetry night. Thankfully, the website for a "Whole in the Wall" was outdated. Instead, it was an open-mike night.

Ethan had gotten there in time to hear some poor guy's terrible standup, and now they were all suffering through an amateur sax player's instrumental rendition of "Careless Whisper".

"He's late." Rivera was backing Ethan up tonight. They'd decided on it a few days ago.

If this was sort of a Russian double-cross, they decided Jason's face would be too familiar. The other agent was hunkered down at the bar, warming a stool while they waited.

Jason was out in the van with Jimenez, waiting in case the meeting turned into a shit show.

Ethan kept his voice to a low murmur. "He'll show," he said into his earpiece. *He better*. Ethan had broken the speed limit to get here on time.

"Bet you're wishing he doesn't so you can get back to your hot tamale."

Only a faint narrowing of Ethan's eyes betrayed his surprise. Otherwise, he didn't move a hair in reaction. He kept sipping his overpriced beer, pretending to enjoy the mangled music. Well, pretending to at least tolerate it with a benign expression.

"I'm Hispanic, too, so I can say that," Rivera argued. "But if you call her that, she should dump your ass."

Ethan rolled his eyes. "Who told you about Juliet?"

"I thought it was Julie?"

Fuck. "Juliet is my pet name for Julie. It's more romantic."

The sound of Rivera gagging filtered over his earpiece.

"Now that you're back on the dating scene, you should consider trying romance. Girls prefer it."

"I thought dating was all about *Tinder* these days."

So, it was like that. Well, whether Rivera found someone after his divorce wasn't Ethan's concern. He only appreciated that the agent wasn't constantly bitching and moaning anymore.

Now if they could just keep random girls from hitting on the guy, maybe he'd be an effective backup.

Ethan sighed as a second hipster babe sat next to Rivera and tried to chat him up. At least the music had improved. The strangled sax had been replaced with a guitar. And the tune wasn't half-bad. It sounded vaguely Eastern.

No. I'm wrong. It's Russian.

"Well, fuck me."

Viktor was the musician. The burly tattooed man towered over everyone in the bar. On the stage, the small spotlight seemed to minimize the worst of the effects, magically transmuting the Russian gangster into another oversized hipster with a guitar.

He heard Rivera snicker, but Ethan guessed he was covering. There was no way the other man wasn't as surprised as he was.

Damn. The giant was rather good. Ethan marveled as Viktor strummed the guitar. In his hands, it looked like a toy. He also wondered how he'd gotten through the song without breaking a string.

The song wound down, and Viktor inclined his head the barest fraction in lieu of a bow. He walked off the stage, breaking the spell that he belonged there.

People scooted their chairs out of the way as he moved to the rear of the bar. Viktor settled into the vacant chair at the adjoining table, facing away from him.

"Not bad," he said, twisting slightly. As far as anyone else could tell, he was simply another patron complimenting the last performer. "Where did you learn to play 'Katyusha' like that?"

"Around." Viktor's kept his gaze on the stage, even though it was empty now. None of the other amateurs wanted to follow him.

After a beat, the man continued. "How do you know Russian so well? You are American, aren't you?"

Ethan shook his head the barest fraction. "My father was career army. We lived in Georgia for a while. Most people spoke Russian as a second language then. Now they speak English."

"You are better at languages than your counterparts," Viktor said, almost conversationally. There was a trace of his homeland in his speech, but if Ethan didn't know better, he might have pegged Viktor as an American.

"How do you know that?" Ethan had done his homework on the Russian, although there hadn't been much to find. But how did Viktor know about him?

His question was answered quickly. "I heard you speak it in the crowd after the incident at the Harvard Labs —with McLachlan's wife."

"You were there?" Ethan highly doubted that. There was no way Viktor would have gone unnoticed in that crowd.

"I was in a car, some distance away. But we had ears there."

Well, that was disturbing, but it explained why Ethan had been chosen over his partner Jason.

Jason was closer to the MacLachlans through his wife Maggie. But the only second language Jason spoke was French, and very badly.

"Why did you pick this place?"

The big man shrugged. "It was far from home."

"No one knows I do this from time to time," Viktor continued, his eyes flicking to Ethan's face. "I'm not watched as much as the others. They don't think I have a brain or ears."

Ethan nodded. It was easy to dismiss Viktor based on his size and obvious strength. He looked like a brute, so his crew treated him like one.

"When did you find out about the girls?"

Another shrug. "Such things…happen. Knowledge of them spills over."

If that were true, there had been more ships with other cargoes. This sort of shit wasn't new for the Komarov crew.

"So, what changed?" Something must have happened for Viktor to turn away from the Komarov.

Russian crews were like family. They demanded loyalty. Dissenters and traitors were punished harshly…or put down.

There was a long silence. "They gave me one."

Ethan blinked. "What?"

"They gave me one of the girls fresh off the boat. As a reward." Viktor rubbed his fingers together. "They forgot."

Ethan wanted to look into the man's eyes, but he forced himself to applaud lightly as a girl in her early twenties tentatively climbed on the stage with her guitar. He waited until she started playing before asking.

"What did they forget?"

This time, the silence was so long he thought Viktor wasn't going to answer. "My mother came to this country that way. On a boat. And then a brothel. I was born there."

Damn. "Is the girl okay? Your…gift?"

Viktor sighed, a strange sound coming from such a big body. "She thought she didn't please me, and she admitted as much to the keeper who delivered her. It was a mistake. They tried to replace her. I got her back in time. She cleans my house now. But when they found out that was all she was doing, they gave me a second, more experienced girl from one of the brothels."

Crap. "I see. Should I assume your help will be restricted to disrupting the Komarov's involvement in the slave trade?"

"Yes...probably."

Ethan raised a brow. Viktor couldn't see his expression, but he acted as if he could. "I've come into new information recently. It's made me reevaluate my position in the organization—specifically what I want it to be."

Okay. Ethan didn't know how to answer that. He decided not to. "What happened to the second girl they gave you?"

"She got bored. Decided to return to her brothel. For her, it beat cleaning."

"All right. So, what can we do for you?"

"I thought you could shut down the house, arrest the brothel keeper."

Interesting.

Unless Ethan was wrong, he would bet anything the local PD already knew about the brothel. He didn't like it, but graft and vice were a fact of life in any big city. So many places flew under the radar, operating with the city's blessing.

Well, fuck the status quo. "Where is this brothel?"

CHAPTER TWENTY-SIX

"Oh, don't look at me like that." Ethan grimaced as Luna batted her long, thick lashes.

She held up her hand, reaching for him. "Play?" she asked hopefully.

"I wish I could kid." He squatted beside her. "I know I promised to take you to the park, but the Angel called while Mama was giving you a bath. He wants the new raid planned yesterday, so I have to go into the office for a while."

Her little nose wrinkled. She grabbed his thumb, wrapping her tiny fingers around it.

Aww. Why didn't she just shoot him? It would hurt less.

"Yeah, I know, Little Moon." He sighed. "But he's the boss. I promise we'll all go if I get back while there's still light out."

"*Cake*," Luna shouted in response, rubbing her teething ring against his mouth.

"Aw, thank you, sweetie," he said, pretending to chew. He kissed her goodbye, lingering to take a sniff of her clean baby scent before putting her back down to play.

"You know she doesn't understand you yet, right?" Juliet asked with a laugh, walking him to the door.

Ethan was indignant. "She's learning fast. I never heard her say 'cake' before."

"It's this week's new word. Last week, it was cookie. I think most of her vocabulary is food related. Junk food specifically—and I think I know why." Juliet cocked her hip, nudging him with it.

Ethan managed to maintain a straight face, recalling an incident with some chocolate-covered Oreos and a new floor rug that had to be thrown out. "But she was so cute, sticking out her lower lip and begging with tears in her eyes."

"Those are crocodile tears. Don't fall for it. Stick to fruit for snacks, please."

He swore to do better, secretly aware he'd cave the moment Luna batted her thick baby eyelashes.

There will be other lazy Saturdays, he promised himself later when he was knee-deep in blueprints.

"So, when is this raid supposed to happen?" Jason asked with a yawn. He spread out the plans for the brothel and the neighboring buildings in Mattapan.

Ethan didn't like coming in on the weekend any more than his partner did, but he was hiding it better. He glanced at his watch. *I should be at home.*

"Earth to Ethan. Paging Ethan."

He raised his head. "What?"

Jason frowned. "I asked when you wanted to do this," he said, gesturing to the blueprints.

"Oh yeah, that. I was thinking mid-week when the foot traffic inside is likely to be lowest. The fewer customers, the better."

"Shouldn't we be aiming for peak business hours? I want to bust as many Johns as we can."

"I considered that, but we're going in to help the women. It's Viktor's priority, so it should be ours. Plus, there's too much of a chance that some of the Johns will be part of the Komarov crew. From what Viktor said, any could be packing. The more guns…"

"The higher the chance of gunfire," Jason finished. "Okay, yeah, I get it. Although, in my opinion, nailing some of the Komarovs would be a bonus."

Ethan grunted. "Charging them with prostitution is penny-ante stuff. It would slide off their back like water off a duck's bill."

"I don't like that. Makes them seem like cute little birds instead of cold-blooded slavers and murderers."

"You think ducks are cute?" Ethan wrinkled his nose.

"Don't you?"

Ethan laughed. "Not a fan, unless they're roasted and served in orange sauce. Outside of that, not so much."

"Don't knock ducks. It's geese that are the fuckers. Those things can double as guard dogs. They bite, too."

Ethan cocked his head. "Do I want to know how you know all this?"

"Hey, I'm an uncle now," Jason pointed out. "My nephew is into baby ducks and bunny rabbits. Mags and I took him to the petting zoo last week. That kind of thing softens you up."

"I think you came pre-softened." Ethan snorted.

"Laugh it up while you can. You're an acting dad now. Or are you going to tell me having Luna around doesn't affect you?"

Ethan pursed his lips. "Actually, I want to finish early so Juliet and I can take Luna to the park."

Jason smirked. "So…are you going to make things official?"

His partner started humming the "Wedding March," making Ethan pause with his hand halfway to his coffee mug. "Juliet and I have been together for less than two months."

"I knew I wanted to marry Maggie in less than one, or have you forgotten?"

"No. I remember exactly how desperate you were."

Ethan ducked the pen that came flying. He leaned back in his chair. "And for now, I'm just going to enjoy having two gorgeous girls waiting for me."

"Ugh, gross."

"Yeah, I heard it, too," Ethan conceded. "But it's not like I have much of a choice but to wait. Until I know more about this Alvaro guy, I can't plan a future, can I?"

Jason grimaced. "Because Juliet is living under an assumed name?"

Ethan nodded. "Luna, too."

"Really?" His partner winced. "I should have guessed that, but I didn't think about it. Poor little thing."

Ethan wanted to correct him. In some ways, Luna was extremely fortunate. She'd certainly lucked out in her aunt. Juliet would do anything for her.

And, someday, she'll do anything for our kids. All right, so maybe he *was* planning a future. He just hadn't figured out how to pull it off.

A thought occurred to him. "Hey, you added known associates to that passport alert for Alvaro, right?"

Keeping tabs on the asshole wouldn't do them much good if Alvaro sent someone else over the border in search of Juliet.

Jason's eyes narrowed. "Err, well, the guy is too well-connected to cover everyone who works with him. We'd be guessing who his closest confidantes are in any case. We don't know enough about him. Unless Julie can narrow down who her ex's BFFs are."

Ethan thought about it. "I don't think she knows. He kept her completely in the dark about his double life. She told me he didn't socialize much outside of work and political events. He spent most of his time networking, rubbing elbows with the city's movers and shakers." He sighed. "We'll have to settle for monitoring Alvaro only."

Jason tossed him another set of plans. "All right, let's get back to our actual work so you don't disappoint your little moon."

"Yeah." Ethan agreed, pulling his chair closer to the table.

Talking about Alvaro made him edgy. He redoubled his efforts, determined to get home as fast as he could.

A few hours later, he headed home, satisfied. He'd somehow managed to condense eight hours of work into four. Still patting himself on the back, he pulled into his apartment buildings parking lot right as Juliet ran out of the building.

Alarmed, he parked and turned off the engine as fast as he could. He was out of the car in a flash.

"What's wrong?" He pulled her into his arms. Something had scared her. He could see it on her face.

"I don't know." Juliet turned her head in jerky motions, scanning the lot with a wild look in her eye. "Did you see another car?"

"No, why?"

She put a hand over her heart. "The electricians were here this morning."

"Were they not supposed to be?"

"No, they were scheduled," she said, her tone shifting from frightened to embarrassed. "But I could have sworn I saw one take a picture of me."

His scowl was immediate. "Are you sure?"

"I think so." However, doubt crept into her expression. "I wasn't looking directly at him. I was talking to their supervisor in the hallway. He was in one of the rooms down the hall, but he stepped out for a second and I heard a click."

"But you didn't see him take the picture?"

"By the time I looked up, he was back in the room." She grimaced. "Ethan, Luna was with me. I was holding her at the time. I took her upstairs and came back down to get a better look at the man, but the crew was leaving. Both of us must have just missed seeing their van."

"Oh." Mentally, he added *'fuck'*. He had assumed Luna was asleep.

A random taking sneaky pictures of a hot woman wasn't all that strange. Creepy—*yes*. Uncommon? *No*. But the fact she had been holding Luna in her arms at the time set off warning bells in his mind. Really fucking loud ones.

He plastered on a smile. "I'm sure it was nothing."

"Are you certain?"

"You are a beautiful woman," he said, pointing out the obvious. "It probably wasn't more than that. I sure as hell don't like it, though."

He put his hand on the nape of her neck to guide her inside the building. "I think I'll call the electrical contractor to talk to him about it."

"I hope I'm not overreacting. I don't want to get anyone in trouble."

"Better safe than sorry." They took the elevator back up, eager to get back to Luna. She was in her playpen, her mouth a mess of chocolate.

"Excuse me... who scolded me about cookies earlier today?" he asked with a grin.

Blushing, Juliet went to wet a paper towel. She wiped Luna's mouth as she apologized. "I know. But I needed a way to keep her in the playpen while I went downstairs."

He kept his benign expression while Juliet got busy fussing over Luna and preparing dinner.

It crossed his mind that against all expectations, he had ended up with a very traditional woman.

Juliet had gone to the best schools in Mexico and Europe. She'd traveled the world, and she'd even spent a semester at Harvard in an exchange program. That was why she had chosen to come to Boston. She was familiar with the city, but she hadn't lived here long. Juliet believed Alvaro would search in Miami or Los Angeles before he would look for her here.

And yet, despite her years of education, she made dinner for him every night. She hadn't even known how to cook a year ago. Julie had grown up with maids to pick up after her and chefs to make her meals. She had taught herself for Luna's sake. And Ethan was reaping the benefits.

It hadn't occurred to him to feel bad about it until now.

If tragedy hadn't befallen her, she wouldn't be fixing their meals. She'd be off at a mixer, still studying for her law degree at the Sorbonne, or at some other exclusive institution.

I should offer to make dinner instead. It was the least he could do.

But then Ethan sniffed the air. *Well, I'll make dinner on a night when she hasn't already started a parmesan cream sauce.* Juliet served it over linguini with scallops. It was a simple meal, but he loved it.

I'll cook every other night, he promised himself before retiring to his office to make a few calls. Twenty minutes later, he was speed-dialing Jason.

His partner could barely understand him because Ethan was talking so fast. Forcing himself to slow down, he took a deep breath.

"I said...there was this guy here today. Juliet thought he was with the electricians, but he wasn't. The electricians thought he was with the plumbers, but they weren't supposed to be in today. And the plumber confirmed he hadn't sent anyone, either."

"And you say he took a picture of Juliet?" Jason made a humming noise as if he were thinking it over. "It could be nothing. You have guys in and out all the time with the renovations. One could have dropped by on his own to pick up something he forgot and decided to snap a pic of the hottie."

Ethan picked up his paperweight, rolling it around in his hand. "If it was just Juliet in the picture, I'd be willing to let it go at that. But she was holding Luna at the time. I don't like it."

Ethan paused. "I'm thinking we should get out of here for a while."

"You want me to get you a room at the hotel?" Jason asked.

"Maybe. Am I overreacting?"

Jason thought it over. "No, man," he eventually said. "Trust your gut. It's saved your butt before. Hell, it's saved mine. But you'll have to have someone else supervising those work crews for a while. Juliet shouldn't be watching them on her own like she has been."

Ethan groaned. "I know. I've been racking my brain, but I can't think of anyone else who can cover for her. I better update Donovan and Mason. They're not going to like it, but I think we might have to shut things down for a while. I can't take time off work anytime soon."

"No, you can't. The Angel would have your ass in a sling." Jason snorted. "But as far as Lang and Donovan are concerned, they can suck it. They left you on your own to do all the heavy lifting."

"Technically, that was the deal with Donovan Carter. Mason and I both knew Carter would be off saving the world for the duration."

"Yeah, yeah. Carter's a saint. But Lang was supposed to be here last month, pitching in." He broke off. "Do you want me to ask Mags about finding someone to take over? The Tylers know everyone in the construction game in this town."

"No, we're trying to keep costs down, remember? Besides, the Tylers work on another level. I don't want someone used to building skyscrapers, slumming it up in here."

"I'm sure Mags can find someone happy to slum it. This town is full of people desperate to be on the Tylers good side."

"As happy as I am for *you* to trade on your wife's connections, I hate doing it myself," Ethan began. "Besides, Lang and Donovan agreed we'd do this on our own."

"Mmm-hmm. This wouldn't have anything to do with the fact Maggie's connections are Liam's connections? Or that he married the girl you lusted after for years?"

Ethan rolled his eyes. When Jason was off, he was way off. "This has nothing to do with Peyton. You know I'm in love with Juliet. But Liam is and always will be an ass. Besides, this is only a small setback for the renovations. It'll be done in time. I just need to shuffle some stuff around."

A small sound made him turn around. Ethan turned to see Juliet at the door. "Dinner's ready."

He covered the mouthpiece. "I'll be right there."

She smiled and nodded, leaving him alone. Ethan watched her go, his chest tightening involuntarily.

He had to keep her safe.

"I have to go, Jason. We won't be coming to the hotel. I thought of someplace else we could go."

CHAPTER TWENTY-SEVEN

She was glad Ethan was carrying Luna because Juliet took one look at the spacious condo around them and tripped.

Ethan's free arm shot out, catching her before she fell flat on her face.

Abashed, she straightened her jacket before realizing she was now too hot. "Who does this place belong to again?" she asked, stripping off her outerwear and pivoting on her heel to take it all in.

The condominium was in the exclusive Beacon Hill area. It was in an old building dating from the 1920s, but the interior had been gutted and reborn into *opulence*.

The walls were a delicate eggshell white with thick dark wood moldings that could only be mahogany. The furniture was antique Louis the XVI, and it was real. So was were the Tiffany lamps and the Harrington commode against the wall. Her childhood had taught her how to spot a fake.

Out of the corner of her eye, she could make out the doorway to a formal dining room with a huge wooden table and an ornate chandelier. *I think this is where mahogany comes to die.*

"This is Donovan Carter's condo," Ethan said. "He's the other partner in our apartment investment."

Donovan was his friend in *Doctors Without Borders*, but perhaps that was a temporary or recent appointment. "Is he a plastic surgeon or something?" she asked, bewildered.

Ethan set Luna on the floor, but she immediately got to her feet, tugging at his pant legs in a silent demand to be picked up again.

He caved, swinging her up into his arms. "No. He's a GP with a background in emergency medicine. When he still lived here, he worked in the ER."

Juliet shook her head. "ER doctor salaries do not pay for this."

"You're right about that," Ethan laughed. "The Carter's are old money. Donovan can trace his origins back to the freaking Mayflower. The entire extended family is loaded. They can find my annual salary in loose change in their sofas."

Juliet cocked her head at Ethan as he began to show her through the rooms. "I thought you said the other partners were moving into the building, too."

"They are."

The doctor was downsizing then. "Is Donovan's new apartment as large as yours?"

Pausing, he turned toward her. "It's a bit smaller. It doesn't have the office space."

The puzzle was deepening. "Did he lose money in the stock market or something?"

"Nope. He just…hates his family."

Ethan shrugged, the expression on his face a mixture of sympathy and exhaustion.

That made sense. It was close to eleven. Luna should have been in bed hours ago, but Ethan had insisted on decamping that very night and coming here.

"Long story short, the Carters have tried to orchestrate Donovan's every move for most of his life. The one time he tried to wrest control away, something bad happened. Now, he doesn't speak to them at all."

Ethan bobbed Luna up and down, trying to encourage the sleepy toddler to nod off. "That's not much of an explanation, but it's all we've got time for today. Donovan will probably sell this place. Knowing him, he'll give the proceeds to charity."

"Are you serious?"

Another shrug. "He's been divesting for years, trying to pull his family's claws out of his backside. I think he took the *Doctors Without Borders* gig as a sort of penance for his family's general shittiness toward humanity."

She huffed. "As motivations go, I understand that one only too well."

He glanced down at Luna. She was finally asleep, one of her little hands curled around the collar of his t-shirt. Very carefully, he transferred her to Juliet's arms.

"I'm going to run down to the garage for the rest of our gear. Tomorrow, I'm going to buy a portable crib somewhere and rent a bigger car."

"We don't need a bigger car," she said, then caught herself. "Sorry, I didn't mean *we*. I meant you. You don't need a bigger car."

"I don't know, I think *we* could use something more spacious. I know the car seat fits, but it's a squeeze. An SUV would make getting Luna in and out of the car a bit easier."

He was so sweet she almost couldn't stand it. *And he said he was over Peyton and in love with you.* Ethan hadn't realized she'd been standing there, though, so she couldn't let him know. Not yet.

"I suppose that makes sense, but I don't want you to put yourself out. I know you love that car."

Before they had met, she had watched him wash it from a safe distance, usually by peeking around the worn curtains of her old studio apartment.

In fact, it had been difficult *not* to watch him. It had been particularly nice when Ethan would take his shirt off to soap up the hood... Of course, it didn't compare to the close-up view she now enjoyed.

"I'm not really attached to the Mustang," he said, blatantly lying to her face. But she understood why.

Standing on her tiptoes, she pressed her lips to his. "You are without a doubt the most wonderful man I have ever met."

Ethan returned the sentiment with a searing kiss before going downstairs for the rest of what they needed for the night.

When he was gone, she set Luna down in one of the condominium's three bedrooms. She picked up extra pillows from the other two rooms, surrounding the bed to make a ring of cushions in case Luna rolled off the bed. Then she went to find the nearest shower.

Ethan would join her there later. In the meantime, she would wonder why she had changed her mind at the last minute.

Why didn't I tell him I loved him, too?

❧

Ethan felt a little bad about what he'd told Juliet as the dealer pointed out the hybrid SUV model he wanted.

It's a white lie.

Trading in the sports car for a more family friendly SUV was a smart move, particularly after the winter they'd had. The hybrid was more economical, too. But there was more to it than that. If anyone was watching them, a nondescript black SUV would be a lot harder to find than his cherry-red Mustang.

There was also the fact he could get away with not putting a license plate on a new car. *Maybe I can mock-up different cardboard dealership signs to swap out every few days.*

"So, are you sure?" the dealer asked, twisting to give Ethan's Mustang another lustful glance.

The dealer was incredibly young, probably quite new to the job. Otherwise, he would know not to say things like that. "I'm sure. I need something with more room. It also needs to fit a car seat."

"The model you chose is LATCH enabled. It's where you clip the baby chair to the seat frame, for more security."

"Great. How soon do you think we can wrap this up? I need to get back to work."

"Well, with your excellent credit score, I think it will take a few hours—minimum."

"I'm hoping we can take care of this in the next forty minutes."

"*Forty minutes?*"

"That's what's left on my lunch hour."

The guy winced. "I'm sorry, but I don't think—"

Ethan put his hand on his belt, pushing his jacket aside to let the badge clipped to his waist show. Hopefully, that would do the trick. He would hate to have to flash his gun.

The guy lifted a shoulder. "I'll see what I can do."

He went around the Mustang to the dealership door, stopping to give the car another admiring glance. "I hope it's worth it."

Ethan's grin came easily. "Oh, she is."

CHAPTER TWENTY-EIGHT

Ethan was at the range when Jason joined him. He wore goggles. His partner slipped on protective earpieces, then aimed at the farthest target twenty-five yards away. He squeezed off five rounds, paused, and then shot another five before pressing the button to bring the target forward.

The brothel raid was tomorrow night. He and Jason had come down to make sure they were in top form.

He slipped off his ear protection before walking over to his partner's cubby. "Not bad," he said, pretending to admire the tight formation of bullet holes on the target. "Why only two to the head?"

Jason was indignant. "It's four to the eyes—twins through each socket. Six to the torso."

"Sure, it is," Ethan teased, pushing the button to bring his target forward. He knew his partner was a great shot and would never lie about something so small, but he was fun to rile.

Swaggering, Jason came over, prepared to gloat. Then he laughed aloud when he saw his target.

"A happy face over the real face," he snorted, admiring the pattern. "That's cool. It's even smiling."

"Should it be frowning?" Ethan smirked.

Jason appeared to mull that over. "I feel like it should. Especially if you try to recreate that on a real perp someday. He wouldn't be happy."

Ethan wrinkled his nose. "It would have to be a pretty evil bad guy for me to want to try. Also, I don't think they'd stand still long enough."

He was fast, but he wasn't *that* fast.

"Hold it up," his partner said. "I have to take a picture of this."

Ethan complied, pointing at the smiling face while Jason took the picture. Then Ethan heard the whoosh of an outgoing text.

"Who did you send that, too?" he scolded.

"Just Mags. Don't worry about it."

"Hey!"

Ethan and Jason both looked up to see Rivera running toward them. "What's up?"

"The shit has hit the fan," the agent panted. He was covered in sweat as if he had run the whole way here. "Our eyes doing preliminary surveillance on the place in Mattapan said there was a gunfight inside *tonight*. Viktor was there. He took one to the chest."

"*What?*" Ethan burst out.

Jason scowled. "What was Viktor even doing in there? Wasn't he staying far away and letting us handle it?"

Rivera shrugged cynically. "Maybe he was blowing smoke up our ass about not being a customer."

"No, I don't think so." Ethan could read people, and his gut told him Viktor had been sincere. "There has to be another reason he went in there. Maybe he thought the girl who went back to the brothel was in trouble or something. Was anyone else hurt?"

Rivera's face soured. "Two girls in the hospital and one in the morgue. You don't want to know how old she was."

Ethan swore, red bubbling up in his vision. What the hell had happened?

"I think Viktor nailed one, though, for what it's worth. There was blood at the scene that didn't match anyone else."

"They took the Russian to Presbyterian Hospital."

Ethan ran to the exit. Jason and Rivera followed him. "Do you know his status?"

"No. I think it's too soon to tell." Rivera grimaced. "I'm heading back to the scene to help Jimenez and the others finish taking statements from the rest of the girls. There's a lot..."

Jason didn't say another word until they were in the garage. "What do you think happened?" he asked as Ethan headed to his new SUV. He stood next to it before he realized he'd chosen the wrong one.

Fuck. Picking an anonymous car was a double-edged sword. He turned around wildly, wondering why the hell he couldn't remember where he parked.

"Ethan, I asked you a question."

He threw up his hands. "I don't know what the hell went wrong." His tone was much sharper than he'd intended.

Jason pursed his lips. He gestured at the garage full of dark SUVs. "Did you forget which one is yours?"

"Yes," Ethan admitted from behind gritted teeth.

If Jason had laughed or even smiled, Ethan might have hit him, but his partner was a smart man and kept his mouth shut. Instead, Jason took the keys from his hand and pressed the unlock button.

The taillights of one of three almost identical SUVs parked in a row lit up. His was in the middle. Sighing, he stalked over, and they climbed inside.

"Do you think someone found out Viktor was working with us?" his partner continued.

"We don't have a leak if that's what you mean." Ethan started the car and pulled out of the lot, trying to stay under the speed limit when all he wanted was to gun it.

"How can you be sure?" Jason asked.

"If we did, the action would have gone down the night of the raid. At the very least, they would have done their best to move the girls, right? No sense damaging the merchandise." He took the next turn with a squeal of brand-new tires.

"Careful," Jason warned. "You'll void the warranty. And it still has that new car smell."

"They bottle that shit nowadays," Ethan said. Didn't they make new car smell air fresheners?

"I think Viktor must have been lured there," he said. "Someone must suspect him. Possibly the whole crew."

"The Angel will be disappointed. Viktor staying in the Komarov's good graces was a big part of his future plans."

"Was it?" Ethan hadn't heard that. "Well, he'll have to impress the higher-ups some other way."

Jason murmured his agreement. They arrived at the hospital shortly after. Ethan stopped Jason before they went through the door. "Hey, try to keep a low profile. No flashing the badge in front of anyone who isn't hospital personnel on the off-chance tonight wasn't about Viktor's involvement with us."

His partner nodded. They went inside, splitting up to look less conspicuous. To his surprise, Viktor was out of surgery. According to the charge nurse, his prognosis was decent, but her expression said that wasn't a good thing.

"From the look of that one, we'd all be better off if he didn't wake up," she bitched before marching away.

Ethan's impulse was to defend the man, but he knew better. The hospital staff saw Russian gangsters like Viktor in here all the time. To them, his body was like a map. They could read his history in the tattoos on his skin.

Plus, they saw a lot of victims. Ethan didn't know how many people Viktor had killed, but his surgeons did. It would have been recorded in ink on his body.

Ethan dragged his feet to the OR recovery room. Viktor laid in bed, naked from the waist up. His swarthy face was a few shades paler than Ethan remembered. The fluorescents certainly didn't help, but he looked better than Ethan would have expected.

"Any news?" Jason entered the room.

He didn't close the privacy curtain. Like Ethan, he faced the glass wall and open door that separated the recovery room from the hallway. The busy nurses' station was at the far end of the hall, but there was a fair amount of traffic outside. They kept their eyes on the passersby, automatically assessing each for threats as they talked.

"The surgery went well. Barring any unforeseen complications, Viktor should make a full recovery. One of the girls who was injured is in critical condition. I don't know what happened to the other one —the one who's not in the morgue."

"I'll call Rivera. Maybe she was taken to another hospital." He glanced at Viktor. "I'm sorry. I know you were hoping we could pull this off without any of those girls getting hurt."

"That was a long shot either way."

Jason winced. "What now?"

Ethan put his hands in his pockets. "You head on home. I'm going to stay here for a bit."

"No, I'll hang here," Jason offered. "You should get back to Juliet and the baby. They've got to be wondering where you are."

"It's fine. I'm texting her about the delay," Ethan said, taking out his phone. "And I'll only stay long enough to get a plainclothes PD out here to guard the door."

"Hmm. All right then. Why don't I make a few calls and get the ball rolling on that?"

"Thanks, man." Ethan sat in the only chair, settling down for what he hoped would be a short wait. After a few minutes, Jason came back in to inform him the protection detail would be along soon. Then, he left.

Ethan messaged Juliet to tell her he'd be at Donovan's soon. She replied with something short and sweet that made him want to leave immediately.

She must be exhausted after watching Luna all day. Even on days when they both were available to watch her, they still went to bed drained.

Well, the toddler wasn't entirely responsible for them falling into bed fatigued and well...sated. A memory flashed through his mind of this morning. He would have been to work on time, but he had lingered in bed after waking up to watch her sleep.

You are pathetic. Despite the situation, a smile teased his lips.

Stop distracting yourself. He had to make some plans. He didn't want Juliet to feel like she had to stay at home all day with the baby, having totally given up on her dreams and goals. She needed to go back to school, to figure out what she wanted to do in life.

Juliet would need time for that. Putting Luna back into her old daycare wasn't an option, but they could find a new one in Beacon Hill, even if he had to take out another loan to do it. In the short time he'd had the pair living with him, he'd learned the price of decent childcare was fucking insane.

He checked his watch, wondering where his relief guard was.

Knowing the attitude of those nurses, they might have redirected his cop elsewhere. Ethan decided to run out for a minute to check.

Outside, the nurses' station was incredibly quiet. The only one there hadn't seen anyone who didn't work at the hospital for over an hour. Resigned, he returned to Viktor's room.

He paused at the threshold. The opaque white curtain had been drawn around the bed. A faint gurgle alerted him there was trouble.

Ethan's gun was in his hand before he could blink. He yanked the curtain, weapon raised, then almost dropped it.

A strange tattooed man was looming over the bed. The tats on his arms identified him as part of the Komarov crew, and he'd been sent to kill. But he hadn't counted on Viktor.

The giant was still half-unconscious. His eyelids were barely cracked, yet he had his big meaty hand wrapped around the slighter man's neck. Despite having been shot, he was somehow managing to strangle the life out of his would-be attacker.

Groaning, Ethan stalked up behind the attacker. "All right, enough," he hissed at Viktor.

He wasn't even sure the man could hear, but Viktor lolled his head in Ethan's direction. The bleary-eyed glance was comprehending, but he didn't let go. The man being strangled wheezed raggedly, his eyes red and bugging out of his head.

"Damn it." Ethan tried to yank Viktor's hand away, trying to get him to let go, but it was as if the oversized hand were a steel vice. "Let go!"

"*No.*"

Frustrated, Ethan took out his gun and hit the hapless assailant. The guy stopped gurgling and slumped, passed out.

"Okay, *now* you can let go."

Viktor gave him a drugged yet baleful glare, but he opened his hand. The other guy fell to the ground.

Fuck. "Did your people find out you were helping us?"

"I don't think so. This is unrelated." The words were slow and hoarse.

Ethan was skeptical. "Are you sure?"

Viktor tried to shrug, but winced.

Ethan tsked. "I guess it takes a hell of a lot of anesthesia to keep you under. The nurse said you weren't due to come out for hours."

In fact, it was lucky there had been enough of the right drugs on hand to do the surgery at all. Viktor could have woken up in the middle of it.

"There...will be more."

Ethan sighed. "If this isn't about you helping us, then why did everything go down at that brothel?"

"I showed an interest. But I don't think they know about the plan. Internal. Coup."

Each halting word was dragged out of him as if they had come from the depths of his soul.

"Huh." It shouldn't have surprised Ethan, but the gang unit had told them the Komarovs were stable. There hadn't been any changes in the upper echelons of the group for years. *I guess someone thought they were overdue.*

"They killed her."

Ethan blinked. "Who? Not your cleaning girl?"

"No, the other one. The one who went back to the brothel."

The girl he had been trying to save with that raid. "Shit. Sorry."

Viktor flicked his fingers in acknowledgment.

Footsteps sounded. Ethan glanced up, but the nurse rushed by without bothering to turn their way.

"You're not wrong. More will come. Many more."

Fuck. This was just what Ethan needed right now.

"I need to get you out of here."

Viktor didn't answer—he acted, tearing out the IV taped to his wrist. He didn't even flinch.

"I guess you're on board with that plan."

The Russian rolled his eyes. Ethan hurried over to help him sit up.

"Wait here. I'm going to find a wheelchair."

Ethan hurried out the door, wondering how the hell he was going to get the Russian version of the Jolly Green Giant out of the hospital without anyone noticing.

CHAPTER TWENTY-NINE

Although he found several, Ethan didn't choose a wheelchair. Viktor was incapable of blending in. Even sitting, the Russian was tall enough to make people turn and stare.

Ethan ground his teeth, wondering what the hell to do when he was forced to step to the side as an orderly with a gurney holding an elderly man wheeled past him down the hall.

Where do I get one of those?

Ethan pivoted, following the orderly. The man disappeared into a room halfway down the hall. He loitered in front of the vending machines as the attendant wrapped up, talking to the patient in a reassuring tone. Ethan couldn't make out the words, but it must have been something about getting tests because he pointed to the bed and left it there before leaving.

A plan formed in his mind, but pulling it off was a lot more difficult than the TV shows and movies made it appear.

Ethan tried to find a lab coat to cover his clothes, but he failed. Next, he tried to secure a pair of scrubs, but there wasn't a stack of neatly folded ones conveniently at hand.

Eventually, Ethan found a pair of extra-large scrubs in a hamper. They weren't clean, but they didn't have obvious bloodstains. Reluctantly, he pulled them on in the bathroom. *Remind me to scour with a Brillo pad when I get home.*

Grinning in what he hoped was a friendly manner, Ethan went back to the old guy's room. He'd hoped the patient would have dropped off in the interim, but luck was not on his side. The old guy was wide awake and watching *Jeopardy.*

"Excuse me, I need to borrow this."

Ethan grabbed the gurney, rushing out the door while expecting the man to protest. Instead, the old coot waved him on. "Fine with me. I'm not in a hurry for that colonoscopy anyway."

Stifling an unexpected laugh, Ethan went back to Viktor's room. The Russian approved of the plan, at least until he heard the rest of it. "We're going out through *where?*"

"The morgue has a separate entrance," Ethan said, helping Viktor climb on the gurney.

Then he grabbed the bedsheet and threw it over Viktor's face. "Just try not to exhale enough to move the cloth. Someone might notice if the corpse is still breathing."

Viktor's head spun, but he forced his eyes open anyway. He was in a large four-poster bed. He squinted at the fancy lamp on the bedside table next to him. There was an equally expensive-looking armoire under an antique mirror on the wall.

Gavno. Panic rushed through him as he took in the sumptuous furnishings. Was he at the Komarov's house?

Two men argued in the hallway. "I can't believe you brought him here, Ethan," an unfamiliar voice said.

Viktor relaxed, collapsing on the down pillow. If the FBI agent was here, then there was no way in hell he was at his father's house.

Ethan said something, but the stranger interrupted. "You were the one who was hell-bent on keeping the girls hidden, then you bring him *here?* You should have taken him to the hotel. We have protocols for this sort of thing."

"If you mean the gold stars, you know those rooms are for women and children on the run, not seven-feet-tall Russian gangsters," Ethan argued. "Besides, this place was closer and he was bleeding again. Donovan stores a lot of medicinal equipment here. Even some drugs because he buys them out of pocket and ships them overseas for his practice in Africa."

"You know you're going to have to move them now, right?"

Ethan's voice was resigned. "Yeah, I know."

The other man said something else, but Viktor didn't catch it. He sniffed. He didn't know what the man meant by moving, but his full height in socks was six foot five. People always exaggerated when it came to how tall he was.

A vague memory came back. He'd gotten dizzy in the SUV last night. The bandage around his abdomen had started seeping, bleeding through until the waistband on his jeans had been soaked.

He'd been awake long enough to climb out of the car in a narrow two-space garage and up some stairs. He didn't remember anything about this house, but he could have sworn he saw a dark-haired woman hovering over him at one point.

And if the pair in the hall were talking about hotels, then the other man must be Jason White, Ethan's partner at the FBI. Viktor knew all about Jason and his hotel heiress wife due to their connection to the MacLachlans, the city's other big crime family.

He closed his eyes, his head pounding. Viktor let the men's argument wash over him. It grew quieter after a minute. He must have slept, but his eyes flew open when he felt a presence.

Viktor started. A small human stood on the bed next to him, staring down as if it were trying to decide what he was. It was wearing a pink shirt that said, 'Future FBI Agent'.

Oh. White hadn't slipped when he'd said girls, plural. There were at least two females here, and one came in miniature.

The little girl gave him a thorough inspection. A tiny finger went up, and she pointed it at him. "Play," she said. She waved a small toy bear in his face. It was also wearing an FBI T-shirt.

"Um…"

"*Play.*" This time, it was an order.

This one could run a crew someday. Viktor shrugged. "Okay," he agreed.

Playing meant getting the toy repeatedly shoved into his face.

Uncertain what to do, Viktor made growling noises, trying to sound like a bear.

That amused the child to no end. Her little chortles brought someone running.

Viktor's eyes widened as he got a clear view of the woman who came in. All he remembered from last night was a cloud of dark hair. In the light of day, the stranger was young and gorgeous. Her features were model perfect with skin that glowed like those Brazilian models in lingerie ads.

"Hi," the woman uncertainly said. She scooped the little girl off the bed, scolding her gently. "Don't bother the nice man."

Viktor's lip quirked. No one in their right mind had ever described him as *nice*. But this girl hadn't even hesitated when she said that. However, she did hurry out the door.

"How do you know I'm nice?" he asked, making her stop. "I don't mean to put you on the spot, but that's not something I hear a lot."

"Ethan wouldn't have brought you here if you weren't," she replied. Her tone was almost convincing. She turned to leave again.

"Is this an FBI safe house?" he asked.

She hesitated, clearly wondering how much to tell him. "No. It belongs to Ethan's friend. We're staying here temporarily."

Because you're hiding, too, he thought, putting together the pieces from the snippets of conversation he'd overheard. Interesting—and fucked up. He shouldn't be here.

Viktor had other places to be and quite a few men to kill. The one who shot him for starters...

Ethan Thomas appeared in the threshold. He leaned in to whisper something in the woman's ear. She nodded in response, telling him quietly she would be packed up and ready after the child napped.

Viktor spent a lot of time in the background in the course of his work. His main job was to stand behind his superiors during meetings of the higher-ups, being large and intimidating. Despite that, most people treated him like furniture. But Viktor paid attention. He was observant, and he could read body language like it was his mother tongue.

These two were sleeping together. Viktor let his lids drift down, but he was still watching as Ethan's hand wrapped around the back of the woman's neck in a proprietary fashion. He didn't kiss her, but he didn't have to. The possessive gesture was mirrored by the heat in his eyes. A flare of jealousy sparked across Viktor's system, but he squashed it.

The FBI agent was in love with his damsel in distress.

For a moment, his mind wandered to Sacha, the girl his superiors had given him, but he ruthlessly cut the thought off. Viktor couldn't afford an investment like that. He had business to take care of first.

The girl disappeared with the little one and Ethan came inside, greeting him shortly.

"Any more trouble at the hospital?" he asked, wondering how many more men his enemies would send after him.

"The guy you almost choked to death was gone by the time the uniforms got there. No one else showed up." He checked Viktor's bandage with a critical eye. "My partner and I have been on the phone. We found a place where you can recuperate. We're going to move you in a couple of hours, once we get a doctor over here to check you out."

Viktor knew without being told this one would be a real FBI safe house with more agents. There would be an offer of witness protection in exchange for testimony he couldn't give.

Feigning exhaustion, he thanked the agent and pretended to fall asleep. Once he was alone, he sat up, carefully testing his body before getting out of bed.

Viktor found formal stationery in the desk by the window. He grabbed a pen, then scrawled a message on the thick paper.

You don't have to move your women. No one will learn their location from me.

Viktor hesitated, debating adding a promise to get in touch. In the end, he decided not to.

From here on out, there would be no help from the FBI. Not that he needed it. Because this time around, Viktor wouldn't be trying to save anyone.

CHAPTER THIRTY

Ethan forced his face to impassivity as his boss tore him a new one. Viktor had bolted from Donovan's Beacon Hill house yesterday morning after they spoke, leaving a short note behind. Now Ethan was being reprimanded for acting on his own and for failing to secure Viktor in a sanctioned FBI safe house right away. Jason, too, although the decision hadn't been his.

According to the gang unit, the Komarov family was in a full-fledged civil war. It had erupted a few days ago out of nowhere.

In retrospect, Ethan should have expected the disappearing act. Viktor's singular reason for coming to him and the FBI had been to help the women forced into prostitution by the family he served. But now Viktor had been shot by someone in that crew.

Ethan knew what that meant. The big Russian was an eye-for-an-eye kind of man. And even though he appeared to be a loner, the man might have relationships and ties Ethan didn't know about. If blood was going to flow, Viktor was the type to wade back in and make sure the right people were doing the bleeding.

"Another thing, where the hell did you take him?" Robert Angel snapped, interrupting his own lecture to switch over to interrogation mode.

"A secure undisclosed location," Ethan hedged.

"He needed a place where he could swiftly be administered medical attention," Jason interrupted, backing Ethan up despite having argued against taking Viktor to Donovan's. "The Russian's wound was bleeding again, and Ethan had his hands full treating him. It was a triage situation."

"That's not what triage means," Ethan corrected. "But I did have to make a quick call. I was getting everything in motion to transfer Viktor to FBI custody when he walked out on his own steam—something any surgeon would say was impossible given the nature of the wound. But he somehow managed."

Ethan may have been exaggerating, but only because Viktor was a beast. The man had shaken off the anesthesia in record time, and he had been on his feet hours after a gunshot wound. Ethan predicted his recovery would be remarkable, which didn't bode well for the guy who had put a hole in him.

"I assume you took him to the hotel?" Angel asked.

"Gold star for you," Jason said, tipping an imaginary hat in their boss's direction.

Ethan pressed his lips together as their boss drew the inevitable conclusion. Coughing, he shook his head. "I wouldn't have moved him at all given the choice, but I didn't have another one at the time."

"That hospital might have ended up a war zone if you'd left him," Jason added, leaving out the part where he sided with the Angel on where they had ended up.

The Angel crossed his arms. "So, our only in with the Komarovs might be lying in an alley somewhere bleeding out?"

"Oh, I doubt that." Ethan sighed. "Viktor isn't stupid, and this can't be the first time he's been shot. He'll hole up until he's better."

"And then?"

Ethan shrugged.

The Angel rolled his eyes. "If you hear from him, I want to know. Day or night—it doesn't matter. I want to know." Then he pointed at the door.

Out in the bullpen, Ethan rubbed his eyes. He hadn't gotten a lot of sleep last night. He'd been too worried. Because of that, Juliet had stayed up with him, too, despite his many protests.

"C'mere." Jason nudged him. "Let me buy you a terrible cup of coffee."

They went to the breakroom, then grabbed two steaming mugs from the communal pot. It tasted vile, but all Ethan cared about was the caffeine.

"Did I tell you Juliet makes excellent coffee? She found this Columbian blend in a little bodega that's cheap as hell but tastes better than any coffee shop drip I've ever had."

"Mmm…" Jason grunted. "And how did she react to your guest last night?"

Ethan huffed. "If not for Juliet, I would have changed my mind about taking him to Donovan's. I *did* change it—like ten times. I was still sitting in the garage when she came down. The condo has a security room. There are camera feeds in the garage and all the entrances. She saw the SUV come in, and she realized something was wrong." He took a large sip of the rapidly cooling brew before continuing.

"Once she saw him half-conscious and bleeding in the backseat, the decision was out of my hands. I even tried to backtrack. I was about to call you to take him off my hands, but she wouldn't hear of it." He managed a smile. "You could have picked her out as a lawyer last night. The woman can *argue*. I'm never going to win a fight against her."

"You make that sound like a good thing," Jason said. "Are you going to bring the girls to the hotel?"

Ethan thought about it. "No. I think we're staying put."

His partner frowned. "Are you sure that's wise?"

"Viktor wouldn't have written that note if he hadn't meant what he said. As long as he's not there, we won't have any trouble from the Russians."

"What if he comes back?"

"He won't." Ethan was sure.

Juliet and Luna were secure where they were for now. He wouldn't have to move them again yet.

"I hope you're right," Jason said darkly.

CHAPTER THIRTY-ONE

Juliet collapsed face-down on the couch, and immediately regretted it. Antique furniture was *not* comfortable. She sat up and rubbed her face, too tired to find a softer chair.

Maybe this Donovan Carter was making the right decision by letting it all go.

She had grown up in a house stuffed full of antiques thanks to her mother's need to surround herself with status symbols. But after living in Ethan's clean contemporary apartment, she preferred his simpler style, one that emphasized comfort without sacrificing quality.

Juliet also preferred the scotch-guardable quality of the upholstery at Ethan's place. She had spent half an hour scrubbing the Persian carpet in the living room after Luna had spilled her milk all over it. Juliet was taking advantage of nap time for a breather, but she couldn't let herself enjoy it.

How long was she going to be living like a fugitive? *Probably as long as you are one.*

Juliet softly snorted. True, the police weren't beating down her door in this country, but that didn't mean she could live like a normal person. All someone had to do was take her picture and she bolted. Only this time, she hadn't done it alone.

Had the threat been serious, or had she been overreacting? Yes, it felt good that Ethan had taken her fears seriously. If anyone would know the right thing to do under these circumstances, it was him. But what if she'd been wrong about the man who took her picture? Was she going to keep jumping at shadows for the rest of her life? And how long would Ethan stand by her if she did?

What if I never clear my name?

Juliet closed her eyes, taking a deep breath. Why did it feel as if losing him would be the worst part of that scenario?

One thing was becoming clear. She couldn't continue to live this way. Juliet had spent her life trying to accomplish every goal her father had set in front of her. Though she hadn't agreed with where he'd wanted her to end up, that drive and ambition was a part of her. Now, she felt...aimless. Purposeless.

Keeping Luna safe had to be her priority, but she could do that and still accomplish some of her other goals. She might even be able to go back to school to finish her law degree sooner rather than later.

Except you'll have to do it under someone else's name.

Juliet groaned aloud. She had to stop having these arguments with herself. Nothing was going to change until she did something about it.

Forcing herself to her feet, she stood and trudged down the halls. Donovan Carter had a home office complete with a fax machine and tower computer with the biggest monitor she had ever seen. There was even a full-sized copier next to the printer.

She powered up the computer under the guest account, then started searching for local law schools.

That didn't last long. After shuddering at the tuition costs, she decided independent study might be in order. It would be difficult with Luna around, but she could at least try to cover some of the necessary reading on her own.

Always so self-sufficient and independent...after Dad has told you where to go to school and what to study.

The mocking was loud enough to be in the same room, but Juliet knew it for the memory it was. Her sister had loved to poke at her, deriding her for following the course their father had laid out for her.

And then there had been that last argument...the one about Alvaro.

In the distance, the door to the garage opened and closed quietly. Jumping up, Juliet met Ethan in the front hall. Without thinking too much about it, she leapt on him, rushing into his arms so she wouldn't have to think about anything else.

The moment her body met his, she relaxed, melting into him in instant surrender.

"Hi there," he said, clearly pleased with her greeting.

"Are you as tired as I am?" Now that he was here, all the tension had drained out of her body.

"I was. I'm not anymore."

She rubbed against him, luxuriating in the feel of his firm muscled body. "That's funny. Suddenly, neither am I."

She lifted her head, going weak-kneed at the expression in Ethan's eyes.

"*I love you,*" Juliet whispered. She had promised herself she wouldn't say it first, but that didn't seem to matter anymore.

"Are you sure?" Ethan's voice was hoarse.

"Yes." Her certainty gave the single word depth. There wasn't a doubt in her mind. Not anymore.

He opened his mouth, but she covered it with her hand. She hadn't told him to force a declaration. She already knew how he felt. When he was ready, he would say it to her face.

She yelped when Ethan nipped her fingers. "I love you, too."

Juliet wrapped her arms around his neck. "Just remember I said it first."

He cupped her ass cheeks, drawing her closer. "Liar. I said it first."

She blinked. "What?"

"At my place, in the office. I know you heard me."

Laughing, she shook her head. "It doesn't count if you're saying it to someone else."

"You know what…you're right. I think it would be better if I showed you." She stifled a giggle as Ethan pulled her t-shirt over her head.

Clothing was discarded, leaving a trail to the master bedroom. By the time they hit the bed, they were both naked.

Juliet moaned aloud as Ethan came down on top of her. Glorying in the feel of his skin, she rubbed her legs over his thighs, wrapping them around his waist.

Ethan made a sound somewhere between a groan and laugh as he stroked against her heated core, finding her already wet and more than willing. He flexed his hips, sliding his hard length against her. The slippery friction drove her crazy, stoking her hunger. Burning, she arched her back, shifting and angling her body so they could come together as one.

Breathing fast, Ethan started to push inside her, but he stopped. Eager for him to drive his length home, she strained against him, but he held her down.

"I do love you. I love you so much," he said. "And I want to spend the rest of my life with you. Will you marry me, Juliet?"

Tears sprang into her eyes. She couldn't breathe.

His brow creased. Ethan was starting to look worried when she found her tongue.

"Yes!" she burst out. "*Yes*. But…how?"

How could a marriage be legal with her circumstances?

Ethan's face was calm and sure. "We'll find a way."

Inclining his head, he pressed his lips to hers—a long, hard kiss that shared without words everything he felt.

His hand reached out to thread his fingers with hers. His eyes fixed on hers, holding them as he entered her, possessing what was his.

A single tear streamed down her cheek as Ethan began to move. He set a slow rhythm at first, but the heat inevitably overcame him, and he began to thrust faster and harder.

Juliet urged him on with her whole body, undulating and caressing his skin, rocking in concert as waves of pleasure built higher and higher. The tight tickling pressure began to throb deep inside, but, this time, she was the one who held it at bay, not wanting this moment to end.

Then Ethan whispered in her ear, promising to always love her. Her climax was impossible to hold off after that. The pleasure crested, kindling into rapture. The convulsions wracked her.

Shuddering, Juliet sobbed as Ethan groaned, grinding against her. She held him, her palms flat against his chest. She could feel his power coiling and then releasing as he erupted, shooting his seed inside her.

Clenching around him with all her might as the last spasms passed, she finally fell into a deep well of sated lethargy.

For a long time, Juliet couldn't move. She couldn't even make a fist. Ethan was almost as weak. Spent, he rolled off her and lay on the bed, panting. His breathing slowed down, then he coughed. "There was no way Luna slept through that."

Juliet listened, but she didn't hear the little girl. "We may have gotten lucky."

Ethan laughed, throwing an arm around her. "I know I did."

She giggled in spite of herself, then cleared her throat. "Excuse me, that did not deserve a laugh."

"How about this?" Ethan tickled her midriff, making her squirm.

She caught a glimpse of the clock on the bedside table. "*Nooo*. It can't be that late. I haven't even started dinner."

Ethan had buried his face in her neck, so his response was muffled.

"I'm sorry, what did you say?" she asked.

He lifted his head. "There's always frozen pizza," he repeated.

"Not for Luna there isn't," she chided. "We have to feed her real food."

His grin could have melted butter. "Frozen pizza is *almost* real food."

Then he sobered. "Sorry, I wish we could order in, but it's too risky. Why don't I hop in the shower, then go grab something? There's plenty of restaurants around here."

"That will be too late for Luna's dinnertime," she said regretfully, sitting up and looking for her clothes—which were scattered all over the living room.

She hopped up, dodging Ethan's hands, which would have dragged her back to bed. "I'm going to fix her some eggs and cut up some fruit and cheese. That should be enough for the two of us. If you want something more substantial, you can get takeout, or I can put in one of the pizzas for you."

"Hmm. There's a great Italian place not far from here. Why don't you make enough for Luna while I jump in the shower? I can pick up something hot and fresh for us."

She leaned over to give him a quick hit-and-run kiss. "Sounds good. I better get started."

But first, I better pick up our clothes. Juliet hurried out of the room.

Sure, Luna wouldn't understand the significance of the discarded garments, but Juliet never knew what the little girl might remember later on. Kids were sponges at her age.

She found Ethan's clothes before hers. Balling them up, she held them in front of herself, scanning the room for her jeans.

She found them behind one of the delicate Louis the XVI couches. Her t-shirt had landed on top of an antique end table. *Now the only thing missing is my...*

"Are you looking for this?"

Juliet spun around. There was a man in a wet wool coat in the doorway, his arm raised. He was holding her bra between two fingers.

CHAPTER THIRTY-TWO

Ethan was in the shower when Juliet screamed. He leapt out of the stall, stopping to grab his service piece from his briefcase before running out to confront the intruder.

He had a quick impression of a tall man in a beige coat standing in front of his naked future bride. Red flooded his vision. Ethan didn't have a clear shot, so he decided to charge. *I'm going to tear apart the bastard with my bare hands.*

But then he heard what the man was saying. "Who are you and what are you doing in my house?"

Hearing him approach, the intruder looked up. Ethan checked his progress, sliding to a stop in the doorway, his gun still raised.

"Holy shit, *Donovan.*"

Dr. Donovan Carter swiveled to him, flinching at the sight of the gun. "*Jesus.*"

Wincing, Ethan put the weapon down. "Sorry, man. I wasn't expecting you."

Donovan looked Ethan up and down, raising a brow at his birthday suit. "Yeah, I gathered," he said with a hollow laugh.

Juliet held their clothes in front of herself, a barrier that was much too small for his peace of mind. Without trying to be too obvious, he moved in front of her, blocking Donovan's view. Her arm snaked around his waist, offering him his jeans and boxers.

Smirking, Donovan turned around while they hurriedly dressed.

"I just got in from the airport. I was going to stop by your place first, but I'm glad I didn't now. What brings you here?"

Ethan tugged his pants on. "I, uh, I'm sorry. I was going to write to tell you I was borrowing your apartment."

Donovan left the keys to the place with Ethan whenever he was out of town, in case of emergencies. His friend didn't have any pets to feed or plants to water, so Ethan didn't need to come over with any regularity. He mostly kept an eye out on the police blotter, making sure no major disasters happened in the vicinity.

"Is the renovation going that badly?" Donovan asked as Ethan turned around to check that Juliet was covered. She was red with chagrin, and her t-shirt had caught on her bra.

He tugged it over her midriff before twisting to tap Donovan, signaling it was safe to turn around.

"No, that's not it," he said, wondering where to start.

In the distance, Luna started to cry. *"Mama..."*

"Um, that's my cue," Juliet said. "Why don't I leave you two to talk?"

Luna cried again, and she hurried out of the room.

Ethan turned back to his friend. "Sorry about the unexpected guests. I can explain."

His friend stared in the direction Juliet had taken.

"It's okay." But his tone said the exact opposite.

"Van?"

Donovan turned. He shook his head, his face clearing. "It's nothing. It's just that when I saw her, I thought...I thought she was someone else."

The reminder was like a kick in the gut. "Shit, now I'm really fucking sorry. I should have realized. I never even thought about the resemblance."

Donovan's lips twisted. It was the saddest smile Ethan had ever seen. "She doesn't look like Sabrina. Not really."

"But she has the same coloring, and she was here," Ethan finished. It would have been enough.

Sabrina had been Donovan's only serious girlfriend. She had lived with Donovan in this house for over a year...up until she died.

That had happened during Donovan's last year of med school, long after Ethan had dropped out and joined the army.

Ethan had only met Sabrina once in real life, but he had stayed in touch with his friend during his tours abroad. Whenever the two had video-chatted, Sabrina had been in the background, a light and sunny presence that offset the sucking black hole of negativity that was the rest of Donovan's family.

"It's Luna and Juliet, right?" Donovan asked, shaking off his memories with a little effort. "I guess your patient is right as rain now."

"Uh, yeah," Ethan said with an abashed grin. He had told Donovan an abbreviated version of his involvement with the girls, but not everything. He made up for that now.

"You are the first to hear this. Juliet just agreed to marry me. But there are complications—the kind that made it necessary for me to bring the girls here, out of sight."

Confusion clouded his eyes, but Donovan put it aside and opened his arms, hugging Ethan. "Congratulations first, explanations second."

He gestured in the direction of the bedrooms. "She's beautiful— you're lucky. *Incredibly* lucky."

"Hmm, I'm going to forget you saw my future bride naked because it was my fault. But if it happens again, I'm sticking both my thumbs in your eye sockets."

Donovan laughed. "I would expect no less."

"Thanks for understanding." Chuckling, Ethan waved in the direction of the kitchen. "You'll be happy to hear I stocked your fridge with beer. Why don't we have a cold one and I'll tell you about...everything."

"Sound good." Donovan lifted his briefcase. "Dinner's on me if you're up for African peanut stew. A patient gave me the fixings before I left for the airport."

"And it got through customs?"

Donovan shrugged. "There's no meat. It's a vegetarian dish."

Ethan hid his lack of enthusiasm, desperately wishing the steak-house down the street delivered. But he pasted on a smile, then followed Donovan to the kitchen after detouring to put his gun in the safe. Then he began talking, starting at the beginning.

"I came home the night the blizzard hit, and there was a tiny pink Michelin Man in the hallway…"

He kept talking as the other man cooked, downing four beers between them—and only one was drunk by Ethan. Apparently, his friend had sorely missed American beer.

"You can stay here as long as you want," Donovan said when Ethan was done explaining. "And by all means, don't move out of the master bedroom. I don't sleep there anyway."

No, Ethan knew that. Donovan didn't sleep in the same room he had shared with Sabrina, not anymore.

"I put Luna in the small bedroom next to the office. Yours, right?"

"No worries. I can crash in the spare room. Or better yet, I can go straight to the new apartment. That's why I came home—to do my share of work on the building. Your emails made it clear you were drowning a bit without Mason."

Ethan wrinkled his nose. "Oh, man, I didn't mean for you to come home for that. We agreed Mason and I would take care of the renovation. Besides, your apartment is still in rough shape. The plumbing and heat work, but the floors are a mess and none of the cabinets are up."

Donovan laughed aloud, stirring the peanuts and other ingredients in a wok. "Ethan, I spent the last three months living in a one-room shack with a dirt floor."

He held up his fingers, thumb and index finger a hairsbreadth apart. "I came this close to getting stung by a scorpion on my unmentionables in the outhouse last week."

Ethan grinned. "Well, in that case, you'll be happy to hear I did manage to install the special Japanese toilet you insisted on. It works, too."

"Then I'm not happy—I'm ecstatic." Donovan pulled a serving bowl from one of the cupboards, transferring the contents from the wok. "And I don't mind coming back to pitch in. I'm overdue for some time off."

"But you're a doctor, not a contractor."

"And you're an FBI agent," Donovan countered. "I daresay I know a bit more about construction now than you do. The last few years involved building not one, but two clinics in the Sudan."

"Not by yourself." It was more of a question than a statement.

There was no telling how much support Donovan had out in Africa. But knowing his friend, he wouldn't have let a lack of manpower stop him. If anything, Van would have stacked and mortared the bricks in place himself.

"I think I picked up enough. I know how to delegate."

Ethan gave in, acknowledging the man's trump card with a bow. "All right then, I stand corrected. Thanks for coming back. But I'm still allowed to be pissed at Mason for being MIA."

"It sounds like he's got his hands full in L.A."

"I guess." Mason hadn't said much about what was holding him up, but it sounded like a friend needed help so Ethan couldn't blame the guy—much.

Juliet appeared with Luna at the threshold. "Someone wanted to say hello."

Donovan smiled at the appealing picture they made. Ethan walked over, taking the little girl from Juliet for a quick snuggle. "Hey, Little Moon, how was your nap?"

"Mama play me."

Juliet ran her hands over the little girl's damp curls. "We took advantage of someone else making dinner to have a bath, complete with the armada of boats you bought her. You have to stop buying her so many toys."

"Aw, c'mon. If anyone deserves to be spoiled, it's this little darling."

Donovan laughed suddenly. "And here I thought you had *confirmed bachelor* tattooed to your forehead."

Juliet blushed, but Ethan simply threw an arm around her and propelled her to the dining room. Donovan followed with the serving bowl. Ethan settled Luna in a chair with a booster, then went back and forth to help set up.

They settled down to eat. Juliet was a little shy and reticent at first, but she soon opened up. Ethan filled her in on Donovan's plan to take over at the apartment building. She immediately wanted to help.

"I know all the crews now and what should be up next on their agenda," Juliet offered. "If you're going to be there, I can go back and be on-site to help out."

Ethan didn't like that. "Maybe we should hold off on you being out in the open just yet."

Donovan cleared his throat. "I don't mind looking after her. You know I can take care of myself. You taught me how."

That much was true. When his friend said he was going abroad with *Doctors Without Borders,* Ethan had undertaken the task of teaching the man, a born pacifist, a little something about self-defense. *And then Mason taught him offense.*

Juliet looked at Ethan, hope lighting up her dark eyes. He wanted to groan aloud. He knew she was chafing under the restrictions of what amounted to house arrest. But he needed to be sure of her safety.

It was only a random man taking a picture, his mind nagged. But Ethan wasn't quite ready to let her go out yet.

"Let's give it another week," he compromised. "If nothing suspicious happens at the new building until then, by all means, you can go back on-site—whenever Donovan is there."

Juliet stifled a happy squeal. Her cheery mood was infectious, but Ethan couldn't help wondering if he'd made the right call.

CHAPTER THIRTY-THREE

"You have to relax. She's *fine*," his partner said.

Ethan swiveled his office chair to glare at him. Jason wore an exasperated expression—one Ethan hadn't earned.

"I didn't say anything," he protested.

His partner scowled. "I can feel you worrying, and it's making me antsy. And there's no reason for it. If anything was wrong, Carter would have called."

Ethan sighed. "I know, but it's her first day back out in the world and I can't help myself." He checked the clock. "Donovan should be dropping her off soon. Once she calls, I'll settle down. I promise."

Donovan had picked her up, too. The door-to-door service was for Ethan's peace of mind. Nothing had happened in the week and a half since Donovan had come home and resumed the renovation work. No strangers had appeared. Every workman was accounted for and had been subjected to a thorough second background check. The companies they'd contracted had promised not to send any unvetted staff to the building.

After he'd finished the background checks, he hadn't had much cause to keep his girl confined anymore.

"You can't keep Juliet under lock and key forever," Jason was saying. "I realize Donovan's old place is nice, but the poor girl must have been crawling the walls toward the end there."

As part of the security precautions, Ethan hadn't had his partner and his wife over, although God knew Juliet would have appreciated the company after Donovan decamped.

"No comment," he said, checking his watch. It was too early to expect an update from Juliet. He better give it an hour. Maybe a half hour. Then he could call her himself.

Jason tossed the file he was holding back on his desk. "You're going to be useless for the next few hours, aren't you?"

They were supposed to be working on a new embezzling case, something not related to the Russians. It was still early days, but it was shaping up to be a fair-sized investigation, which told Ethan he hadn't burned through all his capital with the Angel quite yet.

Although if more bodies keep piling up, I might need to rethink that.

For the last few weeks, the Komarov crew had been roiling—dropping dead guys at an alarming rate. According to the gang unit, there was a deadly internal power struggle going on. The head of the family, Maksim Komarov, had been shot in the street outside one of his favorite hangouts. The old gangster's personal security detail had swept him up and out of sight. Rumors were flying that he was dead, but Ethan wasn't so sure. A crew as large as the Russians had private doctors, including surgeons, on staff. The old guy might have pulled through.

Ethan didn't care if Maksim Komarov was dead or not. But Viktor might be. And if he wasn't, just how many bodies was he responsible for?

Can't worry about that now. Viktor hadn't gotten in touch since disappearing from the Beacon Hill apartment. Ethan had to assume their association was severed. The only thing he could do was worry about his new case.

On that note, Ethan got back to work. He spent the next hour pulling backgrounds and doing research, all the while refusing to look at his watch.

He damn near ripped his pant pocket trying to get to his phone when the text alert sounded.

"Well?" Jason asked.

"Juliet is fine," Ethan admitted sheepishly. "Nothing happened, aside from everyone doing their work. She wants to know if she should pick up Luna."

He texted a reply, telling her that he would pick up the toddler. The new sitter was great, but she was a few subway stops away from the Beacon Hill place and he didn't want to risk it.

Plus, this way, I can swing by and pick up dinner.

Unable to stop himself, he'd signed up for Omaha steaks, reasoning it wasn't delivery because no one came to the house. He had arranged to have the meat sent to a local business down the block.

"Why don't you take off now?" Jason suggested. "We can get away with skating on this case for another day or two."

Ethan checked his watch, then winced. "You know what? That's a good idea. The new babysitter's hours are more flexible than the old daycare, but she charges an arm and a leg for any overtime."

He was out the door before Jason could change his mind. Ethan headed for his SUV, whistling under his breath.

He drove on autopilot, doubling back and using evasive maneuvers to make sure no one followed him home. His mind was on eating a delicious juicy steak, which would hopefully be followed by hot steamy sex with his new fiancée if Luna cooperated and took a nap.

The police cars outside the babysitter's place hit him like a bucket of cold water.

Ethan didn't bother to find a space. He skidded to a stop by one of the cruisers, throwing the vehicle in park before running out to the first uniform he saw, his badge in hand.

"What happened?" he asked, going dark and grim instead of screaming his head off—which was what he wanted to do.

The uniform scanned Ethan's credentials. "The woman who runs the daycare was attacked by two armed men. They took—"

Ethan pushed past him to the sobbing woman standing at the threshold. When she looked up, she began to cry harder. Ethan didn't need to ask what had happened. He already knew.

Luna was gone.

"I'm *so* sorry," the woman cried as he stopped in front of her. "They burst in and hit me, then ran off with her."

"Who did? Did you recognize them?"

A huge bruise was blooming across her cheekbone, the eye above it swelling shut. "No. I didn't see their faces. They were wearing masks."

A plainclothes detective wearing a shield around his neck ran up the steps, alarmed to see a man of his size looming over the hapless woman.

"Hey, who are you?" he shouted. "What is your connection to this woman?"

Ethan took a deep breath. It felt as if his jaw had turned to stone, but he was still able to open his mouth to hiss, "My name is Ethan Thomas."

He held up his badge. "The little girl they took—she was *mine*. They took my baby girl."

§

Juliet hadn't stopped crying since he got home and told her what happened.

She valiantly tried to keep her tears inside, but he could still see her clutching one of Donovan's fine linen handkerchiefs to her face, her shoulders shaking with silent sobs.

His friend patted her back awkwardly. Despite years of living in war-torn countries, Donovan was obviously having a hard time finding the right words to comfort her. But at least he was trying to make her feel better because Ethan couldn't. All he could do was plan and plot bloodshed. The only problem was he didn't know who to direct his rage at.

"Are you sure it's not the Russians?" Jason asked for the third time.

He and Rivera had arrived less than twenty minutes after Ethan had called them—which meant they had broken every traffic law in the book to get here so fast.

Other colleagues were on their way, too. They were going to set up a command center here at Donovan's place. But he didn't know what good that would do.

"I have no idea," Ethan told Jason. "The kidnappers haven't contacted us. There have been no threats and no ransom demands. We're in the dark. It could be them or it could be Alvaro."

His eyes were burning because they were so dry. But he couldn't cry, and he definitely couldn't break every piece of furniture in the room like he wanted to.

Luna may not have been his blood, but he loved that little girl as if she were his own. And he was going to get her back. He had to.

"We need to figure out who took her. We would have gotten an alert on Alvaro's passport if he had crossed the border, so we have to assume it's the Russians—some sort of retribution for helping Viktor. We need to track him down. The only problem with that is if we go in wherever he is, we'll be marking him as a traitor to what's left of the Komarovs and they'll make us."

"I'm still not convinced this is related to him at all." Ethan was getting a splitting headache.

"Can I help?"

He blinked, surprised to see Donovan next to them. "I want to help, but aside from giving Juliet a tranquilizer, there's nothing I can do here. But if you send me to wherever you think Viktor is, I can find him. I mean, even on a good day, no one would confuse me for an FBI agent."

It was true. With his clean-cut preppy looks and gentle eyes, Donovan wouldn't ever be confused for one, but that didn't make it any safer for him.

Scowling, Ethan shook his head. "We don't have any idea where he is. You'd be going in and out of dangerous clubs and gang bars for no reason."

Jason looked behind them at the couch, then turned back, leaning over to whisper. "Actually, the tranquilizer idea might not be a bad one."

"No." Ethan's reaction was instant. He couldn't do that to Juliet. He didn't want her to suffer, but if they heard something about Luna, she would never forgive herself—or him—if she was knocked out or too drowsy to hear the message.

"Well, until we hear something, I think you need to get your ass over there and help your woman deal with this because she's hanging by a thread." Donovan's head drew back. "I know you and Jason here are used to going in, guns blazing, but you can't. What you *can* do is go and comfort Juliet."

Ethan closed his eyes. Of course Donovan was right. Ethan couldn't do what he normally did in stressful situations. He was being an ass.

Grabbing one of the ridiculously overpriced bottles of brandy from the cabinet, he took a single glass and then went over to the couch. He took Juliet's hand, tugging her up and leading her to the bedroom.

She sat on the bed with a thump. "This is all my fault."

He kneeled in front of her, setting the bottle and glass on the floor. "No, it's not. It's mine."

Ethan reached down for the bottle, pouring two fingers into the glass. He drank half of it, then offered her the other half. She shook her head, but he pressed the glass into her hand. "Drink. It won't be enough to get you drunk."

He held the glass up to her lips, urging her to take a sip. She drank it all, shuddering as the alcohol burned its way down her throat.

"You aren't responsible," he reassured her, taking the empty glass from her unresisting hands. "For all we know, this is about Viktor. I should have never brought him here."

"It's *not* about him."

"Until we hear a ransom demand, we won't know. And if it is the Russians—even they wouldn't hurt a baby," he said, hoping he wasn't lying.

Ethan had no idea what the penalties would be for Viktor, but he had to think the Komarovs would be crazy to hurt an FBI agent's baby. They didn't pull shit like that, not unless they wanted the full wrath of the agency coming down on them. Even without the restraining hand of Maksim Komarov, he didn't think the rest of the crew would be that stupid.

"This isn't happening because of Viktor. Alvaro must have found us. He sent someone here. They were watching us. At the first opportunity, they took her."

Fresh tears welled in her eyes. Ethan took her into his arms, pressing her against his chest. "We are going to get her back. *I* am going to get her back."

He was the one who had let this happen. It was *his* fault. Ethan was an experienced agent. Every time he had dropped off or picked up

Luna, he had taken evasive maneuvers, trying to make sure no one discovered the location of the sitter's or where they were staying... but, clearly, he hadn't been careful enough.

Her amazing dark eyes red and swollen, she said, "What if we can't? What if he's taking her straight back to Mexico?"

No. His nemesis wouldn't do that. "If it's Alvaro, he will get in touch. He's going to want that video back."

Juliet shook her head. "Alvaro doesn't even know it exists. I didn't confront him with it. I took Luna and ran, bringing the nanny cam and video with me as insurance."

His head drew back. "Oh, right."

Ethan passed a hand roughly through his hair. Where the hell did that leave him?

"Then we show it to him."

"What?"

He held up a hand. "I've put out some quiet feelers in the Russian community—we're using every CI the office has in those neighborhoods to track down Viktor. If we don't hear anything from him in the next couple of hours, we can assume Alvaro is behind the kidnapping."

Her tearstained face ripped him to shreds. "So, what's your plan?" she asked.

"We'll email him the video," he said, rubbing her back. "You still remember his email address, right?"

Juliet's mouth dropped open. "Yes, but—but what if it's not him? What if he knows nothing about it, but he decides to make a move after he sees it?"

This argument was going in circles.

"We'll make sure it's untraceable. He won't be able to track you here with it. The tech guys will make sure of it. That's if we don't hear something from him first—which I think we will."

Knowledge of the video or not, Alvaro would have assumed Juliet was a witness to the murder he committed. As long as she lived, she would be a threat to him. He wouldn't let his minions take off with Luna without dealing with her.

Juliet put her head in her hands, slumped over, defeat in every line of her body. Then she gasped, her head snapping up. The look of mute horror on her face made his insides twist.

"What is it?"

Raising shaky hands, Juliet covered her mouth. "Oh my God."

"*What?*" Ethan grabbed her hands, frantic now.

"Alvaro isn't ever going to give Luna back," she said, choking on the words. "Because she's his *daughter*."

CHAPTER THIRTY-FOUR

Ethan shook his head. "I don't understand."

The wild look in Juliet's eyes stood in stark contrast to the stillness of her pale face. "I think it's true, or at least Alvaro believes she's his—and with good reason."

She broke off, putting her hand on her stomach. A moment later, she sprang to her feet. She ran to the bathroom, kneeling in front of the toilet seconds before heaving up all the contents of her stomach.

At the sound of someone being sick, Donovan came running. Ethan waved him away. Whatever Juliet had to say, she didn't need an audience.

He wet a hand towel before dropping beside her to wipe her face.

She shuddered. "He never had a kind word to say about her, but I should have believed her—after all, I met him at her party," she said in a shaky voice.

Crap. He knew what was coming. "You think Alvaro and your sister were having an affair?" he asked.

"She said they were."

"*What?*" Ethan gripped the counter next to him for support.

Juliet's lips parted, and she took a shaky breath. "She told me, but I didn't believe her—I thought she was just trying to hurt me. Daniela always said the most hurtful things."

"Okay, I need to sit." Ethan sat next to the toilet while she wiped her eyes. "Please tell me everything."

"I—I don't even know where to start." Juliet gripped the towel, twisting it into a little knot.

Ethan covered her hand with his. "Anywhere you want would be good."

And the sooner, the better.

"My sister was…well, she wasn't the nicest person."

Ethan had gathered as much. Juliet hadn't liked talking about Daniela, but he'd chalked that up to a bad case of sibling rivalry. If this affair had happened, he severely underestimated the extent of the damage.

"If Daniela was carrying on with your fiancé, I'd call that an understatement."

Her lips twisted in a humorless smile. "That's just it. According to Daniela, I was having an affair with *her* man."

"You mean?"

Juliet nodded "She said he—they—had been sneaking around behind her husband's back for years. Or, at least, that's what she hissed at me at the christening."

"This fight with your sister happened the day she died?"

Another nod. "Yes…we were never close. Ever since we were little, Daniela and I were like oil and water. She was more like my mother, and I followed in my father's footsteps. I liked school and always excelled there, while she liked to party and surround herself with wealthy and glamorous friends. But our relationship didn't become truly terrible until I got engaged."

"Did you ever see them together?"

Her brow creased, but she shook her head. "Not very often. Alvaro avoided contact with my family after we met, even Daniela's famous parties unless he knew someone especially important was going to be there. Mostly, though, he didn't mix with them. He said it was bad for his image."

She looked up. "Despite what she said, I honestly never considered the possibility. He seemed to genuinely dislike her. Whenever she came up in conversation, he was dismissive or outright contemptuous."

Ethan knew that didn't mean Alvaro wasn't having an affair with Daniela. A lot of men found it easy to sleep with women they didn't like or respect, but he didn't tell Juliet that.

"So, there were no hints of a relationship," he said. "However, you were working long hours at the café, weren't you? And he was a busy, important man. I'm guessing you didn't see that much of each other."

"That's right," she agreed. "We didn't spend as much time together as I would have wanted. Because his courtship was old-fashioned, I never spent the night with him. Now I wonder if it's because he was sleeping with my sister the whole time. If he is the father, he must have been. Luna would have been conceived *after* we started dating."

He squeezed her hand in sympathy, wondering why the hell any man would want a Daniela when he could have had a Juliet.

Unless he thought he could have both—the good girl to walk down the aisle for his public image...and the bad girl to screw behind the scenes for as long as it pleased him.

Until Daniela threw a spoke in his plans by getting pregnant. Daniela...who was killed shortly after the baby was born. Had she confronted Alvaro and told him he was the father? Or, more importantly, did she make any demands he decided it would be better not to keep?

"We're there any signs of a problem in your sister's marriage?"

"Not that I know of..."

"But?"

She shrugged, and her lashes flickered as if she were ashamed. "Daniela married Xavier for his money. He was from an old family, and he had a great deal of it. There were rumors she was running around on him in the early days, but I think my mother took her aside and warned her not to screw things up. Daniela signed a generous prenup, but it wouldn't have been enough for her."

Ah, so the shame was real. It just wasn't for herself. No wonder Juliet never liked speaking about her family. As for the rest, the scenario unrolled in his mind.

Alvaro probably had wanted Juliet for his wife. She was a beautiful innocent who had connections he could exploit, regardless of how she was getting along with her parents. The news he was Luna's real father would have been unwelcome, particularly if Daniela was using the baby as leverage to get her lover to end his relationship with her sister.

So, he decides to kill her and the rest of her family? It was extreme. Especially since he could have taken out Juliet at the same time.

"Were you supposed to be at the christening?" he asked

Her head drew back as if she were thinking about it. "Well, Daniela didn't invite me, but my mother told me I had to be there. She was tired of her friends gossiping about our rift...and it was for family. There was a new baby. Mother said it was time to mend fences."

"But Alvaro thought you were staying away."

She sighed. "Maybe. I'm not sure anymore. He did try to talk me out of going, and I didn't argue with him. Not much."

Juliet groaned. "If Alvaro is Luna's real father—"

Ethan held up a hand. "Stop right there. At best, he was a sperm donor. *I'm* Luna's real father now, and *you* are her real mother. And we're going to get her back. We *are* going to be a family."

The look of hope mingled with desperation was killing him. Ethan pressed Juliet's face to his chest so he wouldn't have to see it anymore.

CHAPTER THIRTY-FIVE

"Is she asleep?" Donovan asked.

"No." Ethan looked at the darkening sky. Several hours had passed since he'd convinced Juliet to lie down and rest. But he kept checking on her, and she was simply lying there on the bed, trying not to cry.

Rivera gave him a short nod. "We've heard from several of our sources in the Russian networks. They're not all reliable, but there's nothing about a kidnapped baby so far. Not even a whisper."

"Yeah," he muttered. "The Russians weren't viable suspects to begin with."

The other agent grunted. "Also, Jason is on the phone with headquarters. The Angel is tearing him a new one. He wants to know why someone would kidnap your girlfriend's kid."

Rivera winced. "I recommend not telling him about that trumped-up warrant for her arrest if you can avoid it—Jason filled me in."

Ethan scrubbed his face with his hands. "Yeah, good idea."

"Err, why don't I go put on another pot of coffee?" Donovan asked. He headed to the makeshift command center, manned by his friends and coworkers. "I think we're going to need it."

Ethan thanked him, resolving to go find Jason to take over the call with his supervisor. He should be the one doing the explaining.

Donovan ran back in, skidding to a stop next to him. He shoved a paper in his hand. "This was on the kitchen floor—someone shoved it through the window."

Ethan snatched up the sheet. It was thick photo paper. He glanced at the time and place written on the back and then turned it over.

"*Son a bitch*," he yelled. Footsteps sounded. Soon, he was surrounded.

"What is it?" Jason asked as Juliet pushed through the circle of mostly male agents.

Taking a deep breath, he held up the photo. It was Luna. She was making a face—a little baby pout at whoever was holding her. All they could see of the man was his hand.

"The ring…" Juliet pointed a shaky finger at the picture.

Ethan glanced at the picture. There was a thick gold band with a dark stone on the man's hand.

"Now we know for sure," she said in a strained voice. "That's the ring I gave Alvaro. It was an engagement present."

෧

Ethan took the photo and turned it over, skipping over the time and place to read the short message scrawled at the end.

"Come alone or you will never see her again." He looked up at Juliet. "Do you think the ring is a message?"

She took a shaky breath. "I do. Luna is not all he wants. I have to go with him, too."

His scowl was immediate. "You think he still wants to marry you?" Ethan was incredulous.

"It makes sense," Jason said. Rivera nodded in agreement.

"In what world?" Ethan asked with a scowl.

Juliet touched his arm. "He wants the money."

"What money?"

"Mine and Luna's."

Ethan glanced at his partner and Rivera, but they didn't look confused. Even Donovan seemed to be following the conversation better than Ethan was.

"Luna does have money," he said belatedly, catching up. "You said her father was wealthy, but weren't you disinherited?"

Jason nudged Rivera. En masse, the other agents stepped back, taking Donovan with them. They were out of sight, but Ethan knew they were still listening.

He pulled Juliet closer, turning the picture over so she wouldn't have to see the baby she couldn't hold. She studied the message.

"I think it's Alvaro's writing. He must be nearby."

"Juliet, tell me about your money. Do you have any?"

She glanced at a point over his shoulder. "I don't think my father took my little rebellion seriously. Plus, he was a planner. He would have left a will, and my guess is I'm still an heir. Alvaro knows that. I wouldn't be surprised if he doesn't have a copy. He could have easily gotten one through his connections."

"So, let me get this straight—he expects you to go back and marry him so he can claim your dad's money for himself?"

Juliet raised her hand to touch his chest. "Why would he settle for Luna's inheritance when he could have both? He knows as long as he has her, I have to do what he wants."

She wrapped her arms around herself. "And I will have to. For a while, until the money is secure, and then he can safely get rid of me."

Ethan's hand fisted, but he forced it open so he could pull Juliet into his arms. "That is not going to happen. It's time to send this asshole the movie you took. Once Alvaro sees himself in the starring role, he'll realize he no longer has the upper hand."

Juliet's eyes clouded with doubt. "And then what?"

Ethan's grip tightened on her shoulder. "Then we change the rules of his game."

CHAPTER THIRTY-SIX

Isaac Rivera tried to apply the tape to the wires on Juliet's midriff without getting too much of an eyeful. *Damn, her skin is soft.* What kind of soap did she use? Whatever it was, it must have been expensive.

"Almost done?" Jason White hovered over him, reminding him that he shouldn't be lingering like this.

Not that Juliet wasn't worth looking at. But the last thing he needed was to get punched out by Ethan Thomas for having his hands all over his girl—even if he was supposed to be getting her wired up.

They were at the docks. Given the successful op they just had there, Ethan had decided this was where they would confront Alvaro. Personally, Rivera wasn't sure. The location had a lot of hiding places —too many in his opinion. But all the agents in his office knew it backward and forward so they had focused their efforts there.

Putting back the surveillance equipment had been simple. Every available man and woman in the agency was waiting in their old hiding places, leaving strategic openings in their security net the bad guy could exploit. The Angel had cleared it after he had seen the snuff film Juliet had taken. No doubt he'd already figured out a way to capitalize on the Mexican police lieutenant's arrest.

Rivera ripped off another piece of body tape. "Not quite."

"Well, hurry up," Jason said. "And don't forget to put on the vest afterward."

"Yeah, yeah," he replied, annoyed.

Up until his divorce, Rivera had been reasonably tight with Jason and even Ethan, but he could hardly stand them now. Jason was too happily married—always flaunting that gorgeous wife of his—and now this thing with Ethan...

Bad enough Thomas resembled a brunet Captain America, but then he landed a damsel in distress that looked like this. Meanwhile, all Rivera had to show for his love life was a huge hole in his bank account, one created by the alimony payments he owed his ex.

And to top it off, Juliet is rich. Sure, it was blood money, but it was *a lot* of blood money.

Life just wasn't fair sometimes. He huffed derisively.

"What's wrong?" Rivera looked up into Juliet's dark somber eyes, and his bravado shriveled up like a deflated balloon. This was a human being in pain, and, somewhere out there, a little girl was crying for her mother.

"It's nothing." He cleared his throat and straightened, motioning for her to put her shirt back down. "Sorry we didn't have a female agent to do this part."

She leaned in. "A female agent wouldn't give me a gun," she whispered.

Rivera blinked at her. She held up her hands. "Please. Ethan won't give me one either."

"For good reason," he replied. "Do you even know how to use one?"

Not to mention most of the female agents he knew were far more likely to give her a weapon...

Juliet nodded. "My mother acted in several Westerns. She even played a mafia lieutenant in a TV movie. I used to run lines with her and pretend to shoot her."

"Uh..." What the hell was he supposed to say to that?

"I used real guns. They were empty, of course, but real. We—we owned a lot..."

"*Okay.*"

"Really?"

"No!" He shook his head. That would earn him a beating from Captain America for sure. He put his hands on his hips. "Sorry. But pretending to shoot someone is not practice for real life. Plus, most of the time, the inexperienced person with the gun gets it turned on them." Especially if they were a petite woman.

An old memory flashed through his mind, of a girl who bore a strong-enough resemblance to Juliet to matter.

Rivera looked around at the command center. Jimenez had come in. He sat in the corner, manning the trio of surveillance monitors, but he was wearing a headset.

This is a bad idea. But he was going to do it anyway. Rivera bent, then unstrapped the ankle holster on his right leg. The larger one was on his left, carrying his most compact gun, but this one was smaller, almost delicate by comparison.

He transferred the strap to Juliet's leg, tugging the denim down over it.

"It's simple to use. Just pull it out, then press the button." Straightening, Rivera wagged a finger in her face. "Women get knives turned on them even more easily than guns, so this should only be used in dire emergencies."

She cast a cautious glance over at the agent in the corner. "It's a knife?"

"A switchblade and it's illegal, so shh…" He put a finger to his lips.

Owning a switchblade wasn't illegal according to state law. Carrying one, however, was.

Jason came back inside. "Everything is ready, and our people have spotted three men sneaking inside." He turned to Juliet. "It's time to get in place."

"Alvaro actually came?" Juliet wasn't the only one who was surprised. This Alvaro guy was either really stupid or still swimming in a massive power trip from running his own little fiefdom down south.

"Does he have Luna with him?"

"Not that we can tell, but we expected a double-cross. She's probably in the van they drove in on. The team is going to swarm that vehicle as soon as Alvaro and his men are out of earshot."

He put an arm on her shoulder. "He's still expecting to get away by boat, remember? That's why we picked this place. That means he stashed her nearby."

Or the kid could be hundreds of miles away, on her way to Mexico. But Rivera didn't say that aloud. As long as this Alvaro character was here with them, then the kid was safe enough.

Juliet took a shaky breath, visibly willing herself to believe Jason. "All right. And Ethan?"

"He's ready, too."

Rivera handed her the light jacket they had chosen to cover the ballistic vest. "Okay," she said, slipping it on.

Jason tapped the headset strapped to his ear. "Juliet is coming out. *Operation Codename Romeo* is a go."

Juliet hesitated at the threshold of the shipping container. She twisted, nose wrinkled. Rivera rolled his eyes, but he still caught the other man's annoyingly irrepressible grin.

Jason smirked. "I couldn't resist."

CHAPTER THIRTY-SEVEN

Juliet walked down the dock, focusing on the tight planks under her feet. The lapping and swirling of the water around the posts of the pier was the only sound.

But Ethan is close, she assured herself. He wasn't letting her do this by herself.

He chose this place for a reason. Smuggling weapons into the docks by boat via cargo crate was easy enough, but getting them here from an overland route was exceedingly difficult. The entrances were heavily guarded to prevent the dockworkers from coming in and out with contraband too easily.

He's not going to escape by boat. And even if the unforeseen happened and Alvaro somehow got to the craft waiting for him, the Coast Guard cutter lying in wait outside the harbor would ensure he didn't get far.

You need to focus. Alvaro would assume she wasn't alone out here, but Jason had told her no one at the local police precinct had mobilized, so Alvaro would think he was in the clear. He had no idea he was surrounded.

And Alvaro would believe that as long as he had Luna, Juliet would bend to his will...the way she had the entirety of their courtship.

I can't believe you thought he was some sort of hero. She'd been stupid and naive, but she couldn't help but think such a thing couldn't happen a second time.

Everything was going to be okay. She was as safe here as anywhere else in the city. Not to mention the fact she was surrounded by a veritable platoon of FBI agents.

Juliet drew her jacket tighter around herself as a sharp wind swirled around her, lifting her hair. *If I'm this cold, Ethan must be freezing.*

The minutes dragged past, then she felt a frisson run down her spine that had nothing to do with the cold.

Alvaro was here.

CHAPTER THIRTY-EIGHT

Alvaro appeared alone. He walked up the dock with an expression of concern etched on his face.

"Cariño, what is going on?" he asked in Spanish, his tone bleeding with sincerity and confusion. He put his hands up, gesturing around them as if in disbelief. "I have been going crazy searching for you and Delilah. I turned around, and you were both gone."

He broke off, hurt indignation flashing across his face. "How could you leave like that?"

Juliet stared, wide-eyed. Whatever she had expected, it wasn't this.

"Where is Luna?"

This time, the confusion was genuine. "Who?"

"Delilah! I know you took her. And I know you killed Daniela and my parents."

Alvaro stepped back as if she were speaking in tongues. He rushed toward her, hands out in supplication. "Mi amor, you have to calm down—I had no idea you were this...unbalanced by what happened to your family, but it's perfectly understandable."

He broke off, crossing his arms and leaning forward. "This is my fault. I should have realized how difficult it was for you, then had a counselor come and speak to you."

Santo cielo... "Oh, my God—you seriously think I'm stupid!"

She held up a hand when he opened his mouth to speak. "Forget it. I know you do. You think I'm a fool for what—turning my back on my family? Not taking their money? Believing you were a good man?" Her face twisted in disgust. "Well, I admit I made a mistake on that last part."

Alvaro had subsided. He stared at her with narrowed dark eyes, his lips curling. "I repeat, I don't know what you're talking about."

"Yes, you do. I saw you kill that man—over and over," she said. "I know you got the video, so why don't we drop the pretense?"

His face darkened. "I did that for you! Your father made a lot of enemies. I knew those monsters would never stop hunting you until they wiped out your entire family. I took care of the problem for you. Everything I did, I did for *you*."

Ugh. "And how, exactly, was sleeping with Daniela supposed to help me?"

His eyes flared in surprise before he could mask his expression.

"Yes, she told me everything," Juliet confirmed with a nod. "She also told me you were only taking down the cartels in order to take their place—which is why you killed them."

That last was a fabrication, but she was trying to force a confession.

"None of that is true."

"If it's not, then why did you have a warrant issued in *my* name for murder?"

Alvaro closed his eyes, tilting his head back as if he was praying to the heavens. "I did that for your protection, too. I had to use whatever means I could to get you back—and can you blame me? You're clearly a danger to yourself."

Unbelievable. "Murder, Alvaro. The warrant was for *murder*. Any cop in the country could have shot me, and it would have been justified." She held up her hand. "Unless you return the baby, that video goes to every major Mexican newspaper in the country."

He stared, coldness seeping into his expression. "Where is your boyfriend?" he asked.

"My what?"

"The American cop you're fucking. Where is he?" Alvaro looked around, searching for Ethan.

"He's not a cop," she corrected.

Alvaro ignored her. "Where is he?"

She took out her cell phone. The video was already pulled up. It had been pasted into an email addressed to the three biggest papers in their town. Holding it up, she wagged her finger over the send button.

"Tell me where she is," she ordered in a shaky voice.

Alvaro spat on the wooden pier. "She's *dead*. And now...you are, too."

In the second between blinks, Alvaro leapt backward.

CHAPTER THIRTY-NINE

Most people didn't know what a gunshot sounded like in real life. But Juliet was intimately familiar with it. The sound had been burned into her brain on the worst day of her life. And that terrible knowledge saved her now.

When she heard the first distinctive pop, Juliet let herself fall back onto the dock like Alvaro.

He had known they were coming. Alvaro had signaled a sniper, then jumped out of the way.

Crying out, Juliet hit the wooden boards with a pained thump, dropping her phone in the process. The impact knocked the breath out of her as the world exploded around her.

Men shouted, and footsteps pounded. Juliet rolled, opening her eyes to see Alvaro looming over her. When he saw she was unharmed, he bent, his hands twisted like claws. He was going to strangle her.

She didn't remember reaching for the switchblade, but it was there in her hand. Juliet pressed the button, then blindly thrust it forward. It caught Alvaro above the knee.

Blood poured over her hand as he screamed. He pulled abruptly away, digging out the blade from his lower thigh.

"*Pinche puta*," Alvaro hissed, finally getting the blade out.

He lunged for her again, but he disappeared from her field of view in a shower of salty droplets.

❧

Ethan gripped the post under the pier as a larger-than-normal wave, the eddy from an unseen boat, swept over him. He turned his head, shaking the cold water off. Despite the frigid winter weather, he wasn't cold. His rage was keeping him plenty warm.

When discussing where he should wait during *Operation Codename Romeo*—he was going to kill Jason for that—Ethan decided his place was going to be as close to Juliet as possible. So he took a page from Mason Lang's book, and he decided to go commando. He was hiding under the pier.

Above his head, the conversation of his life was taking place, and he wasn't a part of it. He strained his ears, trying to catch every word Alvaro said, but then regretted it.

When Alvaro called Juliet '*mi amor*,' Ethan wanted to leap up and punch the bastard's lights out. But he forced himself to stay in place, adjusting the earpiece he wore. He couldn't move until the second team confirmed they had Luna.

The argument above grew heated. His pulse pounded in response.

Hurry, damn it. What is taking so long? Where is Luna?

Ethan pressed his lips tightly together, so he wouldn't ask the question aloud and give away his position.

The van Alvaro had arrived in was parked less than a half mile away. By now, the second team should have it surrounded. His men should have recovered Ethan's baby girl by now.

Finally, he couldn't stand it anymore. "Update," he whispered, risking discovery.

There was silence. "We've taken the van. It's empty. No driver and no child."

Fuck. "Find them," he hissed. They had to be close by.

Jason's voice came over the com. "We will. You get Juliet out of there."

And not a moment too soon. Alvaro yelled. "She's dead. And now...you are, too."

Reaching up, Ethan grabbed the edge of the pier, rising from the water like Leviathan. The military-grade wetsuit Jason had dug up allowed the maximum freedom of movement, which meant he was able to tackle the asshole with ease.

"Hijo de puta—" Alvaro burst out.

Rearing back, Ethan took great satisfaction in shutting the man up. His fist connected with the guy's mouth, knocking a few teeth loose in the process.

Glass jaw. I should have guessed. Alvaro went down like a ton of bricks, but he was quick. Rolling backward, Alvaro tried to pull a gun hidden in his waistband, but Ethan saw it. He kicked it away, leaping on his adversary when the man twisted to run away.

Ethan threw himself forward, catching him with a restraining hand. Alvaro twisted, landing an unexpected hit to Ethan's solar plexus that stunned him for a second. But Alvaro was smaller, and his punches didn't have Ethan's power.

Recovering, Ethan kicked out, sweeping the other man's leg out from under him. The move, straight out of *Mortal Kombat*, would have made his teenage self proud. Reaching over, he grabbed a fistful of the man's hair.

For all his bluster, Alvaro wasn't a fighter. A lot of killers weren't. When it came to hand-to-hand combat, Ethan was his superior.

"I'm going to fucking kill you," Alvaro hissed as Ethan yanked the asshole's head back sharply.

"I invite you to keep trying," Ethan spat. "Where is Luna?"

"Who?"

Ethan twisted Alvaro's arm behind him, slamming his head against the boards. "I believe you know her as Delilah."

"I'm not going to tell you where my daughter is."

Jaw tensing, Ethan pushed the guy's head, scraping his cheek against the boards. "That's where you're wrong. That girl is my daughter now."

"What the—" Alvaro twisted to look, his dark beady eyes fixing on his face. Behind him, footsteps pounded. Team one was swarming the dock.

"And Juliet is mine, too," Ethan finished, not turning his head. Alvaro was the kind of snake he shouldn't turn his back on.

His nemesis sneered, sitting up. "You're the cop Julietta is shacking up with."

Ethan scoffed as Jason and Rivera appeared on either side of him. "That's another of your mistakes, motherfucker. We aren't cops. We're FBI."

Alvaro waited a beat before leaping up, giving Ethan the opportunity he needed.

He threw another punch. The asshole fell back down on the dock, dazed.

Jason cleared his throat. "Ethan, buddy, I know you're enjoying this, but there's something you should know."

A surge of satisfaction flowed through Ethan as he saw Alvaro was bleeding, too. "What?"

He blinked as his partner's hands gripped either side of his head, twisting it to direct his gaze to the left.

Juliet was in Rivera's arms. Red stained her shoulder, spreading down her arm to her wrist.

She looked up, her eyes like stars that were burning too bright.

"The men didn't reach the shooter in time…"

"I think one got me," Juliet said in a trembling voice. Then she slumped over in a dead faint.

CHAPTER FORTY

Juliet came to as she was placed in the ambulance. She cracked her lids open, wondering why her arm felt as if it were on fire.

Ethan's hand rested on her forehead. He'd thrown one of those FBI windbreakers over his wetsuit, but his hand was still clammy and chilled from the cold water.

Squinting in the bright lights overhead, she tried to sit up. "What happened?"

His smile was too determined to be much comfort. "You passed out, probably from blood loss."

"She didn't lose enough blood for that," the small female EMT said as she cleaned Juliet's arm.

Ethan turned to glare at the woman. "Give it to her anyway."

"Give me what?" Juliet's brain wasn't processing anything properly.

"A transfusion." The EMT's voice was flat. She faced Ethan with an unflinching gaze. "And I told you that your semester in med school does not trump my five years of experience. She most likely fainted because of the shock."

The ballsy woman addressed Juliet. "Have you ever fainted at the sight of blood before?"

"Only once." When her family died. But there had been *a lot* of blood that day.

The woman either didn't notice or chose to overlook the desolation in Juliet's tone. "If she needs blood, they will give it to her at the hospital."

"Then what are we waiting for?" Ethan snapped. "Let's go."

Juliet struggled, breaking Ethan's hold. "No, wait. Where's Luna?"

Ethan averted his eyes. His silence spoke volumes.

"She wasn't in the van?" Juliet cried.

"No, but she has to be here somewhere. The team is scouring the docks. He would have wanted her close by."

Tears filled her eyes. She clutched his hand. "Stay and help them."

"But Jason has it—"

"No, Ethan," she sobbed. "Luna is yours. You have to find her. She —she needs her *daddy.*"

Even the crusty EMT held her breath while Ethan blinked and swallowed. Then he nodded.

"Go," Juliet urged. "I'm fine."

"You will be," he said, nodding decisively. "As soon as I find our baby."

Ethan kissed her, then climbed out of the ambulance. He gave her one more loaded glance before shutting the door.

"I feel bad about giving him shit now," the EMT said with a grimace, signaling for the driver to get moving. "I didn't realize your baby was missing."

Weaker than she had let on, Juliet collapsed onto the gurney. "It's okay. Ethan is going to find her."

He has to.

§.

Ethan could tell Jason was weighing whether to refuse him entry into the interrogation room. He and his partner were cooling his heels while Jimenez and the Angel himself grilled Alvaro Lopez.

That last was the reason Ethan had been forced to stand down. Robert Angel was a fucking master in the interrogation room. If Alvaro was going to make a deal with anyone, it was the Angel.

And if he didn't, there was always plan B—letting Ethan go in there and break every bone in Alvaro's body.

The minutes ticked away. Ethan kept his eye on the clock. It had been almost two hours since they'd hauled Lopez in. He'd had time to shower and change in the locker room, but that had taken him two minutes. The rest of the time, he'd been standing in front of this damn door.

Finally, the tension got to him.

"It's taking too long," he growled. "Alvaro knows we have the video. It's not in his interest to talk. He's not going to tell us where Luna is."

"He will," Jason assured him with faux confidence.

Rivera grunted in agreement. "You know these things take time."

Ethan gritted his teeth, resisting the urge to punch the wall. "Luna doesn't have time."

"He's not going to hurt her. Lopez needs her alive to get her inheritance," the other agent told him.

"Do we know that for sure? Maybe he's already had himself appointed Luna's guardian down south."

If the baby was gone, Lopez could inherit her money now. But Ethan didn't finish that train of thought. The other agents knew what the worst-case scenario was. He didn't need to spell it out for them.

"At least go to the hospital. If the Angel falls short, we'll break this guy for you," the agent told him. "For fuck's sake, your girl was bleeding."

"It wasn't serious," Ethan said from behind gritted teeth. Not being with Juliet while she was hurt was tearing him up. "I can't go to the hospital without Luna. I promised Juliet I would bring her back."

Suddenly, the door opened. The Angel appeared at the door. Ethan fixed his burning eyes on his boss, but Robert shook his head.

Fuck.

"I'm going in."

Wisely, Robert Angel stepped aside to let Ethan pass. Rivera reached out, grabbing his arm. "Just remember Alvaro needs to be breathing to talk."

"Don't worry."

Ethan entered the room with a glower that would make a dockworker flinch. Alvaro was cuffed, sitting at the table. Jimenez was holding up the wall next to the table.

A laptop had been placed on the surface across from the perp, frozen at the moment where Alvaro pointed his gun at his victim.

Ethan gestured at the screen. "Admiring your handiwork?"

Alvaro narrowed his eyes. He relaxed abruptly, leaning back when he recognized Ethan.

Ethan turned the chair around, then sat.

"You know, Juliet had a hard time trusting me at first. After dealing with one corrupt piece-of-shit cop, she was reluctant to put herself on the line for another member of law enforcement. But I'm actually everything you pretended to be...and Juliet's a very smart girl. Smarter than you gave her credit for. She realized what you were, and she left you eating her dust."

He trailed off, pretending to philosophically look into the distance. "I, on the other hand, have benefitted from your fuck-up—Juliet and I are getting married soon."

The minute they got Luna back, Ethan was going to make it official.

Alvaro smirked, placing his hands on the table before shifting his weight forward. "You can have that bitch. I don't care anymore. But Delilah is mine—*my* blood. And you're never going to see *her* again."

Ethan narrowed his eyes at the man. His gut clenched. Alvaro had implied he wouldn't see Luna again, but Ethan's instincts told him that wasn't what the bastard meant.

The smug glint in Alvaro's eyes confirmed it. He was going after Juliet.

CHAPTER FORTY-ONE

Juliet stared at the ceiling as the ER doctor at Union Memorial examined the wound on her arm. "I think your EMT was right. You don't need surgery—although you might start wishing we put you under when I'm cleaning this thing."

Juliet took a deep breath, trying to focus on anything other than the throbbing pain. Her other hand flexed reflexively. She cursed herself for forgetting her phone at the scene.

Juliet asked to use the hospital phone, but she had been told by Jason that Ethan was in the interrogation room questioning Alvaro. He promised to call the hospital as soon as they had news about her baby, but that had been nearly an hour ago.

If they haven't found Luna yet, they may never.

Tears streamed from her eyes, prodding the doctor to ask if she needed something for the pain. "I'm fine. And I don't want to be put under, thank you."

Juliet needed to stay awake and alert. Once she was patched up, she was going back out to the docks.

The minutes crawled with excruciating slowness. The doctor hadn't exaggerated about the pain she would feel when they flushed the wound and began to stitch it up. Even the topical numbing agent they gave her didn't relieve the agony she felt.

When it was over, she was woozy, but she fought to get to her feet. "I have to leave," she told the nurse, her words slurring.

The woman threw her a skeptical look. "Honey, you're not going anywhere. Not only can you barely walk, but the FBI have also been on the horn making demands."

The nurse pointed to the security guard hovering in the background. "This one is going to watch over you in a recovery room until they send one of their men to do it."

Juliet frowned. "Did Alvaro escape?"

"Sugar, I don't know who that is. Just go with the nice man and get out of the way. There was a rollover on the highway, and we have patients incoming."

The reminder that she wasn't the only one in pain got her moving. Juliet allowed herself to be helped into a wheelchair so the harried ER staff could treat the others.

She was wheeled to a different floor, to a tiny room with a single hospital bed surrounded by a curtain. "Wait here," the guard told her. "I'm going to pull up a chair outside."

"All right," she agreed, wishing she wasn't so thirsty.

It almost felt as if her cells were crying out for water, but she needed fuel, too. "Do you think I could have a drink?" she asked hesitantly. "Something with sugar?"

They had passed a vending machine down the hall. "Maybe I can have a Gatorade or something?" she asked, digging into her pockets for spare change.

Naturally, she didn't have any.

The security guard grinned. "It's okay. I have cash. What color do you want?"

"Green."

"A fan of the classics, I see." He left the room, pulling the curtain closed on his way out.

It's so no one can see me through the window. Juliet repressed a shudder. Something must have gone wrong. Was Alvaro sending someone after her?

It made sense. He controlled a small army back home. The idea he would come here with only the two men arrested at the docks had been stupid, but she believed there weren't many people he trusted enough.

What does trust have to do with anything? Alvaro paid people for their loyalty—one of the many reasons he wanted her family's money.

The guard returned a few minutes later, slipping through the small gap in the curtain. He held out a bottle of bright neon liquid. "You're in luck. They had your flavor."

She took it from him with a murmured *thanks*. He leaned against the nearby counter. "So maybe after this FBI thing is over, I could buy you a drink?"

Juliet frowned, her lips parting. "Uh..."

The curtain suddenly jerked open. "I don't think—"

Gasping, Juliet reacted, throwing the bottle in her hand. It flew through the air, hitting the man who entered a split second before she recognized him.

"*Ow*," Donovan Carter staggered backward as the full Gatorade bottle bounced off his cheek. A medical chart fell from his hand.

"Oh, my God!" Juliet sprang up from the bed, but she was too weak. Too dizzy to stop herself, she staggered and swayed.

Donovan and the security guard rushed forward, grabbing her before she slid to the floor. Donovan wore a white coat, and he had a stethoscope around his neck.

He eased her back on the bed with a grimace. "Sorry to surprise you like that. Ethan called me. He knows I still have privileges here. He asked me to come watch over you."

Donovan turned to the security guard. "That's the name of her very muscular FBI agent fiancé by the way. I was going to say he wouldn't approve of anyone buying his girl anything when I got hit with a flying energy drink."

"I am so sorry about that," she said, her shoulders rising to her ears.

"It's okay," Donovan assured her before turning back to the guard. "Why don't you take a break? I can watch over her for a while."

Abashed, the other man excused himself. When he was gone, Donovan reached down to get the fallen drink and medical chart. Setting the chart aside, he twisted the bottle open and handed it to her. "Drink it all. From the look of the blood on your shirt, you need the fluids."

"Did Ethan say anything about Luna?"

Donovan took a deep breath. A flicker of something came and went too quickly in his expression for her to decipher. Then she saw his 'unemotional physician face' settling over him like a mask.

He took her hand. "No, I'm sorry. They haven't found her yet. But they've got the best interrogators in the FBI leaning on Alvaro. I'm sure he will give up her location soon."

The tone was TV doctor perfect, with the right blend of sympathy and surety—a voice designed to calm and soothe. It made her want to scream and smack him in the face.

Juliet tried to tell herself Donovan wasn't doing it on purpose. This must be the way he handled stress.

"Luna is probably halfway to Mexico," she whispered, breaking down. A sob escaped her dry throat. "We're never going to get her back."

Donovan's professional shield cracked. He put his hands on her shoulders, pulling her close. "Yes, you will. Ethan is not going to give up on her, and neither should you. Honestly, I don't know which one of you he loves more."

Juliet blinked.

He drew back, shrugging. "Sorry, was that a weird thing to say?"

She wiped her tears on her bloody sleeve. "No. It wasn't. You're right. We're going to get her back. I'll do whatever I have to do."

Donovan patted her back. "Good. I had an idea that might help. I thought I might call my family's K & R specialist for you. He's local, or at least he used to be."

"K & R?" she echoed.

He sucked in a breath. "It—it stands for *kidnap and retrieval*. I thought it might help."

"Oh, okay. I guess." At this point, she was willing to try anything.

I need to speak to my father's banker. She knew Alvaro had no intention of ransoming Luna, but without him in charge, whoever was holding her might be open to a bribe.

"I need to get something from the old apartment building," she said. "I have something hidden in the air vent of the studio apartment

I used to live in. It's my old address book. I brought it with me in case I was ever in a position to reclaim my old life."

She picked up the Gatorade bottle, then took a long drink. "I need to start making arrangements in case there is a ransom demand."

"Oh." Donovan's face cleared. "It's a good idea regardless, but I also think that might take too long."

Juliet hung her head. Her heart was aching so bad she could hardly breathe. "You might be right, but what else can I do?"

Donovan touched her shoulder. "Let me handle it. I can get my hands on some cash a lot faster than you can."

Startled, she looked up. "What?"

The doctor shuffled his feet. "I have a lot of money," he confessed as if he were sharing a great sin.

"It's far more than I need—than anyone does," he continued. "I didn't earn it. I was born with it. For the most part, I try using it for good. And, well, I can't think of anything better than making sure my best friend and his future wife don't lose their baby girl."

He broke off to place a reassuring hand on her uninjured arm. "Let me make a few calls. I'll call Rainer, the K & R guy, and my bank."

"All the banks are closed."

"I think you know when your account is of a certain size, you get the direct after-hours line."

That was true. She took a shaky breath. "Thank you."

He walked to the door. "I'll try to get an update from FBI headquarters, too. Let me get the security guard back here."

Donovan disappeared out the door. A minute or two later, she heard the guard hail her from the door and the scraping of a chair as it was dragged into place. This time, he didn't come inside, but she was grateful. Her pain was too raw. Exposing it to strangers simply made her more aware of it.

Juliet drew her knees up, wrapping her usable arm around them tight. Eventually, her depleted reserves got the better of her and she lay back on the bed, too drowsy to keep her eyes open.

But she couldn't sleep, which was why the sound of the curtain opening roused her.

She glanced up to see a dark-skinned man in bright pink scrubs smiling down at her. "I'm here to take your blood pressure."

"Oh, okay," she replied, wondering why he had spoken in Spanish.

Maybe Donovan had told him she was from Mexico? He moved toward her, and she saw a boot peeking out from under the curtain.

"Wait, what's that?"

The nurse's hand shot out, grabbing her arm in a painful grip. He raised a syringe up to eye level. "Don't worry, I have another one for you, *puta.*"

Juliet screamed, twisting and kicking at the same time. She landed a lucky kick to his face. Grunting, he fell backward. Pushing off too fast, she fell on the other side of the bed.

Holding up her hands, she yelled in Spanish, "*Stop.*"

He ignored her, shifting his weight as he prepared to lunge.

Enough. "I can pay you," she hissed, pointing.

The man hesitated, then his lip curled. He bounced his body weight from foot to foot, transmitting the intention to jump her.

Juliet drew herself up, arrogantly holding up a hand the way her mother had in *Venganza de Amor.* Like everyone on that set—including the crew—he froze.

"I know you," she continued, schooling her voice to sound like her mother's. "Your name is Gonzalo, and you work with Alvaro."

She hadn't met him, but he'd always been there in the background of Alvaro's life.

The man hesitated. He lifted the syringe. "So what if you know my name? You're not going to tell your new cop boyfriend. You'll be in Mexico."

She shook her head. "No, I won't, and neither will you."

Scoffing, she drew herself up, refusing to retreat.

"Alvaro wants me to go home so he can marry me, then kill me because of my family money. Remember that? The *money.*" She emphasized the word, drawing it out.

The man shrugged as if to say, '*so what*'.

She rolled her eyes. "Well then, why settle for a small cut when you can have it all?"

"All?"

"Well, a big chunk—enough to live like a king. All you have to do is call whoever has Luna and have her brought here to me."

Gonzalo appeared to think about it, but then he shook his head. "Alvaro will kill me. He says the girl is his, too."

Juliet briefly closed her eyes. "Well, it's not true. Daniela told me the truth the day she died. She said she couldn't jeopardize her marriage for Alvaro. If her husband suspected the baby wasn't his, he'd divorce her. She would never risk that, but she told Alvaro the baby was his so he would end things with me."

The lies flowed freely now.

Something like vindication flitted across Gonzalo's face. "I knew it," he said smugly. "Daniela...she was always a bitch."

"Alvaro is in FBI custody," Juliet reminded him, lowering her voice and leaning forward.

It was another little trick she'd learned from her mother. Her parent had used it frequently on reporters during interviews, manipulating them into believing they were sharing a confidence.

"The FBI is going to bury him for what he did. He's not going to be able to help you. If you want to get anything out of this, you should take my offer. Forget about him and bring me Luna."

Gonzalo finally put the syringe down. "Alvaro is my cousin," he told her quietly.

Shit! Juliet hadn't known that. "Forgive me for being crass, but isn't a fat pile of cash thicker than blood?"

She held her breath. Gonzalo's head pulled back. He brought his phone to his ear, then pressed a button. "Carla," he said.

When the curtain blew aside and Gonzalo went down hard in a blur of white, Juliet raised shaky hands to her mouth.

She ran around the bed to find Donovan on top of a prone Gonzalo. The doctor had a wild look in his eye, and his face was red and flushed with victory.

"I did it! I saved you." He scrambled to his feet. The man underneath him didn't move.

Donovan turned to face her. "Are you okay?"

"No," she cried, throwing her hands up. "He was going to tell me where Luna was!"

The doctor shook himself. "*What?*"

"I was talking him into a bribe. He was going to call the woman who has Luna—Carla something."

Donovan's face fell. "Oh, shit." He glanced down at the man at his feet, kneeling to check him. "Uh, he hit his head on the bed frame when I tackled him."

"Can't you make him regain consciousness?"

He winced, moving Gonzalo's head around as he examined the wound he'd inflicted. "I can't give him something without a full examination."

"We don't have time for that!"

Donovan's chest heaved. His eyes darted back and forth. He swept his arm out, fishing a cell phone out from under the bed.

"Then we'll call her," he said, "She's not on the line now, but maybe we can return the last call and make her the same offer."

Juliet hopped over Gonzalo's legs, glancing over his shoulder as he scrolled through the phone. "There isn't a recent call—no calls at all today."

She gasped when he opened the messages. "Why aren't there any texts?"

Donovan groaned. "I've seen this with militia soldiers and insurgents I had to treat. They communicate via apps that destroy their messages after a few minutes. We just need to find the right one."

His finger swiped over the screen.

She frowned. "But he was talking. He said 'Carla' into the phone."

"Umm, well then, maybe it was a walkie-talkie app."

"Those exist?"

"Yes, and certain groups use them for the same reason they use apps that destroy texts—to avoid having a record of what was said."

Her lips parted. "Do they have a limited range, like real walkie-talkies?"

If they did, could Luna be close to her now?

He scratched his head. "Uh, I don't know. They could have the same limit as a cell phone."

Disappointed, she stared at Gonzalo. Why wouldn't he wake up?

"Would he know that?" Perhaps he was an underling for a reason. Most people assumed walkie-talkies were short range. Even if the app wasn't, he and whoever Carla was might not know that.

Donovan understood. "I'm going to get security. We'll start

sweeping the floors." He headed for the door, hesitating at the thresh-old. "Do you have a picture of Luna?"

She shook her head. Ethan hadn't let her carry her bulky wallet to the meeting with Alvaro on the small chance she needed to run and it would impede her movement.

"Don't worry. I'll get one from Jason." He disappeared through the door, but he reappeared a split second later. "Stay here. There might be more."

She waited until he was gone to spin around toward Gonzalo.

"Like hell I am," she muttered. Juliet wasn't going to sit here on her hands doing nothing. Her baby could be in this hospital.

Juliet knelt beside the fallen man. "Tell me you have a weapon."

She didn't anymore. Rivera had quietly recovered his switchblade from her at the docks.

Gonzalo didn't have a gun. *C'mon!* There was no way she was sitting here doing nothing, but she wasn't stupid. She needed something.

The syringe!

She knelt, then crawled around the floor in search of it, but there was no sign. In desperation, she went through Gonzalo's pockets. She came up with a single empty backup syringe, still in its wrapper.

Putting her hands on her head, she wracked her brain for other ideas. Maybe she could find something else to use in the hall or one of the other rooms—a loose walker or an IV pole. One of those would make a decent battering ram, provided it still wasn't attached to a patient.

She hurried to the door, kicking the bottle of Gatorade on the way. It had landed on the floor in the scuffle.

Juliet straightened and picked it up, caught by a sudden idea.

CHAPTER FORTY-TWO

"Drive faster!"

Jason ignored him, focusing on the road as he whipped around the corner. "Enough. We're going as fast as humanly possible."

"The hell we are. You should have let me drive."

"If you wanted to drive, you shouldn't have traded in the Mustang."

Ethan braced himself as his partner whipped around the corner. "I can't believe you didn't give Juliet back her phone."

Jason grunted. "Again, not my fault. Someone must have misplaced it in the command center. Besides, I had to watch over you. Otherwise, Alvaro might have taken an unplanned dip in the harbor. We might have never recovered the body."

Ethan covered his face with his hands. "Just drive."

"We'll get there in time. Try Carter again."

"He's not picking up." But Ethan lifted his phone to try again. Jason turned another corner before braking hard.

His arm shot out to brace himself on the dash as his head whipped forward, giving him whiplash.

"What the—"

The road in front of him was a parking lot.

"Back up."

Jason twisted to look behind them. "Can't. We're already blocked in."

"Fuck." Ethan slammed his hand on the dash. "Pull up here," he said, pointing.

"Ethan, that's not a lane. It's the sidewalk."

"Yeah. *Park*." The hospital was six blocks away. "We run from here."

Jason shook his head, but he did as Ethan asked, jumping the curb and pulling the car up on the raised concrete. The vehicle's front grill stopped a few short feet from the nearest table of a sidewalk café.

People started shouting. Jason whipped his shield out, waving it at the nearest irate customer. "We're going to get in so much shit for this."

Ethan got out, ignoring the clamor. "We'll deal with it later. Start running."

The shouts faded in the distance as their feet hit the pavement.

Please let Juliet be all right. Please.

&

Juliet had searched her entire floor and the one above it without success. Tears blinded her, but she scrubbed at them ruthlessly in case anyone stopped or called attention to her.

She needn't have worried. Nothing made a person turn away faster than the sight of a crying woman.

Taking the stairs, Juliet headed down to the floor below. She emerged to see a different color scheme on the walls, one that included painted teddy bears and ducks.

She was in the maternity ward.

There wouldn't be many places to hide here. Juliet didn't know much about American hospitals, but she assumed the babies would be the one thing they guarded more closely than the drugs.

The waiting room...

OB/GYNs met the mothers for checkups on this floor, didn't they? It would have a waiting room—maybe one with a few toys to occupy those children while they waited for their appointments.

Tension filled her chest as she walked down the hall with

measured steps. She stopped, spotting a sign for the space she was looking for.

She peeked around the corner.

Luna.

She drew back, flattening against the wall. Her chest felt like she might explode. Juliet was torn, wanting to charge like a kamikaze, but she wasn't sure her legs would even support her.

Bracing herself, she risked another peek. The woman with Luna—Carla, presumably—was turned away from her. She was checking her phone as if willing it to ring. Luna sat at a little table painted in bright primary colors.

The expression on her little girl's face would haunt Juliet as long as she lived. The toddler was drawn, unsmiling. She also looked tired and scared.

If Luna was tired, she would cry or scream until she was changed or put to bed, whichever she needed. If she wasn't doing either, it was because someone had taught her to be afraid to.

Suddenly, Juliet's legs weren't weak. Rage propelled her across the waiting room floor, uncapping the syringe as she went. She grabbed Carla's head from behind, jabbing the needle in her neck.

Carla gasped and began to struggle, swearing in English. Juliet pushed the syringe deeper into the woman's neck. "I wouldn't move. You don't know what's in this needle, but I do."

Sensibly, the woman stopped struggling.

Juliet smiled at Luna, tears in her eyes. "Hi, baby."

Luna rushed over, hugging her knee. "*Mommy.*"

Her heart couldn't decide if it was swelling or breaking open.

"Mommy missed you," she cried, staring down at her little girl. "I'm right here with you, and we're going to find Ethan."

Juliet turned her attention back to the kidnapper.

"*What is it?*" the woman hissed, straining to see the syringe. It was long enough for her to spot the bright green and yellow liquid.

What sounded bad enough?

"It's cancer drugs," Juliet said, making it up on the spot. "But since you don't already have cancer, it's going to *give* it to you instead. That's what chemotherapy drugs do—they're poison."

Without further hesitation, she depressed the plunger on the syringe, then shoved the woman away.

"*Hey,*" Carla yelled, grabbing her neck.

Juliet ignored her, picking up Luna. She crushed the little girl to her chest, but Luna didn't complain.

Across from her, Carla raised a gun.

Juliet faced the weapon with her heart in her throat. "If you shoot us, you'll bring everyone running," she said. "They're searching for you. But you're not going to shoot. You're going to run down to the ER so they can flush your system. You only have a few minutes left before the drugs do permanent damage."

The woman's face creased as she hesitated. But the sight of the syringe on the floor with its trace of almost-fluorescent liquid convinced her.

Carla ran away, disappearing down the hall.

"Luna, baby." Juliet sobbed hysterically now. She pressed her lips all over Luna's face, rocking and hugging her.

"*Daddy!*"

"What?" Confused, Juliet wiped her eyes. But Luna wasn't looking at her.

"Over here."

Juliet whirled around. "Ethan!"

He looked like an angel in his jeans and white t-shirt—the warrior kind who came from Heaven to kick the devil's butt.

Jason stood behind him, bent over and trying to catch his breath. But she didn't get a chance to ask them where they'd come from before Ethan wrapped his arms around both her and Luna.

"Did I miss the action?"

"You can find the bad guy—or girl, in this case—in the ER, probably asking for dialysis or for her stomach to be pumped."

Ethan drew his head back in confusion. "Never mind. You can explain later."

Always averse to being ignored, Luna reached up to touch his face with grubby little fingers.

Ethan laughed, but it caught in his throat like a sob. "Hey there, Little Moon. I missed you."

"Hi, Daddy," she said, slapping his face in her enthusiasm.

This time, Ethan did sob. He took Luna in his arms, kissed her head a few dozen times.

When he was done, he turned to Juliet. "I didn't train her to say that. Really, I didn't. The babysitter called me her daddy in front of her a few times, and I thought the truth was too complicated to explain. That's why Luna is confused."

Juliet put an arm around his neck, resting her weight against him. "Oh, she's not confused. Not at all."

EPILOGUE

Ethan made a big smacking sound, pretending to smooch the smelly owl puppet that was Luna's current favorite toy.

The little girl giggled, grinding the owl's face into his nose. "More, Daddy."

I need to throw this toy in the wash. Luna dragged it everywhere. It had acquired a very particular and not altogether pleasant scent. But he grinned, then kept kissing as loudly as he could.

Fortunately for him and Juliet, the toy Luna had chosen as her supreme ultimate must-have-at-all-times plaything was machine washable, and it could be found in bulk at Ikea. He and Juliet had half-a-dozen more waiting in the closet. The minute Luna's back was turned, he was going to swap this puppet for a clean one.

And the guys said parenting would be hard, he smugly thought, tickling his baby.

Sure, being a dad wasn't always easy. There were good and bad days. Potty training had been no picnic, but it was going much better lately. That ear infection last month had been damn rough, too.

At least Luna had stopped having nightmares. For weeks after her ordeal, the little girl had woken up screaming and crying every night. She had been impossible to calm down. It had gotten so bad that

Ethan had crashed on the couch for a few days to let Luna sleep with Juliet.

But the sleepless nights hadn't ended until he'd gotten into bed with them both. His presence had finally soothed the little girl back into the sense of security and safety she needed. It was something all babies deserved to have, and Ethan was going to make sure she never had to go without it again.

Luna was the daughter of his heart and soul. Even if he and Juliet never had any biological children of their own—and he planned on at least two more—Ethan knew he had been blessed. He was a father.

His sleep was a lot easier for another reason as well—everyone who had hurt Juliet and Luna was in jail.

Despite rumors to the contrary, the video of Alvaro committing murder had been proven authentic by experts on both sides of the border. It had been more than enough to put him and his lieutenants away. The Mexican authorities had been chipping away at his miniature empire ever since.

The bigger shock had come when Juliet—or rather, Julietta Diaz—had reclaimed her name and her life.

"You're worth how much?" he'd asked after she'd met with her father's lawyers.

North of thirty-five million dollars? What did that even mean? He couldn't wrap his head around the sum.

Juliet's small smile had been sad. "It doesn't matter. I'm not keeping it. Not most of it, anyway," she said, cuddling against him on the couch after the meeting. "I'm only holding onto enough to finish law school and settle my family's affairs."

"What are you going to do with the rest of it?" he asked. "Give it to charity?"

"Yes, but I'm not sure which one. I want to make sure I use it wisely, where it will make the most difference."

Ethan had wholeheartedly agreed with Juliet's decision to give up her millions. Despite the size of his government salary, he felt financially secure. His apartment venture was starting to go well. Last month, the first tenants had moved in. The investment was still far from being in the black, but it was starting to pay dividends.

Despite the fact money wasn't an issue, Juliet had decided not to give up Luna's legacy. Regardless of Alvaro's claims to the contrary, she was the child of Daniela and Xavier Acevedo—at least on paper. As such, the little girl had inherited her legal father's rather sizable fortune.

"I don't feel right taking it from her," Juliet explained. "I may not have gotten along with my sister or been close to Luna's father, but their money is hers now. Xavier inherited most of it in any case. I don't think it's dirty. She should decide what to do with it once she's old enough."

The lawyers had set up a trust for Luna, one which would allow her to go to any school she wanted to. As for the rest of the cash, she would get it when she was twenty-five—ample time for Ethan to teach her the value of hard work. By the time she was able to access her fortune, she would have the knowledge to handle it.

Also, he and Juliet had blocked Alvaro's request to have Luna's DNA tested—and they always would. That evil man would never be allowed to have a tie to her.

"Can have more cookie, Daddy?" Luna asked, interrupting his trip down memory lane by tugging on his sleeve. She gazed up with hopeful brown eyes.

"Sorry, Little Moon. I shouldn't have given you the first one." Ethan sighed. "Your mother is going to kill me when she sees your dress."

As if on cue, Juliet hurried into the living room, her dark hair cascading down her back in stylish sable waves.

A hot flash coursed through his body at the sight of her red dress. A midsized diamond solitaire winked in the light next to a platinum wedding band. He had put both of those on her last month—to his everlasting satisfaction.

Ethan forgot what he was doing. He was too distracted by watching his beloved wife move. The red figure-hugging tailored number wrapped around her body like a second skin. Curves that should have come with a warning label glowed against the backdrop of the dark wood paneling.

Lord have mercy. The outfit wasn't even revealing. Juliet could have worn it anywhere.

And the eyes of every man in the room would follow her. But they did that regardless of what she wore. Ethan had already had to teach more than one man a quiet but firm lesson over touching what was his.

Juliet reached up to her ear, putting on one of the diamond earrings he had given her for her birthday. "Are we ready?"

Ethan blinked, giving himself a little shake. "Uh, almost."

He gave her his most winsome grin before helping Luna to her feet.

Juliet's face fell when she saw the front of Luna's gold-embroidered gown. "Oh, Ethan. This is why I said no Oreos." She groaned. "And she got your sleeve, too!"

Ethan grimaced at the mark on his sleeve. He picked Luna up, then started to carry her out of the room. "I'll change us into something else. Two minutes. I promise."

"Hurry. We can't be late. It's her big day!"

Five minutes later, he was dressed in a fresh shirt. Luna wore a less stylish but much safer black velvet dress. They hustled out to the car, and he only had to break the speed limit twice to get to the judge's chamber in time.

Making someone a citizen should involve more pomp and circumstance and less paperwork, he thought as he signed document after document.

"That's the last one," Judge Kenisha Washington pronounced after Ethan and Juliet worked through the stack. "Luna is officially a naturalized United States citizen. Congratulations!"

Applause broke out from their small audience. Jason and Maggie were there, of course, but so were Patrick and Thalia Tyler as well as Sergei and Eva Damov with his godson, Ethan Thomas. Even Rivera was there with his latest girlfriend. Donovan Carter was back overseas on yet another *Doctors Without Borders* mission, which was the only reason he wasn't.

"Yay!" Maggie squealed, waving a tiny American flag in front of Luna. The little girl took it, adorably shaking it just long enough to take a picture. Then she jabbed it back in Maggie's face, almost taking her eye out with the pointy end.

Laughing, Ethan confiscated the flag, signaling to Maggie she should step back. "We're still not done."

"No," Juliet agreed, pressing into his side. "We still have to do the most important part."

They turned back to the judge, who laid out a final set of papers. She handed Ethan a pen with a gracious nod.

Bending, he began to sign the adoption packet.

Luna was already Juliet's. The authorities in Mexico had granted Juliet custody right after they dismissed the warrant Alvaro had falsified for her arrest.

Normally, naturalization and adoption procedures took a lot longer. It might have taken years before they got settled. But Ethan was a highly decorated FBI agent with a sterling service record—that...and he'd made friends in high places.

Finally, Ethan reached the last page. He signed with a flourish, returning the judge's pen before taking Luna from Juliet's arms. "Come to Daddy, Little Moon."

She was too small to understand why his voice was so scratchy. Wrinkling her nose, she carried on being adorable.

Juliet wiped her eyes before hugging him and pressing a hot kiss to his cheek. "I can't believe it's finally official."

He threw his free arms around her, pressing her to him. "Better believe it, Mrs. Thomas. We are officially a nuclear American family."

She laughed with tears in her eyes.

"That's enough of that," Jason interrupted, handing her a tissue. "We have a party to get to."

Hours later, long after the celebration bash at the Caislean was over and Luna had been put to bed, Ethan hustled his new wife to their bedroom with a bottle of wine and two glasses.

Sometimes, their coupling was fast and rough out of necessity. Having an active little girl made them make the most of what time they got. But tonight, he wanted to take his time.

Ethan waited until Juliet had finished her glass before kissing the nape of her neck, unzipping the back of her dress and pushing it down to the carpet. Her lingerie followed in short order while she helped him strip.

His mouth drank in her skin, feasting. Her little whimpers fueled his hunger. He lay her on the bed and drove into her wet heat, caressing her with his cock and hands.

Fingers threading with hers, Ethan used his body to please her the way she liked best. His every move was a dance—part instinct, part hard-earned knowledge. Very *hard*.

Wordlessly, Juliet kept pace with him, taking him into her body with fervid and ardent moans that kept him rock hard long enough to make her come three times.

Afterward, he collapsed next to her, pulling her into his side. Then they talked, making promises and vows about the years to come.

"I've been thinking about my future," she said after he had asked her when she wanted to restart law school. "When I go back to school, I think I want to change focus, but not to environmental law."

Ethan braced his head on hand, lying on his side to study her. "To what then?"

She rolled to face him. "I want to be like Judge Washington. I'm going to go into immigration law."

Ethan smiled. "I don't blame you for being inspired after today, but are you sure?"

She nodded. "I've been thinking about it for a long time. I was lucky enough to be born here. Luna was lucky to have you and your connections, but I can't help thinking the only reason she is home safe with us now is because I got lucky and rented the right apartment. That and she has a fortune of her own."

Her face grew serious. "There are a lot of people in this world that would turn their backs on a baby like her just because she wasn't born here. In fact, they do it every day. Mothers, fathers, sons, and daughters—all are in danger, running for their lives like I was, yet people here are still determined to turn them away. Their circumstances do not matter to them."

Ethan stroked her hair. "I know and I'm sorry, but not everyone is like that. I know circumstances aren't ideal given the current culture, but I have faith that people are basically decent and things will change on that front."

"So, you don't think it's a bad idea?"

"Oh, I think it's a great idea. Especially your other plan—you figured out what to do with your fortune, didn't you?"

She smiled softly, reaching out to stroke his cheek. "You know me so well. Yes, I've decided to use my parent's money to set up a legal defense fund for immigrants and asylum seekers. I can't think of a better way to use that money for good. I can be there for people the way you were there for me."

Pride filled him. Juliet had the potential to do so much good in the world, but the size of her heart never ceased to surprise him.

Taking her hand, he rolled over, covering her body with his. "You have my full support, of course. Always."

He pressed a kiss to her lips, a silent vow to stay by her side. It was a promise she returned wholeheartedly...

Now and forever.

THE END

Check out the next installment of Rogues and Rescuers!

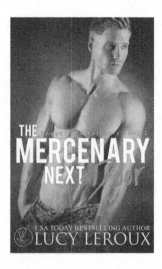

Falling for the girl next door...

Mercenary Mason Lang never intended to go into this line of work, but with pay this good, he can't turn it down. The only challenge is getting out with all of his limbs still intact, which is a lot harder than he realized. And when he does, Mason is going to have it all—including the shy and sweet girl next door.

Laila James knew her crush on the gorgeous next-door neighbor was hopeless. And following a humiliating incident, she'd rather just forget him completely. However, when Mason comes back to town and tries to claim her for his own, Laila keeps her resolve. After all, she's moved on and is even dating someone else.

But Mason isn't giving up so easily. His instincts go into overdrive as he suspects that the rich, frat boy who latched onto Laila is trouble. Determined to prove that they're meant for each other, the mercenary has a new mission. Missing his chance the first time around, Mason refuses to lose the only woman he's ever really wanted. Can he make the girl next door fall for him *again*?

ABOUT THE AUTHOR

Lucy Leroux is another name for USA Today Bestselling Author L.B. Gilbert.

Seven years ago Lucy moved to France for a one-year research contract. Six months later she was living with a handsome Frenchman and is now married with an adorable half-french toddler. Her family lives in California.

When her last contract ended Lucy turned to writing. Frustrated by the lack of quality romance erotica she created her own.

Lucy loves all genres of romance and intends to write as many of them as possible. To date she has published award-winning paranormal, urban fantasy, and gothic regency novels. Additionally, she writes a bestselling contemporary series. The 'Singular Obsession' books are a combination of steamy romance and suspense that feature intertwining characters in their own stand-alone stories. Follow her on twitter or facebook, or check out her website for more news!

www.authorlucyleroux.com

- a amazon.com/author/lucyleroux
- f facebook.com/lucythenovelist
- twitter.com/lucythenovelist
- instagram.com/lucythenovelist
- BB bookbub.com/authors/lucy-leroux

Made in United States
North Haven, CT
25 April 2024

51770264R00146